Margarit Wel... (handwritten)

W9-BFT-349

"AN AMUSING NOVEL OF MANNERS . . . THAT RARE COMIC NOVEL—A WARM COMIC NOVEL—ABOUT THE TEMPORARY DISHABITUATION OF AN INTELLECTUAL." —*The New Yorker*

"A ZESTFUL SATIRE . . . A BRAINY ROMANTIC COMEDY . . . [with] dilemmas of lust and learning." —*Chicago Tribune*

"A SCREWBALL SEND-UP OF NEW YORK INTELLIGENTSIA." —*New York*

"Cathleen Schine elevates the academic novel to heavenly new heights of intelligent silliness. . . . It's hard to stop giggling." —*Village Voice Literary Supplement*

"OPINION, JUDGMENT, TRUTH, PERCEPTION, DOUBT, FAITH . . . A NOVEL OF IDEAS DRESSED UP AS A MANHATTAN MARITAL COMEDY . . . It's a witty book, deceptively so; the undercurrents are serious, dealing with the tricky contours of identity and authenticity." —*Los Angeles Times*

"SHREWDLY OBSERVED, OFTEN RIBALD, AND ALWAYS SMART . . . A BOOK OF MANY PLEASURES." —*Lear's*

CATHLEEN SCHINE's two previous novels are *Alice in Bed* and *To the Birdhouse*. She lives in New York City with her husband, the critic David Denby, and their two sons.

Books by
Cathleen Schine

Alice in Bed
To the Birdhouse
Rameau's Niece

Rameau's Niece

CATHLEEN SCHINE

A PLUME BOOK

To Margot Hentoff and Leon Tec

PLUME
Published by the Penguin Group
Penguin Books USA Inc., 375 Hudson Street, New York, New York 10014, U.S.A.
Penguin Books Ltd, 27 Wrights Lane, London W8 5TZ, England
Penguin Books Australia Ltd, Ringwood, Victoria, Australia
Penguin Books Canada Ltd, 10 Alcorn Avenue, Toronto, Ontario, Canada M4V 3B2
Penguin Books (N.Z.) Ltd, 182–190 Wairau Road, Auckland 10, New Zealand

Penguin Books Ltd, Registered Offices: Harmondsworth, Middlesex, England

Published by Plume, an imprint of Dutton Signet, a division of Penguin Books USA Inc.
This is an authorized reprint of a hardcover edition published by Ticknor & Fields.
For information address Ticknor & Fields, Houghton Mifflin Company,
215 Park Avenue South, New York, NY 10003.

First Plume Printing, April, 1994
10 9 8 7 6 5 4 3 2 1

Excerpt from "The Night" from *Selected Poems* by James Schuyler. Copyright © 1972, 1988
by James Schuyler. Reprinted by permission of Farrar, Straus and Giroux, Inc.

Excerpt from "Letter to N.Y." from *The Complete Poems* 1927–1979 by Elizabeth Bishop.
Copyright © 1979, 1983 by Alice Helen Methfessel.
Reprinted by permission of Farrar, Straus and Giroux, Inc.

℗ REGISTERED TRADEMARK—MARCA REGISTRADA

LIBRARY OF CONGRESS CATALOGING-IN-PUBLICATION DATA
Schine, Cathleen.
  Rameau's niece / Catherine Schine.
    p.   cm.
  ISBN 0-452-27161-4
  1. Women authors, American—New York (N.Y.)—Relations with men—
Fiction. 2. Women translators—New York (N.Y.)—Fiction.
3. Manuscripts, French—Fiction.   I. Title.
[PS3569.C497R35   1994]
813'.54—dc20   93–36528
                                                          CIP

Printed in the United States of America

PUBLISHER'S NOTE
This is a work of fiction. Names, characters, places, and incidents either are the product of
the author's imagination or are used fictitiously, and any resemblance to actual persons, living
or dead, events, or locales is entirely coincidental.

My ideas are my trollops.

— DENIS DIDEROT,
Rameau's Nephew

One

THERE IS A kind of egotism that shrinks the universe; and there was Edward's kind. It dominated the world not by limiting it, but by generous, almost profligate recognition of everything, like sunlight, illuminating whatever it touched, and touching whatever it could.

Margaret's husband was a wonder to her, a loud, handsome Englishman, a Jew from Oxford with gray hair that stuck up in tufts, like an East European poet's, an egotist whose egotism was of such astonishing proportions that he thought the rest of the world quite marvelous simply because it was there with him.

Margaret Nathan was herself a person of no mean ego, although she knew her own egotism shone less like the sun than like a battery-operated flashlight, swinging this way and that way, lighting short narrow paths through the oppressive darkness of other people. Margaret was a demanding person, hard on herself, certainly; harder by far on everyone else.

But turning her restless beam toward Edward, she could find nothing there to be hard about. As to Margaret's demanding nature, she felt immediately that here was a safe haven for it. Edward seemed to demand demands, so that he might have the joy of satisfying them.

Margaret marveled at her husband, awed that he had come to be hers at all. They met in New York when he was visiting an old friend of his and her boyfriend at the time, Al Birnbaum, a Marxist graduate student who spoke, in so far as he was able, like William F. Buckley. It occurred to Margaret that at some secret, buried level Al aspired not to change the world, not really, but to present the opposing view on "Firing Line" — to costar. She could envision him quite clearly: slumped, languorous and slack, in one of those low-backed chairs, right beside Bill, his own head rolling back on its own pale neck, the evil twin of the evil twin.

She took one look at his friend Edward, who was looking rather closely at her, and she saw that he was looking at her in that way that suggested that his old friend was not, after all, *such* an old friend. And she looked back at him in a way that she hoped said, Nor of mine.

"Why, you must come with me, of course," he said when he heard she was writing her thesis about an eighteenth-century female philosophe. He took her hand in both of his. "What a wonderful idea. We'll visit her château. Did she have a château? Surely the woman had a château! I was planning to go in the autumn, through France to the Alps, into Italy. A long and leisurely trip across Europe by car. We'll stop at Venice. Then we'll turn around and come back. Will you come with me? Of course you will. Oh God, what luck."

They were joking, playing around in front of the Boyfriend. But the Boyfriend wasn't paying much attention (he was sick of Margaret, who had become increasingly unpleasant, subscribing to *Dissent* and reading long, liberal anticommunist articles aloud to him); and Margaret and Edward, fooling and flirting in that self-conscious and ostentatious way one employs when one is indeed joking or when one is wholly in earnest, made a mock promise to meet the next night (ha ha ha, went the chorus), which they both breathlessly kept.

Madame de Montigny's château had long ago turned to dust, but Edward Ehrenwerth did take Margaret on a trip across Europe that fall just the same. They drove in a gentle, gray mist from London to the ferry, where Edward then had a long and apparently satisfying chat with one of the crewmen about model trains, then on to their first stop, a renovated farmhouse in a village just north of Paris, belonging to some friends of Edward's. Jean-Claude and Juliette, two exquisitely thin persons in identical, droopy black cashmere sweaters, were French academics who studied and taught American literature: he specialized in neo-Gothic romances written by former housewives; she in slim, laconic novels of a style she referred to as *minimalisme*. They pored over paperbacks and called them texts.

"You don't mind that these books are, you know, shitty?" Margaret asked after several glasses of the wine that had been brought ceremoniously from a cool cellar.

"But on the contrary, American culture, this is its vitality, life's blood, this" — *thees* is what he actually said — "aah, how shall I say it, this, this —"

Sheet, Margaret thought. Thees sheet.

"And you know, such judgment," Juliette interrupted, "such criticism is so patriarchal, so very, very logocentric."

"Margaret, Margaret, literature is, is what?" cried Jean-Claude. "The acquisition and distribution of cultural capital!" Jean-Claude, having warmed noticeably to both the wine and to his subject, slapped Margaret heartily on the back. "Good? Bad? Pooh! The project of the Enlightenment is dead! Invert the hierarchy of judgment!" He raised his glass and laughed. "Long live the liberation of the signifier!"

"Well," said Edward, after joining the toast, "the wine is awfully good. Thank God, my dears, you haven't inverted that particular hierarchy."

"Ah, well, the wine," said both the host and hostess, grin-ning with pride, shrugging in their lovely, loose sweaters. "The wine — of course."

IN HONOR OF the visiting American, Juliette had adapted her cuisine, making hamburgers. Then Edward and Margaret retired to the guest room, which was the entire top floor of the house, a beautiful room, and when she saw it, Margaret thought, with some envy, Ah, the French, so much taste, so little brain, for the room was decorated in the most luxurious velvets and brocades and tasseled cabbage-rose drapes and a Herman Miller sofa and butterfly chairs and original Eames and Knoll pieces, a marvelous, elegant, witty combination, a happy marriage of *minimalisme* and Gothic romance.

Outside, the wind howled, rattling the shutters. Margaret sank her head into the square feather pillows and listened. Creak creak. Clunk clunk. "Is this the attic?" she said. "Are we in the attic?"

"I suppose it is. The attic. That sounds a bit portentous. What will happen here? What will happen here tonight? This very drear and drafty night? Perhaps the enraged Enlightenment will haunt us, armed with sharpened quill. 'I have been wronged!' Ah, Juliette and Jean-Claude — they open cultural doors. They *are* cultural doors."

"Did you see the door of their refrigerator?" Margaret said. Juliette and Jean-Claude had proudly shown them the refrigerator, a high-tech, extremely wide, remarkably shallow apparatus behind a door of elaborately carved wood.

"Yes," Edward said. "Theirs is a very pure and cerebral socialism."

Creak creak, said the shutters.

Margaret picked up a paperback from the bedside table. The cover showed a dark-haired (raven-haired, she corrected herself) woman, her head thrown back, and beside her a beautiful black woman, head thrown back too, both of whom seemed to be bound, in an indistinct way (perhaps they were just sort of tangled) on a dock. The book was called *Desire's Dominion*.

"Well, they're very considerate, your friends, aren't they?" She lay back, closed her eyes, and listened to the wind outside. "Do you like France, Edward?"

Edward leaned down and whispered, "'Thanks to the human heart by which we live, thanks to its tenderness, its joys, and fears, to me the meanest flower that blows can give thoughts that do often lie too deep for tears.'"

"To whom is that addressed?" she asked. "Who is the meanest flower that blows? Me or France?"

"Neither. It's my manifesto. Neither of you is in any way mean. I just like Wordsworth. And you. And France."

"How very un-British of you."

But Edward had spent most of his childhood summers in France. It was where he'd met Jean-Claude, on one of those summer holidays. Margaret thought of Jean-Claude and Edward, skinny boys in skimpy but still baggy bathing trunks, digging among the rocks on the Normandy shore. She thought of the "Immortality" ode. Now, whenever she thought of Jean-Claude, she would think of Wordsworth's lines, she would remember a boy she never met, until he'd become a considerate, fatuous postmodern man, on a beach she'd never seen, and tears would come to her eyes. How annoying, to be so vulnerable to poetry, to Edward.

"Did you ever see *Splendor in the Grass*?" she said, as some kind of revenge. "*That* was a post-Gothic romance."

BEFORE THAT TRIP, Margaret never drank, not even wine; and she rarely drank after it. But during those weeks, she was quite thoroughly drunk every day.

The sun came up each morning to find her snoring in the starched white sheets of some plump little pension bed. No, she thought, when Edward tried to wake her. No, you see, I've moved in, I'm quite settled here and cannot be shifted, not ever, certainly not by you, Edward, whoever you are. And through half-open eyes she watched him get dressed, marveling at how the British could have conquered the world with such skinny, sunken chests.

"Maybe you should wear tight pants tucked into boots, you know?" she said. "Like Mick Jagger."

"Undoubtedly."

Sometimes she could pull him back to bed, sometimes not. She didn't care. She didn't care about anything except scenery and wine and food and pictures in echoing galleries and churches in echoing squares and Edward in the same ill-fitting brown suit.

Driving through the Rhone valley, passing a party-cake castle in the distance, rushing to make a reservation at a four-star restaurant, still hours away, Margaret leaned her forehead against the cool glass of the window and thought, This is the last phase of my long, long childhood. This is the last time I will sit in a car, still drunk from lunch, staring at fairy castles while someone else drives and worries and frets and checks the road map and the odometer. It's the first time, too, but I know what I mean.

Rows of poplars lined the road. The sun had come out from the clouds, which now glowed and reddened. This is bliss, Margaret thought. No wonder Edward likes Juliette and Jean-Claude. No wonder people drink wine, so red and velvety, rolling on your tongue. Margaret let her head fall back. She closed her eyes.

"*Tu baves, ma chérie,*" Edward said gently, patting her knee.

"I'm what?" Margaret said.

"Drooling, darling."

*

THE RESTAURANT was dark and quiet and seriously comfortable. Yum, yum, Margaret thought, gazing lazily at the menu. Yum, yum. Little lambs and little bunny rabbits and little fluttery quail — all manner of gentle, innocent beasts. I will have pork, the forbidden flesh scorned by centuries of my ancestors, but big and ugly. Yum, yum, yum. Medallions of pork with chestnuts.

"Too many pets on the menu," she said. "If I ran this joint, I would offer *boeuf sous rature*. Get it, Edward?" She heard herself laughing.

"Yes, Margaret, I get it," Edward said.

He was not laughing, but looking at her rather dryly. Still, she could not stop herself. What was the point of having read so much incomprehensible Derrida if one could not make philistine deconstruction puns? "*Sous rature*," she continued. "'Under erasure.' And then they'd serve you — nothing! They'd take the beef *off* the plate!"

"Is this what they teach you poor children in graduate school these days?"

"And then on the menu you could draw that line through the word *boeuf,* as the deconstructionists do in order to denote when a word is, well, when a word is whatever it is that makes them draw that line through it . . ."

As she rambled on, drunk and delighted with her erudition, Edward ignored her and ordered the wine, which was even better than what they'd drunk at lunch. She held the glass to her lips and drank slowly. If she was not mistaken, Edward was talking to the waiter about medieval husbandry. She could see the lights in the dim restaurant reflected in her wine glass, in the wine-dark wine. Wine-dark wine. She giggled. She could see the lights twinkling there, like stars, like stars on a dark night. Oh, how banal. Oh, how sublime.

She staggered to bed that night and lay staring at the ceiling as Edward untied her shoes and recited in Latin a Catullus poem about a stolen napkin, and she thought she would marry him, would have to marry him, that it was a necessity, a rule of nature, like gravity. If, of course, he would have her.

"'Give back my napkin!'" he shouted, straddling her, pinning her arms to the bed. "'Or await three hundred hendecasyllables!'"

THE NEXT DAY they drove to Les Baux, the cliff-top ruins of a castle where some medieval nobleman had grilled the heart of a poet and served it to his wife for dinner. When that lady had finished her meal and was told the ingredients, she said the dish had been so sweet that she never wanted anything else to pass her lips, and jumped off the cliff.

"Ah, the goyim," Edward said.

They drove to Vaucluse, where Petrarch had written his love poems to Laura, and to Avignon, where Margaret came down with a fever and stayed sweating and shivering in the little low-ceilinged hotel room within the city's high walls; and from her damp, febrile pillow she wondered if she would die right now, right here, dissipated with drink and lovemaking and museum-visiting.

When she recovered, they drove to the Italian Alps and spent the night in an almost empty ski resort where she read while Edward held a long, quiet, serious discussion that Margaret could not understand with the Austrian chef's eight-year-old son. Edward knew seven languages, and accepted only with the poorest grace that he could speak just one of them at a time. The others were always waiting, eager and impatient, shifting from foot to foot like children, until, at last, one of them would be allowed to thunder out, full speed ahead. Edward spoke with resonant, distinct enjoyment, loud and clear, savoring each word, as if the different languages tasted good. He was a show-off, talking, laughing, sometimes singing loudly, without fear, sharing his own wonder of himself. Margaret was so fully in love with him now that she never knew if the flushed confusion she was experiencing was from the wine or her boisterous companion.

"For our honeymoon," he said the next morning as Margaret drove the left-handed English car on the right-handed Italian road, "I propose —"

"But you never have proposed, you know."

"I propose Sri Lanka — Ceylon, as we old stick-in-the-mud imperialists prefer to call it. We shall discover the meaning of life on the scented isle. When bored with copulation, we can go up to Kandy and regard the Buddha's tooth."

WHEN MARGARET woke up in the Alps, the air was so clear she blinked. Driving on the winding road, toward Italy, toward a whole new land of new wines and new paintings and new beds to share with her new fiancé, she stared ahead at the narrow, climbing vine of a road, and her heart pounded with disbelieving pleasure. Edward, in the mountains, was required by nature to recite Romantic poetry. He recited poetry as habitually as other people cleared their throats. Verse was preverbal: a preparation for speech, an ordering of one's thoughts and feelings, an exquisite sketch, a graceful, generous, gratefully borrowed vision. Margaret understood this and listened to his voice, as clear as the air, as self-consciously grand as the surrounding peaks, as happy as a child's, and then she drove off the mountain. Not all the way off the mountain, she noticed. Just *aiming* off the mountain, really.

"Shortcut, darling?"

Margaret never forgot driving off the mountain, and she never forgot how Edward pretended she wasn't shaking, how he made quiet jokes that guided her back to the road and back to the world where cars were aimed at Turin rather than at a heavily wooded abyss.

She drove slowly, with determination, ecstatic that she had not rolled hideously to a foreign death, and for a moment she felt about the world the way she thought Edward always felt about it, for thirty honking cars trailed irritably behind her, and, glancing in the rearview mirror, all she noticed about them was how brightly they sparkled in the mountain sunlight.

BEHIND THEIR LIVES stood Edward's schedule, a firm yet supple structure that gave to each day a thousand opportunities. If there were only twenty-four hours, then let them begin! Edward rose not only with the sun, but as if he were the sun. I am here, he seemed to be saying. The day may, indeed must, begin. He ate the same breakfast each morning, but what a breakfast — kippered herring and pumpernickel bread, bacon and eggs, fried tomatoes and mushrooms, Cheerios and sliced bananas, toast and jam and muffins, too. It was a labor-intensive meal, which was perhaps how he could stay so thin and eat so much. He presided over this ecumenical array of bowls, dishes, pots, and pans with smooth efficiency, then, finished, turned to his coffee and his newspapers, sometimes reading aloud to Margaret, unless she objected, which, foul-tempered and puffy-eyed, she often did.

"I don't care, Edward. I don't care about the Czech Philharmonic just yet."

"Margaret, one of the things I love about you, and there are so many it fills my soul with joy, but one of the most endearing qualities you have is how sincere you become in petulance." He smiled.

Margaret, her senses blunted by fatigue and the rich pot-pourri of breakfast odors, would nevertheless experience his presence then, acutely and pleasantly — the look of him and his touch, without looking or touching — and she would feel rising within her the familiar tide of gratitude and astonishment that she had come to recognize as love.

Margaret put her hand out and touched his across the table. Far away in Prague, the Czech Philharmonic was actively participating in a democratic revolution. In New York, she was happy and married to Edward. Both of these occurrences seemed equally improbable to Margaret and nearly miraculous. Edward was right: the world was a marvelous place.

"You really don't mind me," she said. "You like me."

"Our marriage is a putrid sink of festering lies; a vile, infested prison house into which we have been flung by a careless and callous fate."

Edward had married Margaret and moved to New York, to Columbia's Comp. Lit. Department, adapting as enthusiastically as the English sparrow, shifting effortlessly from an ancient, orderly university town to the great noise of urban decay. An Americanophile, Edward was a scholar of (of all people and against all academic fashion) Walt Whitman, and he adored the home of his poet.

Mannahatta! "'A million people — manners free and superb'!" Edward was a man at peace with New York.

For the next six years, each morning at 7:00, Edward ventured forth into Mannahatta to run around the reservoir. He maintained that it cleared his head, but Margaret noted that running was practically the only exercise that would not affect pectoral muscles in a positive way, and so she was convinced that he underwent the ordeal merely to assure that his British chest would remain sufficiently concave. When he returned home, at exactly 8:40, sweating and loquacious after so much time deprived of both students and books, he would quickly shower and change, eat his extensive breakfast, then walk up to Columbia for his 11:00 class. Home for lunch and a twenty-minute nap. Back to school, for conferences or research or petty, backbiting department meetings, each of which he embraced warmly and without reservation, for they belonged to his life, and therefore to him, and so beamed with a pleasant and interesting reflected light. Home for dinner at 6:30 sharp, whether he had an 8:00 class or not. When he did, home at 10:15. If not, work at home until 11:00. Asleep at 11:30. Up at 6:30 for another round.

If there were exceptions to this routine — a dinner date, a lecture to give, a concert — the schedule rippled effortlessly and made room. Margaret had never met a more orderly, less rigid soul. Edward's mind, nearly promiscuous in its passionate interests, opened to every new possibility, with one exception: the possibility of failing to do what he had planned to do when he had planned to do it, and of failing to do anything else he wanted to or was required to, as well. And so, every day, like the spinning of the earth, like the silent journey of the stars from one curved horizon to another, Edward's day followed its course. If "willful" and "blessed" were synonyms, they would describe Edward and the gentle, unvarying rhythm of his days.

Vigorous and effortless, the weeks passed and his life was full. Margaret gazed admiringly, for she herself had no schedule to speak of. Her contributions to the family income, while considerable, came irregularly and from far away. Margaret was almost famous. She had written a biography — a plain, sturdy little biography, a biography as unfashionable, as modest and unassuming as an aproned housewife, which had nevertheless caught the public's fickle eye. The subject, Charlotte de Montigny, had been assigned to her when she was a graduate student in intellectual history looking for a dissertation topic. Wife of a dissolute and ill-tempered minor eighteenth-century aristocrat, Madame de Montigny had consoled herself by becoming an amateur astronomer, an occasional portrait artist, and an avid autodidact of anatomy. "Oh, *you* might as well take *her*," Margaret's adviser had said. An aging, eminent professor who drank too much and married too many of his students, he ordered up dissertation topics as if they were dishes at an unsatisfactory restaurant, the only restaurant in town. But this time, the meat loaf had won a prize, several prizes. Margaret was the recipient of grants and royalties, of a postdoctoral sinecure, of a little office at Princeton that was too far away to use.

But grants and royalties and an unused office across the river did not require a schedule or regular habits. Margaret eavesdropped on Edward as he argued amiably on the telephone with a magazine editor for whom he was reviewing a book.

"Do you like James Schuyler?" Edward finally asked into the phone. "I do. So American. 'The night is filled with indecisions, to take a downer or an upper, to take a walk, to lie down and relax. I order you: RELAX.'" And then, with great satisfaction, as if that certainly settled the matter, he hung up. Sometimes, when Margaret saw a poem on the printed page, with all its punctuation, its short and long lines, its verses, she would be startled. Living with Edward, she had come to regard poetry as conversation.

At her desk in the study they shared, Margaret turned back to Voltaire. Voltaire and his mistress had worked together for years, she thought. But they shared a château, not a spare bedroom. They worked in separate, elaborately appointed quarters, a prudent arrangement that made it quite impossible for Madame du Châtelet to waste her working time by listening in on Voltaire's undoubtedly brilliant and entertaining telephone conversations — although she had regularly steamed open his mail. Still, she showed far greater independence than I do, sitting around gawking at my own husband as if he were my first beau, my secret lover, my only friend, and my lifelong mentor.

Sometimes the depth of her feelings for Edward annoyed her. Am I a domesticated household pet, to take such pleasure from the physical presence of a man reading the *Mississippi Review*? She got up and put her arms around his neck, burying her face in his silver unmowed lawn of hair. Who does he think he is, strutting around, being happy and punctual all the time?

"Let's go to Prague together," she said then. "Let's hear the Czech Philharmonic."

MARGARET SPENT the day at the library. Even the sunlight stepped carefully here on its slow, heavy journey down from the dusty windows high above, whispering to itself, Do not disturb, do not disturb.

Margaret did not disturb. No one disturbed, which also meant no one disturbed Margaret. Margaret lived in constant fear of casual conversation, in which invariably someone would ask her about something she had written, and she would not know what they were talking about. Margaret was an authority on many things, with this one qualification — she had forgotten those many things as thoroughly as if she swilled daily from the river Lethe, morning, noon, and night, gulping, gargling, brushing her teeth with the waters of oblivion. Margaret suffered short-lived but all-consuming intellectual passions to which she gave herself over completely, becoming expert enough to be thoughtful. After she wrote about whatever it was that preoccupied her for that moment, she forgot, forgot everything, forgot it altogether, retaining only a pleasant feeling of accomplishment and completion.

While working on her dissertation, which became her first book, *The Anatomy of Madame de Montigny,* Margaret had discovered an intriguing eighteenth-century manuscript. She could find no evidence that it had ever been published, and how it had arrived at Midtown Medical Library, she could not yet say.

It was in the form of a dialogue. Gradually, she came to realize that whole passages of works by Helvétius, Diderot, Kant, Condorcet — everyone who was anyone in the eighteenth century — as well as considerable portions of John Locke's *Essay Concerning Human Understanding,* had been lifted, unacknowledged, and scattered through the book. This was not in itself unusual. There were no copyrights, and pirated editions of philosophical works, anthologies of unattributed excerpts, often considerably altered, were common.

But was this a philosophical work? she wondered. For, in addition to the philosophical content, the story, like much of the literature of that libertine time, was one of seduction.

Was it then a libertine novel? And if not — if not a philosophical tract and not a libertine novel — what was it? What manner of beast? Margaret was translating it from the French. Her new book, on underground Enlightenment literature, was centered on this bawdy, didactic dialogue. She turned to it each day with increasing pleasure and curiosity. A hybrid creature, feathered, furred, and pink-complexioned, it lay before her, open, waiting, a mysterious coquette, waiting for her, for Margaret. It was called *Rameau's Niece.*

RAMEAU'S NIECE
by Anonymous
Translated by Margaret Nathan

It is my custom to whistle while I work. I adopted this habit at
a tender age and have found it to be a pleasant accompaniment
to the exertions of my occupation, an occupation already so delightful that this further adornment sometimes lifts my spirit to
such an unaccustomed height that I thoroughly forget what, in
fact, my delightful occupation is.

On one such occasion, as I whistled merrily, the sounds flew
from my pursed lips to join, somewhat humbly, the magnificent song of a lark perched in a tree beneath which I strolled.
I turned my eyes toward that delicate creature of heaven and
so, my attention averted momentarily from my earthly path, I
stumbled.

My foot had rubbed against a thick, protruding root, causing
me to lose my balance, and I thus was flung against a passerby,
hitherto unnoticed by me, engaged as I was in my habitual
whistling and the aforementioned glance at the feathered mes-
senger of Venus; for the lark's song was indeed a song of love
that day, an idea by which I was struck even as I was struck by

the beauty of the passerby whom I inadvertently, but rather forcefully, struck.

SHE: You have lost your footing.
MYSELF: I have indeed lost my footing. But let us hope that I have not lost my head, for surely, just this moment, I have lost my heart! What a lovely apparition to appear before me, here where I expected only solitude.

She was indeed lovely. Lovely? She was exquisite, a girl whose many qualities, each one remarkable on its own, created together a sense of harmony, of consistency, of perfect unity — in short, of beauty! I felt all of this immediately, before even I realized I was experiencing anything at all, for her grace was of such subtle power that the effect seemed to be obtained without any effort. And so too, effortlessly, was it apprehended, and welcomed, by me.

MYSELF: Will you forgive me?
SHE: I cannot forgive you for an act instigated not by you but by chance; nor would I forgive you for an act that gives me the pleasure of meeting again, after all these years, the friend of my uncle and a philosopher of such brilliance. For let me confess, sir, I have often desired to see you again. Your *Treatise on Sense and Sociability* has been my most intimate companion this past year.

How extraordinary. A little girl (she was no more than sixteen) had chosen for company a work of mine, a rather difficult one, too. Why, it was in her small and delicate hand at that very moment! She pressed the book — my book — almost reverently to her breast.

SHE: I have so many questions.

As did I, the first and most pressing of which was, Who was she?
   This I knew not. But, yet, I felt I knew something of greater weight, for her desire to struggle toward the freedom to make

use of her reason was clear to me. And so too was my obligation to accompany — no, to lead her on her journey. Without my knowledge, I had been chosen to be (indeed, judging by the book in her little white hand, I already was) her guide on a journey toward enlightenment. Here was an innocent child, unspoiled, seeking an education.

MYSELF: But how is it that you know me? And who is your uncle?

I tell you now, dear reader, that I addressed these questions to the lovely girl in a state of agitation, for in my distress at disturbing an innocent young lady by clumsily bumping into her on a deserted and narrow garden path, and in my excitement at discovering a pupil so eager, I had quite forgotten to step aside to let her pass, and so was standing in such intimate proximity to her that I felt her breast heaving, in shock at the surprise of the initial encounter, no doubt, against my own chest, her little hand clutching still my modest treatise on sociability now pressed between our two hearts.

I longed to teach her then, to be her friend, to be employed incessantly in promoting her felicity and increasing it by every sort of pleasure.

And, longing thus, foreseeing the pleasure and happiness of such an arrangement, and standing thrust against her as I was, I became conscious of another feeling — a sudden and enormous surge of emotion on my part.

Recognizing my inability to control this swelling of sentiment in a situation of such delightful propinquity, and fearing that the girl might herself sense this sudden fullness of feeling and become alarmed, I moved back a pace.

SHE: Don't be startled, sir. I am not a stranger to you, only a stranger in this figure, for you have not seen me since I was a child. I am Rameau's niece.

∾ ∾ ∾

EDWARD HAD NO difficulties at dinner parties. If he had been seated beside a rock, he would have quickly begun an animated discussion of its layers of granite or sandstone or lime, its life underground, its ocean journeys and aspirations for the future. Intoxicated by this encounter, he would regale Margaret with tales of the rock's history, which he would tell with such enthusiasm and such grace that she would laugh and hope that some day she too might sit beside a stone at dinner. And the stone? It would sigh and bask in its newly realized glory, its importance and beauty, necessity and dignity — I pave roads and build towers, I form mountains, I rest on the throats of gracious ladies!

Margaret, on the other hand — well, sometimes she thought about what it would be like to sit next to herself at a dinner party. She would have nothing to say. And neither would she.

Unable to ask the initial dinner-party question (the question to ask at a dinner party, at least at the kinds of dinner parties she attended, was either "What is your field?" or "What are you working on?" depending on the degree of familiarity between participants in the exchange), unable to ask the question because of a feeling that she ought already to know the answer but didn't, or that the answer was "Nothing" and would make the question seem aggressive and cruel, she would sit in an agonized silence that she, in the next chair, also paralyzed and mute, would interpret as disdain, boredom, or, worst of all, stupidity.

Edward told her that her appalling memory was cleansing, that she came to everything fresh, and so it was a virtue. But he was wrong. A poor memory robs a person of dignity, Margaret knew. She had some standing in the world, but none of it had been achieved at dinner parties.

But here we are, Margaret thought, as she and Edward entered a large West Side apartment, the walls around them enameled, glistening, slick as ice. The ceiling, she thought, looking up — you could skate on the ceiling, gravity aside.

Edward whispered in her ear, " 'And most of the jokes you just can't catch, like dirty words rubbed off a slate, and the songs are loud but somehow dim and it gets so terribly late.' " Edward had taken to quoting only American poets since moving to New York. "Elizabeth Bishop," he said gently, answering her helpless look.

The couple giving the party were named Till and Art Turner. Margaret had roomed with Till in college, an unforgettable experience that involved witnessing constant rehearsing of Till's roles in various avant-garde student productions, many of them musicals.

Till's husband, Art, a tall, handsome man with a short beard and lovely teeth, stood at the door. He was a highly regarded writer who never seemed to write anything, which somehow only added to his reputation. He was a man of integrity. He smiled, shook hands, smiled, smiled, and smiled. He whispered to some, loudly announced others, his attentiveness calling attention to itself.

It was Art who, in a flurry of self-importance, had insisted on taking Margaret's doctoral dissertation to an editor he knew, only to see it become the best-selling *Anatomy of Madame de Montigny*. Art and Margaret had never forgiven each other.

He is a monster, Margaret thought, watching him greet his guests. An unholy monster of manipulation guarding the castle gate, a man who has learned the meaning, the secret, of other people's vanity and uses it to feed his own. Come, he seemed to say, submit to excessive flattery, *my* excessive flattery, come along. And as you sheepishly (shucks, you really mean it?) accepted his invitation, the gate slammed: clank. And you were — still outside.

He rolled back his head and exposed his very good teeth. "Ah, here's my little discovery."

Margaret looked down at the thick forest green carpet, guilty. But it sickens him, too, she thought. It sickens him too that his help helped.

"You're marvelous, Margaret, marvelous," he said. "Open, simple, lacking all affectation."

What Margaret had said, the inspiration for his effusive welcome, was "Hello." She tried to smile in a friendly, grateful way, but felt immediately that she had failed.

"A conceptual breakthrough in the critical biography," he was saying. "The field can never be the same, never recover from this onslaught of . . ." He paused. "Well. How modestly you carry your genius, Margaret. I'm sure no one would ever suspect it was there at all." And he turned his shining smile to his next guest.

Not only didn't people observe genius in Margaret — they detected very little intelligence at all. It was Margaret's fate, or misfortune as she saw it, to have inherited from her mother a face that was pleasant and decorative enough, but that in no way expressed her temperament or personality. As she suffered from panic, shyness, and critical disdain for her fellow man, all her fellow man saw was a pretty young woman with undignified Shirley Temple curls, a spray of freckles across her nose, and a wide eager look in her brown eyes which might easily be interpreted as cheerful self-confidence.

Would that I were sallow and severe and haughty, she thought, my thin hair in a tight French knot. But Margaret looked jolly and content instead.

She sat down, turned, and noted that she was mercifully not sitting next to herself. She was beside a man known to her slightly, and only by meetings at parties such as this one. There he sits, she thought, patiently waiting to be unable to strike up an interesting conversation with me.

He was a writer, a fairly fashionable one from the East Side with a brownstone and a table at the sort of restaurant at which writers had tables, a best seller or two in his past, and a small, lingering portion of celebrity that she found particularly intimidating. He was just famous enough so that she ought to know some basic facts about him but not famous enough so that she did. She, on the other hand, had written a famous book, and enough had been written about her book so that she expected people to know what it was she had written about, but it was the kind of book that assured that no one had.

She glanced around, looking for Edward, listening for his voice, hearing only other voices gliding stylishly through the topics of the day. This is what people did at dinner parties: talk. But the talk existed on some level beyond communication. It was decorative.

Margaret saw Edward walking toward her. He put his hand on her cheek as he passed by but said nothing, and she felt almost forlorn. If Till had seated him next to Margaret, she wouldn't have to worry about making smooth flourishes of talk, or trying to follow it. She wouldn't have to be clever.

She would listen instead, and she would hear Edward. His loud, exuberant talk would swoop her up, filling her deliriously with information and observation and line after line of American poetry.

But Edward was destined for other parts, and Margaret sighed and took stock of her situation. On her left side, a highly perfumed girl slid in. Across from her sat a man who looked familiar, but perhaps it was just his eyeglasses; next to him was a woman whom Margaret might or might not have known; and so on around the large table, until Margaret met the pale blue eyes of her husband and she smiled. Some woman or other was next to Edward, then Till's appalling husband smirking and nodding ("You've created an entirely new vocabulary, a new critical language . . ."). Really, Margaret thought, Art's habit of thrusting greatness about, as if he had just this instant, and *that* instant, too, as if every instant he had just discovered a continent and were planting the flag, was becoming increasingly trying. Margaret detested Art and she liked Till very much, in the way that one likes a friend and no longer knows why. That Art and Till came together as a package was unfortunate, but they did come together and always would. Couples were miraculous, odd, ill-formed things that grew without reason and without grace, like double ears of corn. Still, she thought, Till should discipline him.

Beside Art sat Lily, a friend of Till's from college whom Margaret hadn't seen in years but remembered liking. With her short, tousled black hair and red, pouty lips, she looked like a girl on the cover of a 1950s bohemian paperback.

According to Till, Lily had traveled with one or two hangers-on, a motley collection of chic but unproductive artists, ever since college. The most loyal of them was with Lily tonight, a wiry middle-aged man named Pepe Pican who exhibited such contempt for his surroundings at all times that all he could bring himself to do was dine. He dined wherever and whenever he or anyone he knew was invited.

"Hi," Margaret said to Lily. "Hello, Pepe."

Pepe looked at her darkly and turned back to his plate.

"Margaret! I haven't seen you in, I don't know, a century! I had a dream about you last week!" Lily said, then turned back to the man next to her.

All around Margaret there were faces, more faces, smiling and laughing, their mouths opening and closing, easily, in the formation of words, the mystery of conversation. Margaret wanted to cry. She tried to recall which Eastern European government had fallen that day. Was it really Romania? She wished she was at a dinner party in Romania, beneath the family's single forty-watt light bulb, a spotty boiled potato on her plate. What a trivial person you are, Margaret, she thought. All the Romanians want to be here, where we're free. Free to be trivial.

Margaret put her chin in her hand and watched Till. Till reached for her wine, and a joyous rattling chorus rose up, a choir of bangle bracelets. Her jacket was iridescent green, her long crimped hair jet black, her teeth white and large. At the head of the table, she jingled and sparkled as a goddess would, omniscient, powerful, confident.

Till Turner was first and foremost a hostess, but she found time to write, too. She was a playwright whose enormously popular body of work concentrated on small groups of women sitting in large moving vehicles — there was an airplane play, another on a bus, a train, a ferry — jouncing along, chewing the old bones of their lives until whole skeletons of marriage and divorce and aged parents and teenage children, an ossuary of relationships, lay gleaming white around them, clickety-clack.

Till Turner was nicknamed Turner Off by one critic, but

most of them welcomed her ability to churn out a new play every single year. Her apartment was old and the rooms large and square, not narrow and rectangular as in most New York apartments. Although Margaret was perfectly happy in her own apartment, when she went out she found herself inattentively, but invariably, appraising, and wanting, someone else's. She would stand, panting from the six flights of stairs, in a narrow garret in the East Village, trying to keep her balance on the slanted floor; or step out onto a balcony not much bigger than a shoe box from an apartment on Second Avenue and Sixty-eighth Street and listen to the traffic bray below; or search the dark, endless hall of a railroad flat near Columbia, looking for the dreary bathroom. It didn't matter where she was — every apartment had something, a leaking but romantic skylight, a view, a shower fixture. She vaguely wanted all of them, and of all of them the one she vaguely wanted most was this one, Till Turner's. Sunlight streamed through the treetops to the broad windows during the day. Beyond the trees was the park and then the river. At night, the lights of New Jersey twinkled merrily through the leaves: you over there may ridicule us over here, the New Jersey lights seemed to say, but look, just look who you're staring at, and look who we get to watch!

Now Till was leaning over the back of Lily's chair, speaking rapidly and softly to Lily, and Margaret watched them with envy, wishing someone, anyone, would at that moment speak rapidly and softly to her, or even loudly and excruciatingly slowly. Till looked up and saw that Margaret was watching. She pulled away from Lily with a little laugh.

"I haven't seen Lily in a long time," she said. She laughed again and moved on to another guest.

"Margaret!" said Lily from across the table, her head tilted to one side as if Margaret were a very rare bird indeed. "In the dream, we were reading Ovid together. Translating for a course. Wild? In straight-backed chairs. Just like Mr. Griswold's class, remember?"

"I've never studied Latin," Margaret said. "I never read Ovid."

"Of course you have," Lily said reassuringly. "And you're absolutely scandalous, with your best seller and all your prizes. I'm so envious I could spit." She reached out and put her hand on Margaret's and patted it and didn't seem the least bit envious, only amused.

"Don't spit," Margaret said.

Maybe I should hone my poor socialization skills with Lily, Margaret thought halfheartedly, noticing Lily's vintage white silk suit. She's exotic. She looks like a post-quickie-divorce Las Vegas bride.

Till, in and out of the room, up and down in her seat, back and forth and round and round among the guests, now approached Margaret's vicinity. Thank God she won't wonder at my magnificent simplicity the way her unbearable husband did. Margaret thought she heard Art discussing his SAT scores. He was forty years old. "It was an onerous burden. I cheated to bring them down, of course."

Till stood beside Margaret now. Her appearance had a biblical quality, flowing in various ways and directions — skirts, hair, scarves, and sleeves. In her deep voice, a hoarse, gravelly melody of slightly Southern intonation, she said "Telephone" to the girl beside Margaret with such resonance and respect that the telephone ceased all at once to be a convenience and returned instead to its early, almost mythic stature — it was again an invention. As the girl beside her silently rose and wafted away, Margaret wondered anew at Till.

"Margaret," Till said, and she looked at Margaret with such evident interest and approval, such enthusiasm. This, Margaret thought, is a kind of power. To make other people feel they are important to you. "Margaret," Till repeated, as if her very name were a joy to the senses and the intellect both. "What are you working on?"

"A sequel."

"Ah. Margaret the scholar. I admire you, Margaret. I mean, your work actually has stature. You don't know that because you're so absurdly self-effacing, but you have an impact on people, on the way people think . . ."

Margaret said, "*Marchons, marchons.*"

But her work did march victoriously, and she sometimes watched its odd popularity with alarm. *The Anatomy of Madame de Montigny* had been reviewed on the front page of the *New York Times Book Review* as "an unusually accessible, one might even say readable, work of scholarship that addresses issues as relevant to twentieth-century women as to the women of the Age of Enlightenment," and had crept onto the best-seller list, where it settled in for nineteen weeks.

"By the end of the eighteenth century," the review said, "the sturdy peasant had replaced the delicate aristocrat as the physical ideal. Breast-feeding, says Nathan, became a national obsession: 'The bosom metamorphosed from decorative bauble to natural wonder. Charlotte de Montigny, a student of anatomy and therefore conscious of these changes in sentiment, recognized them as revolutionary and sought to name them. She did this by renaming the human body in a little-known tract called *Anatomie sans culotte*.'"

Who cares? Margaret had wondered, reading the review. Only I care. Only I, who have spent so much of my adult life with this woman and her body parts. No one else could possibly care.

But they did. They cared that the feet were named *lafayettes,* the erector penis the *crescam ut prosim* (words, meaning "Let me grow, in order to benefit mankind," engraved on Lafayette's sword by Benjamin Franklin, while the testicles, the *cur nons,* or "why nots," were named after the other motto on the sword); it intrigued them that the sigmoid notch had become the *vainqueur de la Bastille,* that the mammary glands were dubbed the *citoyens bienfaisant.*

The book was hailed by every publication from *Savvy* to *Dyke: A Quarterly* as a feminist breakthrough. A woman had written it about a woman who had turned the body upside down, literally, beginning her anatomy at the feet and working her way up past *le quatorze juillet* (the heart) to the *voltaires* (the eyes). The feminist theoretical journal *Enclitic* praised it as a seminal work in the study of the politics of the body in an article called "Feet First: Inverting the Anatomical Hierarchy." An HBO TV movie, called simply *Anatomy* and starring Mariel Hemingway, was in production. And in a special issue of *Diacritics,* devoted entirely to Margaret's book, Jacques Maridou had written a highly influential essay revealing Charlotte de Montigny's tract on the anatomy to be a precursor of postmodern *bricolage.* Margaret was a popular pedant.

"Now, Margaret, listen," Till continued in a somber whisper that conveyed both urgency and special, exclusive trust. "Be especially nice to Dominique. She just got in from Paris and she doesn't know a soul." She kissed Margaret on both cheeks, in honor of Dominique, no doubt, and returned to her duties.

So the girl who'd been sitting beside Margaret was named Dominique and came from France. No wonder her scent was so, so — scented. Well, certainly I know what it feels like to sit on the outside looking in. But will I be able to do my part for the foreigner with the overdeveloped taste for perfume? Margaret asked herself.

She was becoming increasingly uncomfortable. The room was warm, the talk noisy. The gossip about craven producers and publishers, about billionaire real estate magnates (the popes and monarchs of this particular circle of urban courtiers), the revelations and snickers about other writers, all floated tantalizingly by. She couldn't keep the names straight. Ron Perelman and Richard Perle; she knew she disapproved of them both, but which one for which reason? She could not recall. Well, yes, now she could, now that the conversation had turned to something else. Harold Brodkey or Joseph Brodsky? Saul Steinberg or Saul Steinberg? Oh, where was that perfumed Parisian, who had none of these worries, who knew that every American was a gangster, a cowboy, or an arbitrageur?

I have forgotten even more than I ever knew, Margaret thought. Names and dates, faces, theories — she sought them with a kind of desperation. She could never possess them, not really, and so they had become for her precious, moving, full of wonder. Margaret had become a connoisseur of these treasures, they were so rare, so delicate, so easily destroyed. Insatiable, she had studied history in college and then in graduate school, plunging into dusty libraries and dreary indices as if they were pools of clear, cool water.

Margaret was considered an important new voice after the publication of her book. But by those who met her, at conferences or even at dinner, she was considered a mute, and so a fool. I don't want to be a mute fool, she thought. I want to be witty and wise. Like Edward. If only Edward were a ventriloquist. I could move my mouth and not worry about what came out. And I could sit on his knee!

The man next to her was still next to her, wasn't he? Well, perhaps she could say she had loved his last book. She hadn't read it. But it's possible she would have loved it if she had. Her mother had read it over the summer, and she had loved it. She could say that.

Across from her, beyond the baskets and bowls and platters of fashionable food, there was a skinny man who, with his red, shiny, bald head, reminded her of her Uncle Harry.

Maybe, like Uncle Harry, he would let her puff on his cigar and then, when it was bedtime and she had to go to her room, slip her a new, crisp dollar bill. Next to him, Lily discussed life-size human figures, knitted and stuffed with cotton rags, which she referred to as sculptures. Margaret thought of the toy monkeys made from gray and red socks. She wondered if Lily actually knitted sculptures, clicking her needles in a SoHo rocking chair, or if she merely admired them. And then she remembered — Lily was a critic of something. Art? Yes, sort of. She was the editor of a trendy feminist art journal. *The Gaze.* And she wrote a column about women's health issues, "Body Text," for some place like *Harper's Bazaar.*

Margaret stared miserably at her plate. I am too self-centered, she thought. Too vain and too easily bored.

"Well," the author said in response to something Margaret had, as usual, missed, "if men have no close friends, and that's what they say, that men have no close friends, then why are there so many buddy-buddy movies? I wonder if the reason is just that, that men have so few close friends. American men have created this myth . . ."

Margaret mused on her own self-absorption. If people expect anything of me, I resent them and feel incompetent and ill at ease. And yet I expect so much, and if I don't get it, I feel only contempt. I'm sort of an asshole, she thought.

"Politically, the myth of the American male had its strongest expression in Ronald Reagan."

"Do you really think so?" she blurted out, determined suddenly to join in, her voice sounding loud to her. "Eisenhower is my idea of an American male."

"And that is why she married me, isn't it, darling?" said her husband in his most affected imperial British (she rules the waves!) accent. I say, said the accent, what a funny little colony it is.

No, Margaret thought. I married you because I'm greedy

and you're generous, because when I'm with you I don't notice that I've forgotten everything because you have forgotten nothing.

For years she had toiled in the library, willful and superior, tolerating this boyfriend, then that boyfriend, for a while, then abruptly dumping the current one to take up unenthusiastically with another, proud of her detachment — one false move and you're out, buster — all the while waiting. Waiting for Edward, of course, with whom the fog of her life took on a discernible shape, an elegant, exquisite shape, like Jove when he had abandoned his cloudy disguise after seducing Io.

Of course, poor Io turned into a heifer, didn't she? Maybe I had really better tell the American male how much I loved his book, she thought, looking at the author, because really I'm sure I would have; or ask him what he's working on, although that probably was reported by Liz Smith and sold to the movies in a record-breaking deal months ago, or worse, this morning, and reported on page one of the *Times*.

He wasn't as well dressed as he was reputed to be, though, was he? Didn't they write magazine pieces about his wardrobe? Then, suddenly, Margaret blushed, thanking God for the inability to speak at dinner parties, which thereby covered up her inability to think at dinner parties, and admitted to herself that she had spent all this time under the impression that the sportswriter beside her, whom she had met so many times, was a novelist whom she had never set eyes on.

She could hear her husband. He was talking about Walt Whitman. I wish I could talk about Walt Whitman. I wish I was Walt Whitman, a drunken homosexual American genius. What cachet. Then I could say whatever I wanted. But I don't want to say anything.

"Excuse me," said the perfumed girl (Dominique, was it?), squeezing back into her place.

Remembering Till's injunction to be nice to Dominique,

Margaret tried to smile, then, slowly, careful to enunciate clearly, she said, "Do-you-read-American-poet? Whitman?" She gave the name a slight French intonation: Whit-mahn. "Walt Whit-mahn?"

"No," said Dominique.

"So, Bonnie," said the sportswriter-who-was-not-a-novelist to Dominique, "What're you working on?"

"I'm in turnaround," said Dominique-who-was-really-Bonnie and had never been Dominique at all, or even French. She went on about her latest project, a screenplay called *The Private Life of Squeaky Fromme*.

Well, now it is time for me to go home, Margaret thought. Go home and read a book. A book by Walt Whit-mahn.

"*Zut alors*," she muttered to herself. Then abruptly, to the sportswriter, "Do you have a lot of friends?"

She had interrupted him. He was still talking to Bonnie. "Do I what?" he said.

"Do you have a lot of friends?"

"I suppose I do."

"Oh."

"Do you?"

"That's a rather personal question," she said severely.

EDWARD had gone out to hear a friend of his at a reading, but Margaret disliked readings, embarrassed if the work was bad, too distracted by the author's physical idiosyncrasies and the audience's hairstyles to enjoy it if it was good. She stayed home and tucked herself into bed with her manuscript.

∞ ∞ ∞

The girl was a guest of the Marquise de——, as was I, and our paths crossed many times during that month. At dinner, I often found myself glancing at her as I attempted to resolve some problem of philosophy, turning it over and over in my mind. And it soon became apparent to me, from her own glances, as well as a sudden and remarkably becoming flush that appeared on her cheeks during these exchanges of looks, that she too pondered these philosophical questions. At least so I hoped, and as the days passed I grew more and more curious to ascertain whether my perception was correct.

At these times, too, the question with which I was grappling began to take on a new urgency.

Is corporeal sensibility the sole mover of man?

Eagerness to establish the truth burned in my breast, fueled by the looks I exchanged with Rameau's niece.

One morning, I came across her walking in the gardens. She carried a book which, when she saw me, she held out to me as she approached with her habitual grace and delicacy. I took it from her, from her fingers agile and exquisite, and opened the volume, whereupon she turned the pages with such a lightness of touch that I marveled and felt almost weak with admiration.

She pointed to a line.

Understanding that I was to read it aloud, my voice trembling with involuntary emotion, I began.

MYSELF: "When a man enters into himself, when he examines the bottom of his soul, he perceives nothing in all his sentiments but the development of bodily pain —"
SHE [her eyes closed]: "— and pleasure!"

In the days that followed, we often found ourselves alone in the gardens, discussing philosophy. Was it really true, she asked, that interest and want were the principles of all sociability?

Her arm brushed quite accidentally against mine, stimulating my own interest and want to a degree I declare I had never yet experienced. I composed myself as best I could and answered.

MYSELF: Men exaggerate the force of sentiment and friendship.

She looked away with a suddenness I found surprisingly gratifying. For did not this gesture suggest disappointment at my words? And did not her disappointment suggest the force of her own sentiment, of her own feelings?

Wanting to discover the validity of this proposition, that she was experiencing a forceful sentiment and desire for friendship, I continued.

MYSELF: Men exaggerate the force of friendship. They represent sociability as an innate affection or principle. But there is but one principle of this kind.

We had stopped walking and I was speaking softly to her.

MYSELF: That principle is corporeal sensibility.

Her eyes widened then. Her complexion, pure and white as a pearl, glowed with a sudden rosy hue. She tossed her head in anger.

SHE: I admire your wisdom, sir. But heaven forbid that I should copy it. If all your friendships are nurtured in a sunlight as harsh as this, then your garden must be a dry, insipid place indeed. I myself must seek a little cooling shade. These walks of ours expose us too much to the glare of Apollo's gaze without the serenity of his gentle song.

She began to walk away, and when I attempted to accompany her, she turned and walked in a different direction.

Was this to be the course of my careful tutoring? That it should end before it had in truth begun? That my student should flee her teacher, untouched by understanding?

MYSELF: Please! I meant only to suggest . . .

But Rameau's niece strode on, deaf to my entreaties. Nor, for days afterward, did she take herself again to those garden paths. "I feel the sun so acutely," she would say when asked by some member of the company why she had forsaken her earlier regimen of exercise and fresh air. She avoided my eyes as carefully as she shunned the garden. Never did I surprise her in a room alone; always was she attended by the marquise's retinue of old women.

For days, and then a week, and two weeks, this inhumane treatment persisted. My sleep was uneasy, my appetite uninspired, and it was only small comfort to notice the same symptoms in the gentle girl who steadfastly refused to respond to my sighs and glances. In the company of the other guests, I would address bitter speeches to my lost student, speeches she and only she could recognize as being meant for her, and only for her.

In these speeches I rendered accusations:

MYSELF: Seeing that life is but a motion of limbs, the beginning whereof is in some principal part within, why may we not say that all automata (engines that move themselves by springs and wheels as doth a watch) have an artificial life? If that is so, is it not true that the heart is nothing more than a spring?

I implored mercy:

MYSELF: It is a law of nature, is it not, that a man ought to pardon the offenses past committed by them that, repenting, desire it? For pardon is nothing but the granting of peace; and not granting it to those who repent is a sign of aversion to peace, and refusing to forgive is therefore contrary to the law of nature.

Sometimes, when I was near her, all my senses were strangely ravished and my eyes did not dare to rest on hers; all my body felt languid and oppressed. But my pupil appeared to notice nothing regarding her teacher.

Only after two weeks of existence in this arid desert devoid of feeling, of charm, of beauty, did I see the first sign of budding life, a mere shoot, a tender sprig of attention, but enough to cause my heart to beat with renewed vigor. Rameau's niece on this day, truly a spring morning, allowed her glance to fall on me.

MYSELF: The understanding is like the eye. While it makes us see and perceive all other things, it takes no notice of itself; and it requires art and pains to set it at a distance and make it its own object.

Her own eyes, large and luminous, looked into mine as if seeking there understanding, the sight of the mind. For a moment, I was unable to continue and remained where I was, silent and trembling in the unaccustomed glory of her gaze. She lowered her lashes then, plunging the world back into the darkness of her indifference. But that one moment gave me hope, and I continued.

MYSELF: But whatever be the difficulties that lie in the way of this inquiry, whatever it be that keeps us so much in the dark to ourselves — and to each other — I am nevertheless sure that all the light we can let in upon our minds, all the acquaintance we can make with our own understandings, will not only be very pleasant, very, very pleasant . . .

And here I sighed, and really I could not go on. As my voice trailed off, the other guests remarked with sympathy on the rigors of philosophy and suggested I take some wine, while Rameau's niece retreated silently from the room with a quick, shy glance at me that worked simultaneously as both cure for my sudden infirmity and the cause of a debilitating relapse, so that I felt it necessary to take myself weakly to my chamber for the restorative balm of sweet solitude and repose.

In the days following, Rameau's niece began to offer to me more of these slight glances, at first shyly, then with greater intensity and frequency, looks almost of tenderness, certainly of curiosity, until one evening after dinner, as she walked past me toward the card tables, I felt something pressed into my hand, and in my excitement at this undreamed of felicity, I stuttered some words attesting to a headache and took to my room. There, I opened a note written hastily but in a beautiful hand. It said, "From the dim candlelight of these sad weeks, I long for daylight, for the sun to illuminate my way to greater understanding. It would be unpardonable to undervalue the advantages of knowledge, to neglect to improve understanding when given an opportunity to do so. You are my teacher, I see that now. And I? If you will have me, I am your student."

ॐ ॐ ॐ

MARGARET PUT down the manuscript and turned off the light. A teacher and his student, bound together, locked in the giddy embrace of pedagogy. Margaret sighed and remembered when she had first seen Edward teach, remembered sitting at a desk in the back of the room, listening; remembered a line from the Whitman poem ("Does not all matter, aching, attract all matter?"); remembered what he wore; remembered that one of his shoelaces had been untied, remembered a hazy space between his body and hers, a crowd of students and desks and chairs, none of which existed. Only Edward existed. Edward and Margaret and the words and the silence that ran between them.

She never went to hear Edward teach anymore. She was too busy, he told her everything he wanted to discuss ahead of time, at home, and it seemed undignified to follow one's husband around listening to him lecture when perhaps one ought to be lecturing oneself. But recalling the early days, when she sat before him, waiting and listening in the uncertain ecstasy of anticipation, she thought perhaps she ought to resume her studies with Edward.

Still, it was blissful to be alone sometimes, she thought. Like now, the whole bed to herself, the whole apartment to herself, no one blasting into the room with a new interpretation of an old dog of a poem. Edward was wonderful, it was true, but sometimes his wonder weighed heavily.

Where was he, anyway? It was past twelve. The reading was over at ten. Unlike him to be so late. They probably went out for a drink afterward. Still. She considered what she would do if Edward ever had an affair. Make him stop.

WHEN MARGARET had been very young and single, people, also very young and single, had constantly dropped by. They would telephone from the street corner or just ring the bell and come and sit on the couch with her and discuss how much they hated being so young and so single and, more often than not, so unemployed. Margaret sighed. What golden days those were, sitting in the gloom. The dimming afternoon light. Slouched on the sofa until it was really quite dark. Too lazy to reach up and turn on a light. Drinking coffee, having lunch delivered from the coffee shop across the street, dinner delivered from the coffee shop across the street from the first coffee shop. (She was too ashamed to get both meals from the same place. She had once almost ordered a poached egg for breakfast and had it delivered, but decided at the last minute that it would be decadent.)

Since marrying Edward, Margaret's social life had taken a peculiar turn. She went out more than she ever had in the past but seemed to know fewer and fewer people. She met people — Edward's colleagues, Till's chattering circle. She met other historians, too, although she had managed to keep her academic activities to a minimum. She hated to teach, and after the success of *The Anatomy of Madame de Montigny* she had not needed to. She belonged to a group, a seminar of pseuds (as Edward, who also belonged, called it) which brought her into contact with people from other disciplines. She had lunches with magazine editors. And so her universe, once the narrow university, was now slightly broader, perhaps, but considerably more ephemeral. And the comfort of friendship — the kinds of casual, open-ended encounters she had once had with friends — now occurred almost exclusively between her and her husband.

Margaret didn't really mind the change; indeed, for a long time she didn't even notice. Edward made up for a great deal. He filled a lot of space. Listening to him, she was busy. She struggled to recall names, dates, everything she had firmly believed in two hours before. Edward remembered vigorously, joyously, as if the act of remembering was itself a magnificent physical pleasure.

Sometimes she wondered if he didn't fill up a little too much space, for she was aware of him even as she thought her own thoughts. And every once in a while the rhythm of those old, long days, when she and her thoughts were alone, would come back to her, like a song, and she would feel a sense of nostalgia for a time when all was expectation and nothing was expected from her.

HER OLD FRIENDS, or at least her old ways of friendship, seemed to have slipped away when she wasn't paying attention. Had she simply forgotten them, along with their names? Had her forgetfulness hardened to callousness? Margaret didn't like to think of herself as a callous person — it wounded her vanity — and she disliked the idea of losing anything, anything at all. Thinking this way, she felt a familiar urge, a compelling desire, not for something specific, just for more. Seek, and ye shall find. Then ye shall forget. So, ye'll just have to seek again.

Forgetfulness was the engine that moved her. And if it compelled her to frenzied gathering of facts and ideas into books, surely she could gather friends to her bosom, too.

Being a methodical as well as a suggestible person, and having spent the morning reading Francis Bacon, she decided to test the inductive method of reasoning by making lists of former friends and looking for a characteristic common to all of them by which she might arrive at a general law of friendship gone awry.

The names fell into two categories: those she had lost interest in, and those who had lost interest in her. She looked briefly at the column of names of people she had lost interest in, considered calling one or two, then lost interest. The other list, those who had lost interest in her, was baffling, and the only general law she could arrive at was that they were disloyal. This was of course a tautology and surely not what Francis Bacon had been driving at, but then he died of a cold caught while testing his theories of refrigeration by shoving snow into a chicken.

Margaret called Richard, her editor. In a way almost unheard of for the editor of an academic, he watched over her like a hen, clucking and fussing and proud. He admired her, protected her, manipulated her. He actually edited, too. Margaret recognized that she was smiled upon by fortune, even if this blessing came to her by way of Art Turner and was itself of a highly irritable, even petulant, nature.

Was he her friend? Yes, she supposed he was, if your benefactor could be your friend, if someone you saw a couple of times a year, in a small dusty office, in order to determine whether your prose was tripping over your ideas, or your ideas tripping over your prose, if someone who laughed out loud with pleasure when you improved a sentence and then peevishly wondered why you hadn't written it that way to begin with could be your friend, yes, he was her friend.

She thought fondly of him, the way his pink finger tapped at a word (his fingers were oddly flat on the pad, probably from all that tapping), a direct, visceral code of irritation and disapproval. She thought of his hands when she thought of him because that's what she knew best, sitting beside him and watching him tap. He would hop up periodically and bustle away in irritation to look after other books in other stages of production. He would purse his lips and snort in annoyance when the phone rang, reach for it with a severe swoop of his arm, and then, in his soft, insinuating, melodious voice, as if he welcomed the call, and knew who was calling, too, he would say, so gently, "Hello?" Margaret wondered which reaction, the preliminary show of fury, or the gracious, musical greeting, was sincere. She loved his voice and called him often, braving the flourish of anger she could always picture as the phone rang, rewarded by his hello. His finger pressing against a page, his seductive voice, the nape of his neck. Only when he saw something he liked did he lean back from the table and turn his face to hers, and she was always, even after so many years, startled to see his perfectly pleasant, ordinary face.

They spoke on the phone almost daily. He had discovered her, or so he liked to say. In fact, she had attained her odd crossover success while under his tutelage, to his surprise as much as hers. Art had given him the manuscript of a graduate student of intellectual history. He liked it and agreed to publish it; there was a meager advance, a token printing the next spring. She was thrilled, and then one day, or so it seemed, it happened so fast, she was suddenly reading about her "theories," first in little magazines, then in big ones. No one actually read the book, but it had somehow hit a nerve and people talked about it — and bought it. They discussed it at the cocktail parties and dinners that Margaret disliked; they argued about it on the phone. She was Margaret Nathan, author of the best-selling biography, *The Anatomy of Madame de Montigny,* did you ever read it, I have it at home, it's marvelous, I'll lend it to you, but give it back, I've never actually finished it.

Everyone had never actually read anything she'd written, and yet everyone knew who Margaret was, every member of the little circles that for her overlapped into one large, bulging, media-academic-literary-political-Washington-New York ring.

I know no one, she thought. I remember the jangle of a woman's bracelet rather than her face. I know nothing. I remember gossip but forget whom it is about.

She called Richard. The phone rang twice and she imagined him, pushing his chair back with an outraged clatter, thrusting his hand at the phone, pulling it violently off the receiver and to his ear.

"Hello?" he said, so gently, a caress.

"Hello. Busy?"

"No, I'm just stretched out here on my chaise longue doing my nails."

Oh, how very clever, such repartee, she said to herself. But his sarcasm, however tired and predictable, always delighted her and made her laugh, in much the same way puns did. "I'd like to have lunch with you."

"Why?"

"Richard, really, people do have lunch together. Frequently. Particularly people like you, editors, and people like me, writers. I'm sure I'm right about this."

SOMETIMES Margaret wondered at her good fortune. She, Margaret Nathan, who knew nothing, who experienced ideas the way other people experienced landscapes, who drove through them admiringly and wrote scholarly articles about the view, snapshots that became more real for her than the memory of the original — was she a fraud? Or was her success the reward for her hard work, for the loyal, desperate clicking of her camera?

Edward's reaction to her success was a mixture of pride in her and in his choice of her, pride in the outside world's confirmation of his pride, and the simple excitement he always showed when something good occurred, for he was proud of goodness itself, as if it originated with him. In fact, he took the whole thing so much in stride — my wife, Margaret? Well, naturally! — that Margaret herself began to feel comfortable with the situation. It was, she concluded, a freak of nature, a happy fluke, like being born a strawberry blonde. No one deserves to be a strawberry blonde, no one earns it, it is not the reward for virtue. But on the other hand, no one deserves not to be a strawberry blonde either.

The seminar Margaret belonged to met four times a year, a group composed primarily of academics, with some poets, novelists, and highbrow journalists thrown in. For Margaret, it was a rather intimidating group, especially after she'd been discovered by writers, like Jacques Maridou, whom she couldn't even bear to read. Would she now have to discuss Maridou's theories of narrative? Weren't they hopelessly passé yet? She had not escaped critical theory altogether but had ignored it as much as possible, even in France. Her many visits to France, spent mostly in libraries, had made that country seem only more foreign to her: the fashions oddly distant, like costumes in an old James Bond movie; the food fetishistic; the intellectuals enthusiastically cynical. But now, *she* was a fashion in France. It was the bicentennial of the Revolution, and Margaret's book had been reprinted under the title *Anatomie sans culotte,* with Maridou's essay as an introduction.

One of the seminar's quarterly meetings was a Christmas party held in the large university-subsidized, West Side apartment of the group's chairman. The chairman herself, a colorful woman who taught Italian literature and claimed to have been Rossellini's production assistant during the filming of *Open City* (as a *teenager* — she was as vain about her age as she was about her avant-garde credentials), stood at the door to greet Margaret and Edward. After a flurry of *ciaos* and kisses, Edward threw an arm over the shoulder of a dapper man and wandered off, speaking German.

Margaret watched Edward walk away and thought that he was like a drug, a dangerous, potent, exhilarating drug, that the more she had of him the more she seemed to need him and want him. Did that mean she had too little of him, or too much? She noted the apartment's ornate cherry moldings with envy and turned her attention to the roomful of her colleagues. Which name went with which face? And then, which idea went with which name? Margaret thought there ought to be nametags with a person's discipline, political bent, and latest publication printed neatly beneath the name. "Timothy Shiller, economist, neoliberal, *Why I Am Not a Socialist — And Never Was, Either.*" "Leonard Winks, medieval historian, far left, *The Importance of Cross-Dressing in the Symbolism of the Eleventh-Century Promissory Note.*" But of course there were no labels, and anonymous bodies drifted past her as she leaned forlornly against a bookcase, listening to an enormous, effeminate art historian discuss rap music with a middle-aged woman she didn't recognize. Was it an indigenous art form? Or a commodity? Margaret didn't really care, but she felt the warmth of academic familiarity comfort her in her distress.

A pleasant-looking girl smiled in delight when she saw Margaret.

"Hello!" Margaret said. I know you, she thought. And I like you. Who *are* you?

"Yes, I read it," said a tall, pink man with a slight English accent to the young woman. "You were *laboriously* fair."

"You gave my book a nice blurb," said a man with a beard whom Margaret recognized as a professor of American history.

"I did?" Margaret said.

"My dear young lady," said a graying old man with a heavy Eastern European accent, "I have just written you a letter."

He was a professor of philosophy, she thought. The New School? No, Brooklyn College. Very partial to the thought of someone no one had ever heard of. Seventeenth century? And he was a translator, too. Czech, was he? Or Polish? He was a neat and compact man, as if he'd been specially designed to fold easily for travel. Jan! His name was Jan something. Comenius? Jan Comenius.

"I have invited you to Prague. That is, the Comenius Society has invited you to Prague to speak."

Ah. Jan Comenius was his philosopher, not his name. She remembered. A Bohemian protestant.

"I read your article in *Quod,* my dear young lady. 'The Satin Underground.' Very amusing title, very droll. And timely, too, this article. Don't you think the dissemination of revolutionary ideas through popular, underground art such as pornography is an interesting antecedent to the *samizdat* publications of my country? *From the Satin Underground to the Velvet Revolution!* What do you think?"

"Well . . ."

"What fun you will have, my dear young lady. I have just come back. 'Havel in the Castle'! That is what all the posters say! There are people dancing in the streets."

"Yes, I'm sure. I mean I've heard —"

"The Comenius Society will pay your expenses, there is a small honorarium —"

"That's very generous, and I would love to go to Prague —" Prague! Where whole editions of John Ashbery sold out in a single day! Where playwrights led revolutions! Where ideas rose up as if on their own, pure and untainted by market research! Where even popular culture was culture! "Especially now, my God! But don't you think my work is, well, in light of what has happened, almost trivial? Why would anyone in the middle of a real-life democratic revolution want to hear old plagiarized smut and watered-down empiricism?"

Jan wagged his finger at her. "But that's how revolutions are made!" he said. "And that's what real-life revolutions are for!"

Margaret laughed, flattered. "Thank you," she said. "Thank you for thinking of me. Prague! Do you have any idea when? Is there a date yet?"

"It's rather short notice. Impromptu, you might say. This is a revolution, after all! Next month? To return there, after so many years in New York — for me it was a miracle, my dear young lady. A miracle."

Margaret listened to the old man, who now fell into a comfortable monologue, obviously his favorite monologue. Teachers are wonderful, Margaret thought. They take full conversational responsibility. She leaned against the bookcase, half closed her eyes, and basked in someone else's knowledge and confidence in sharing it.

"It is fashionable now to say that truth is just a convention," he said. He took out a cigarette, lit it, and continued, waving his hand as he spoke, leaving a soft, silver trail. "But in Prague, where people have had to live a lie for so long, truth is no convention. It is a moral reality."

Comenius believed in educational reform, he explained, and smoke wafted from his mouth and nostrils. Margaret watched it evaporate, politely nodded her head, and waited in a pleasant state of excited passivity for him to continue. Everyone knew that. Everyone in Czechoslovakia, anyway. He touched her arm every now and then, a gentle emphasis. She smiled and listened and watched as he spoke. But more important, he continued, reaching with both hands for both her arms now, his cigarette dangling from his lips, more important, there was a direct philosophical line from Comenius to Václav Havel, one that bypassed completely the Cartesian thinking that dominated Western thought. As Margaret listened, she thought, Only Eastern Europeans and teenagers can smoke without shame anymore.

"I love to speak," he said, interrupting himself apologetically.

"I love to listen," she said. Then she added, "To you." And his words and pale cigarette smoke surrounded her again: For Descartes, truth and beauty were not a part of objective reality but were subjective, lesser, opposed. But in central Europe, Comenius understood that reality was meaningful in itself, that truth and beauty were intrinsic values, the very structure of reality. For Havel, for Czechoslovakia, truth had a moral urgency; truth had the force of reality.

"But I am so sorry, Miss Nathan," he said suddenly. "I am warm on this subject and really have been lecturing you, shamelessly lecturing you. Let us talk about beer. In Prague, the beer has the force of reality, too, you might say. It is worth the trip, my dear, for the magnificent beer alone."

MARGARET MOVED through the rooms of the shaggy old apartment, looking for Edward. She wanted to tell him that she had been invited to speak in Prague. They could drink beer there, together. They could encounter truth, beauty, and witness a revolution all at the same time. Why, they could go to the Czech Philharmonic after all.

And she imagined walking with Edward through a city she had never seen. Had she even seen a picture of Prague until the newspapers began running photographs of students huddled around candles at the foot of the statue of King Wenceslaus on his horse? She imagined walking beneath King Wenceslaus, gently stepping over flickering tapers and brave students wrapped in knitted scarves.

Next month. That was soon. She would have to start preparing something to say immediately. Next month. Well, if it was next month, she realized, she would have to meet truth and beauty and the transcendent pilsner on her own. For that was the beginning of the new term, and Edward, the Virgil to her wandering Dante (and to everyone else's), would have to stay home and teach, teach other people, teach students. That was a pity. Edward was always good to have around. In case she forgot something. Like her name. Well, she could always make one up. She hadn't traveled alone in years. And after her trips with Edward, orgies of food, sex, and culture, it didn't seem quite possible to travel alone. What would she talk about? And with whom? And Margaret hated to give lectures, suffering from stage fright, losing her place in her notes, forgetting the subject of the talk in midsentence. But still — Prague! Kafka's city! Havel's city! And Comenius's city, too, of course.

"Oh, you wrote that book," a young man said to her.

Margaret reddened but stood her ground. She nodded bravely.

"Oh." He smiled and walked away.

A woman began talking to Margaret about the difficulty of assessing the relationship between the forms of popular culture (by which she meant images, she considerately explained) and their consumers. Margaret wondered if she was referring to the Nielsen ratings system, but then the woman noted with some conviction that "pop had never really signified with one discourse," and Margaret knew that she was not. Oh, Prague! she thought. Where are you when I need you?

She thought how much she would miss Edward, even for a week, how much she liked him, how often she saw him, how little Kafka she had read. She found Edward chatting in Russian (It sounded like Russian, but then, who knew? Perhaps he'd learned Polish on the sly, or Czech) with a skinny, handsome man with bad teeth, and when there was a pause, Edward introduced her, she smiled, did not even take in the man's name long enough to forget it, waited till he'd drifted away, and then told Edward she'd been invited to Prague. "To talk about traditions in underground literature," she said.

"Dirty books? That's marvelous. Shall I join you? No, of course I can't if you're off so soon. The term will be just beginning." He offered her a glass of some sort of spiced wine. "What a grisly business Christmas is," he said. "I have been thinking of a plan for calendar reform which would improve matters immensely. It is obviously incompatible with the exciting educational advances of today for children to be expected to remember complex rhymes such as 'Thirty days hath September, April, June, and November,' don't you agree? So I propose that ten months be of thirty-one days each, leaving just two exceptions: February, with its twenty-eight, and December, which would have only twenty-seven days. Consequently, New Year's Eve would come forty-eight hours after Christmas Day and only twenty-four after Boxing Day. The gain for sanity, the boost to production, the sheer beauty of the scheme from all points of view, make me wonder why it has not been promulgated before." He put his arm around her. His hand squeezed her shoulder. "You haven't been away from me, Margaret, in such a very long time."

"Let's go home," Margaret said softly.

"Yes," Edward said, and he kissed her head.

"I'll be lost without you, Edward. Like Virgil without Dante. I mean, Dante without Virgil."

"No, darling. Like Joseph K. You're going to Prague, you see, not to hell."

Margaret frowned, embarrassed, and walked off.

" 'Then my leader went on with great strides . . .' " Edward recited the lines from Dante at the top of his lungs, following her as he spoke. " 'Her looks disturbed somewhat with anger; so I left these burdened souls, following the prints of the dear feet.' "

A WEEK or so later, Till called to invite Margaret to a dinner party in honor of a young unproduced playwright she had taken up. Till discovered young unproduced playwrights. It was a hobby. She was much admired for her generosity, although Margaret had noticed that she then proceeded to give the young unproduced playwrights advice like, Why not take a couple of years off and go to medical school? or, Your work is much too important to be produced in such a small theater, which pretty much assured they would become old unproduced playwrights.

Margaret did not think she could face another evening at Till's large, busy table just yet, so she suggested they have lunch together instead.

"I'll bring Lily, too," Till said.

Yes, Margaret thought. Why not recreate an earlier era, when lonely girlfriends gathered together over coffee shop tables, covered wagons briefly turned away from the wilderness toward the warm fire? Sometimes Margaret wondered if she missed being lonely. There had been a certain down-and-out vigor to her plight which appeared lean, almost glamorous, compared to the round contentment she experienced now.

They met at a hamburger place in the neighborhood. Margaret got there first and watched Till clatter in on gold sequined high heels, rings on her fingers and bells on her toes, or very nearly. Till, like John F. Kennedy, did not wear a coat. It was a gift, she said, her inner warmth.

Together they watched Lily make her entrance. Her cheeks were, as always, just barely flushed, her short wavy hair in easy disarray. An open, beckoning, corruptible-peasant-faced sort of person, she maneuvered through the tables with her lips slightly parted and her eyes slightly glazed. Lily always looked as if she had just been fucked. This look appealed to Margaret. How did one achieve it?

"Oy, what a day," Lily said, sliding into the booth with a motion so fluid and so revealing of the many positive features of her figure that Margaret wondered if she practiced sliding into coffee shop booths, if she went to a health club specializing in coffee-shop-booth-sliding workouts. And one, two, three, sliiide!

"Notice how the menu says 'We,'" Lily said immediately, pointing to Till's open menu with one hand while unzipping her motorcycle jacket with the other. "'*We* have a meat loaf special today'! Do you think that 'we' includes us? Of course not. The 'we' refers to them. Hello, doll." And she kissed Till on the cheek, then leaned across the table and kissed Margaret.

Margaret now remembered why she hadn't seen Lily much in the years since college. Because she disliked Lily. At least, she disliked a good thirty percent of the words that tumbled happily from Lily's red, cherub lips.

"It's just a menu," Margaret said. And she ordered the meat loaf.

"We have no meat loaf today," said the waitress.

Lily giggled. "Never trust the transparency of meaning, Margaret."

"Now, girls," Till said in the fey, show-biz tone that had been popular among them in college, but that she alone had kept up.

"It's still just a menu," Margaret said irritably.

"I wrote my dissertation about menus," Lily said. Then she turned the sultry warmth of her gaze on Margaret, smiled, squeezed Margaret's arm, and seemed so genuinely pleased to see her that Margaret smiled and knew she must forgive anything Lily said because of the way she said it — the flirtatious, absurdly good-natured warmth; her voice, the whisper of a starlet; and the way she giggled deliciously. And then, perhaps most important, Lily had always seemed to like Margaret so much. That was greatly in her favor.

"They leave their telltale signs everywhere," Lily continued, looking at her own menu in its dark green plastic cover. "The text of their exclusion is so public. Oh, I like your do, Margaret," she added, patting Margaret's hair, which had just been cut. Then she leaned forward, and continued, "You know, I wake up in the morning and I feel like a sex object."

Because she thought this sounded glamorous, Margaret examined Lily more closely. The tight black leather skirt was de rigueur for a feminist art critic, she supposed. But the red lace bodice seemed a more personal statement. Well, if one had shapely shoulders and beautiful breasts, the left breast blessed further with a beauty mark, why shouldn't one display them? If this caused men to leer at one and treat one as a sex object, it was a reflection on them, the men, wasn't it? There was something wonderfully innocent and nearly tragic about Lily, Margaret thought, like a flower, bursting with gaudy color and health, swaying in the garden breeze, alluring by nature, but shy of every admiring glance, seeing there its own — pluck! — mortality.

~~ ~~ ~~

We determined that we could do no better, in the pursuit of enlightened understanding, than to examine the nature of friendship using our own growing friendship as a model. My pupil, my "friend," had already set for herself a course of reading of such a noble and ambitious tone, a road leading to such heights and yet lined with such pitfalls, that I felt compelled, as a friend, to accompany her, to act as her guide, to take her hand and lead her.

MYSELF: Education determines a man. Men are born ignorant, not stupid. They are made stupid by education. But you, you have somehow escaped and remained as unstained as a child.

Now your education can begin. First, your senses will awaken. You will see and hear and smell, you will taste and you will touch.

And then, ah! As your senses awaken, all the inlets to the mind are set open; now, now, all the objects of nature will rush thither.

SHE: Thither?

MYSELF: Thither.

SHE: To the inlets?

MYSELF: They will rush into the deepest inlets. To all the inlets of the mind.

Rameau's niece, formerly a wretched, sniveling infant (as I vividly recalled when once she identified herself), an indefatigable nuisance, petulant, weeping, quarreling with other little nuisances, a graceless, unruly thing, who had yet been worshiped as a goddess by her parents, blinded as they were by nature, was now truly a goddess. Please, do not deceive yourselves that my judgment was likewise clouded by parental sentiment. I felt not at all like a parent to this exquisite little girl whom any man of discernment would have described, as I often did to myself, as a figure of such elevating charms that just to look at her, the way her shoulders curved in relation to the equally elegant curve of her white neck, and the manner in which her waist, with its own, quite unique little curve, yet was bound up so eloquently with the rest, was to experience that these curves achieved a most pleasing unity of effect, an effect of beauty so powerful that I confess that during one of our meetings (this time in the library, for it was raining), before I could even realize what I was doing, I had flung myself to my knees before her.

Alone in the room, the others having retired, we faced each other, she seated, still clutching the volume she had been reading, myself at her feet, wondering what I had done and fearing more than anything her displeasure at my intemperate behavior, when suddenly the silence was broken by her soft, pure voice. My pupil began to read aloud.

SHE [reading]: When I observe the relation objects have to me [here she glanced at me, then lowered her dark, bright eyes to the page], I am in like manner attentive to the impressions I receive. [She paused, and I, heeding what I took to be the import of her words but even more her agitated expression, placed my hand on hers. She trembled, dropped the book upon her lap, then quickly recovered it and resumed reading.] These impressions are either agreeable [her breathing seemed to change to a rhythm of particular intensity] or disagreeable. Now, in either case, what is judgment? [She closed her book, put it aside, took my hand in both of her own.] To tell what I feel. [Reciting now from memory, my pupil drew my hand to her breast.] To judge [she was whispering now] is to feel. To judge is to feel.

∽ ∽ ∽

"SO YOU had lunch with your lady friends," Richard said. "Did you wear hats?"

"Yes, and we counted out the change and loudly discussed how we would divide it." It was her evening call to him, when she lay back in bed with pages piled beside her and reviewed the day that was nearly done. She smiled, accidentally pressing several of the phone's buttons with her cheek, triggering a long series of clicks and beeps through which she could hear Richard muttering.

"Richard," she said, when the phone was quiet. "Men are born ignorant, not stupid. But what if you remain ignorant?"

"I wouldn't know."

"It's very difficult being an ignorant intellectual."

"Well," Richard said thoughtfully, "I suppose it's better than being a stupid intellectual."

Margaret sighed. Then she read to Richard from *Rameau's Niece*.

"'I must compliment you on the great care which you take of my education,' says the little girl, 'and on your unwearied perseverance, my dear teacher, and the pains which you bestow on me. You are no more wanting, I am persuaded, in skill than in industry.' That's Hume, Richard. My author stole that from Hume, from *Dialogues Concerning Natural Religion*. Just listen to what he's done to poor Hume! 'By continual precept and instruction,' replies the philosopher, 'and I hope, too, by example, I shall imprint deeply on your tender mind, and your equally tender lips, an habitual reverence for these principles of kissing. Then at last, having thus tamed your mind to a proper submission, I will have no longer any scruple of opening to you the greatest mysteries of all.'"

"No one ever speaks to me like that," Richard said.

"I am," Margaret said. "I do." The pillow was cool against her cheek. Richard's voice was soft and alluring, and she felt suddenly very tenderly toward him, always there on the other end of the phone when she needed him, when she wanted him. She felt tenderly toward him and toward the world at large, she realized when she'd hung up, as she lay in wait for Edward, toward whom she felt most tenderly of all, most tenderly indeed.

"I have no longer any scruple," she said when he came in looking for a pencil, "of opening to you the greatest mysteries of all."

"Reading that smut again, eh? That's a good girl."

∽ ∽ ∽

So that our thoughtful discussions should be neither hindered by inclement weather nor interrupted by other, less philosophical members of the household, we began to meet indoors and at night, and in our search for privacy decided on my bedroom as the best location.

Philosophy was a pursuit that came naturally to her. Having taught herself Latin at a tender age, she was knowledgeable of the classics and eager to learn more. I was eager to teach her.

MYSELF: Take nothing on trust. That is the first lesson. Seek whatever instruction is to be obtained from observation and experience.

SHE: Let me begin, then, to observe and to experience. I long to begin, for all have an equal right to be enlightened respecting their interests, to share in the acquisition of truth.

My pupil, seeing no other piece of furniture on which to rest her charming figure, had sat upon the bed and, then, recognizing how unnatural was that position in that place and seeking, as always, to achieve the harmony and balance necessary to beauty, she lay down.

Seeing her thus attending to the laws of aesthetics so dutifully, it occurred to me that I could do nothing less than join her in order to help her to acquire whatever understanding she sought in any way I was able to. I began to contemplate those various ways, thoroughly enjoying the exquisite anticipation of the intellectual exchange I foresaw. For it is often true that foresight of an approaching pleasure is in itself an actual pleasure, and I was soon transported by my imagination.

But presently, as I stood and pondered these lovely issues, I noticed that she, on the bed, seemed to become what I can describe only as agitated, her cheeks taking on an unnatural but nonetheless delightful flush, her breathing quick and strained, so that I feared she might faint and quickly bent over her reclining figure and loosened her garments, whereupon she gratefully pulled me to her and expressed again her impatient desire to begin her lesson.

This without further mental preparation I therefore commenced.

MYSELF: I will begin with the senses. I must, naturally, consider the objects of my sensations. Recognizing the necessity of experience for understanding and hoping to impart this important value to you, my pupil, I will now consider the particular objects before me with great attention.

As I began carefully to investigate the immediate objects of my sensations, that is the ravishing graces and delights of a young girl reclining upon my bed, this activity seemed to stir her intellectual faculties in a highly agreeable manner, just as I had hoped and anticipated. Our lesson had at last begun in earnest.

MYSELF: There are two kinds of perception. First, I will demonstrate to you the meaning of 'impressions.' Impressions are perceptions that are forceful and violent, external objects pressing in upon you.

SHE: At this moment, not only do I sense a glorious external object forcefully pressing in upon me, but in truth I feel myself to be nothing but a bundle or collection of different perceptions . . .

MYSELF: . . . which succeed each other with inconceivable rapidity?

SHE: Yes! Exactly! They are in perpetual flux and movement!

After some time, during which we continued our investigation into the nature of perception with a mutual interest and single-minded devotion to experience which precluded for the time being any discussion other than the occasional cry that signified the perception of a particularly forceful impression, I felt true friendship to be within our grasp, and I experienced a flash of understanding, of sublime illumination (a flash, I concluded from various observations, that I thoroughly shared with my pupil), and in my sudden enlightenment, I cried out these words:

MYSELF: The end of the social art is to secure and extend for all the enjoyment of the common rights which impartial nature has bequeathed to us all!

She answered in a voice thick with understanding.

SHE: Your logic, sir, is rigorous, your assertions sublime.

෨෨ ෨෨ ෨෨

"DON'T YOU GET tired of all the stuffy academics you hang around with?" Margaret asked Edward one morning. She lay in bed, turned on her side, looking at him.

"Are *you* tired of them?"

"No. But I like stuffy academics. That's why I married you."

Edward smiled.

"But what about the trendy ones?" Margaret went on. "Like my friends? Like Lily? Imagine Lily as a colleague. She's bad enough as a friend, but at least I don't have to take her seriously. I don't have to argue with her at department meetings. Your department is crawling with Lilys. How can you stand it?"

Margaret was actually envious of Edward, envious of the regular, comfortable world of academia. If only one didn't have to teach! She too could be a professor with a little office, with rumpled colleagues and spiteful intrigues and adoring students. But one did have to teach, and Margaret preferred to live in unstructured solitude rather than face a sea of students, arrogant and needy.

"Stand it? I live for it!" Edward said. "'All men by nature desire to know,' said Aristotle. And I am in a place dedicated to the desire to know. I fulfill the desire to know, I satisfy it. Even Lily, the eminently silly Lily, desires to know. She's wrong about everything, isn't she, but on she rushes, determined, lusty, indomitable in her quest, a creature of desire, of the desire to know. Ah, Lily. How many of her students desire to know little Lily, I wonder."

"Oh, please," Margaret said, and then she cupped her chin in her hand.

Sometimes she felt as small and aloof as a spider, hanging by its thread. No ground beneath its several feet, nor water. But at least a spider could spin a web, a frail sticky gathering place for stray passersby. Till had spun a web, drawing people to her simply by the strength of her desire, her desire to have them there. Edward had spun a web of enthusiasm and pleasure for all around him. Of course, this was a perverse and counterproductive way of viewing friendship: as a trap for struggling, buzzing prey. Still, Margaret thought, shall I spin a web? Isn't that better than being the struggling, buzzing prey in the nets of others?

"Margaret, you're so competitive," Edward said when she voiced these ideas on the nature of sociability. "And you're so serious. You're even more earnest than I am, and no one is more earnest than I. Friendship! It's not a commandment, my darling."

"Yes, but you hear people talking of falling in love, don't you? When you talk of friends, though, you don't fall at all. You make friends."

"Well then! To work!"

Margaret sighed.

"Anyway, I'm your friend, aren't I?" Edward said.

"That's just the trouble, Edward." She looked at him and

thought how large he loomed in her life, filling it with interesting talk and real understanding and tender exchanges and good sex and irritating habits and jokes and obscure quotations. He helped her in her work and liked her and cherished her. She wanted nothing else. It didn't seem right. "It doesn't seem right. To be satisfied. Don't you want more?"

"'I exist as I am — that is enough; if no other in the world be aware, I sit content; and if each and all be aware, I sit content.'"

"Oh, Edward, for heaven's sake. You go ahead and sit content. And get obscenely fat on oysters like Walt Whitman. Is that who you quoted? Well, he's dead now. And I'm not."

"Margaret, bless you, you've gone mad at last. How I've longed for this moment. A mad wife! Lock her in the attic. Chain her! Feed her oysters — *against her will*. Ravage her till dawn. Till noon! Quite my ideal, a mad wife."

Oh well, Margaret thought, as Edward pulled her to him. Dissatisfaction can wait.

EDWARD SOMETIMES brought students home for dinner, and Margaret had always welcomed these gatherings, for they pitted her against amateurs only, an enemy far more frightened of her than she was of them. At one of these pleasant, unthreatening dinners, Margaret listened with some interest as a student of Edward's, a boy from Oregon, described his father's mink farm, and as she listened she watched the other student guest. She was from some suburb of Boston, pretty, a little shy, and she had not taken her eyes off Edward all evening.

I used to be a girl from some suburb of Boston, pretty, a little shy, and I used to gaze with longing at my professors, Margaret thought. Have you come here to haunt me?

Edward smiled indulgently at the girl, but then Edward smiled indulgently at the world. Still, Margaret thought. And she turned away from the girl with a sinking feeling, as a man turns hopelessly from his fate, and then stared at Edward without realizing it, until he turned and smiled at her and reached for her hand and squeezed it.

MARGARET had been talking to Till for almost forty minutes, which for her pretty much obviated any need to see Till for at least two months, when it occurred to her that people like Till and Edward didn't let that happen. They never allowed the comfort of the telephone to overwhelm the pleasure of companionship, never let the phone keep them from their duty to appreciate all around them, to celebrate the existence of their friends by glorying in their company, never sunk to that enervated state in which one wondered if going out to keep a date might horribly disturb the aimless tranquillity of one's day.

"Have you and Lily gotten together again?" Till asked.

"No."

"Oh. You seemed to hit it off. Are you planning to see her soon?" Till said.

"I don't know," Margaret said. "What about you? Do you want to have lunch again? I think I'm becoming an eccentric. I think I have to become a better socialized person."

"No, no," Till said in a determined voice. "You and Lily have lunch without me. That will be better."

"Ah. You think I should strike out on my own, blaze new

trails. But I never know what Lily is talking about. Still, there's something sweet about her, don't you think?"

Till said, "Like fruit."

"Fruit?" Margaret had not thought of fruit. But there was something so charming about Lily, an utterly benign person chattering happily about the oppressive, phallocentric monstrosity that was modern existence. What a mess, she seemed to be saying. Isn't it grand?

"So you like Lily?" Till said.

"Don't you? She's your friend."

"You know that Lily and I lived together for four years?"

Margaret was puzzled. Of course she knew that. They had been roommates after she and Till had been roommates, and had shared an apartment for one year after school.

"Anyway," Till went on, "when will you two get together? I think this week would be fine. Do you want me to call her for you? I have to call her anyway. If you like her, and she likes you, I think this is a good thing. This friendship."

"Well, I don't know. I can call her, I guess. If I want to. Thank you for taking such an interest in me and my socialization."

MARGARET DID MEET Lily that week, at the same coffee shop. Why not? Lily blew in wearing a short swirling coat held closed by one large button and black spandex leggings, her complexion tinted by the cold, fresh air. Margaret noticed her teeth, which were small, all the same size, and white, like little tiles.

"Hello, doll," Lily said, lighting a cigarette and exhaling a cloud of smoke straight up into the air, 1930s style. "Have you read your Ovid, yet, Margaret?" She reached for a menu. "The menu!"

"The menu."

Lily was smiling, smoking, and thoughtfully examining the

daily specials inserted in a special narrow plastic page. Was she pondering the menu as a reification of woman's role, a paradigm of organized control over woman's life, the repressive figuration of woman's qualities and skills?

"I think I'll have a bacon cheeseburger," Lily said. She took off her swirly coat with its big round button to reveal a tight suede tunic laced up the front in medieval peasant fashion, her breasts spilling over the top. She ran her hands through her short hair, fluffing it.

"Funny," she said, tilting her head and staring at Margaret. "Funny we didn't really know each other at school." Her whispery voice gave way to a little sigh. She put her hand under her chin and pouted slightly.

"Well, I guess I didn't see too much of Till or her friends after the first year. I retreated to the library."

"The library," Lily said softly, "is one of the mechanisms of discipline, capturing the individual in a system of registration and accumulation of documents."

The way she said it, Margaret thought, in her throaty whisper, sucking on one dainty finger, she made the library sound like soft-core bondage. Oh! Discipline me with your mechanism! More, oh, more!

"So what are you working on?" Margaret asked, not sure how else to respond to Dewey Decimal de Sade.

"I'm thinking of writing something about music, for a change. Rachmaninoff," Lily said.

Margaret sighed. Poor Rachmaninoff. What crime had he committed to cause him to fall prey to this pretentious sexpot fraud?

"He's not a woman," Margaret said. "Is he?"

"Ah, but he might just as well have been a woman," Lily said tenderly. "Poor Rachmaninoff."

"You *like* Rachmaninoff?" She herself loved Rachmaninoff but saw no reason to tell anyone about it.

"Look," Lily said, "a case must be made for the second tier. Genius is an oppressive male construct. Genius, genius, genius. Enough with the genius."

"You like Rachmaninoff because he's *second-rate*?"

Lily smiled and began to hum loudly a particularly lush passage from the Symphonic Dances.

Margaret, though sorely tempted, forced herself not to hum along. One had one's pride. But she did regard Lily with a new respect and with a growing warmth.

"Do you like Trollope, too?" she asked hopefully.

INSPIRED BY Lily's description, Margaret went to the mechanism of discipline the next morning, but it failed to live up to its reputation, and she felt restless after only an hour and began to stare into space. The anonymous author of *Rameau's Niece* had lifted passages from so many philosophers, and with such abandon, that Margaret knew she would be spending months tracking down sources. The author was well versed in the literature of the age. Was he some provincial boy who had come to the glamorous big city to be a philosophe? There were plenty of them in Paris during the Enlightenment, failed intellectuals writing smut and peddling it to get by. Or perhaps he was a bored clergyman passing the time between nones and matins. And why "he"? Couldn't the author have been a woman like Madame de Montigny? Margaret sometimes wondered if *Rameau's Niece* was written as a hoax, like Diderot's *La Religieuse,* which Diderot and a friend began as a series of letters to another friend, signing them with the name of a fictitious nun. Or it could have been meant as a vehicle for edification, like classic comics. She had once read a fanciful description of the living quarters of Crébillon *père* and *fils* which had the two of them in a garret filled with large dogs drooling and shedding immoderately, and it was thus that Margaret liked to imagine her own author, pen in hand, animals sprawled and snoring on the Louis Quinze chaise.

She finished the translation almost with regret, the way one finishes a Victorian novel. For now she was torn from the bosom of the manuscript, or it was torn from hers, and she would have to present it to the world. She planned to drop it off with Richard and then have lunch with him that afternoon.

In the subway, she bought a *Street News* from a homeless man and read how Marianne Faithfull had been homeless when she was a drug addict, except that sometimes she went to her mother's house to have a bath.

She was still half an hour early. She looked in some stores, then stood around for a while in the dirty cold, then called Richard.

"Hi, can we have lunch yet?"

"Margaret, I've been trying to call you. I'm sorry, dear, no lunch. Where were you off to so early in the morning? An affair with the milkman? At his place? I'm sorry, Margaret, I really am, actually, but it's an emergency. I have an engagement at the Simon Gleason Residence for Senior Citizens."

"Moving?" Margaret said.

"Uncle Herbert is moving. Uncle Herbert must move, must be moved, with the greatest dispatch. Uncle Herbert arrived on my doorstep in his pajamas this morning. I left him with my landlady while I find him a suitable place to move to, preferably by this afternoon. Would you like to have lunch with Uncle Herbert, Margaret, since having lunch looms so large in your imagination these days?"

Margaret put another quarter in the phone as she thought. The path toward socialization seemed to her strewn with insurmountable obstacles. If she wished to have friends, she would have to be a friend, or at the very least approximate however it is that friends behave. But how is that? I am very much downcast, she thought, as they said a century or so ago. And how did friends behave a century or so ago? She seemed to remember a lot of noble withdrawing going on in all those novels, men nobly withdrawing from women to preserve reputations, women nobly withdrawing from men, leaving them to other, more — or less — needy, women. Maybe Margaret should nobly withdraw. Then she could go home.

"Do you want me to come with you?" She said it impulsively, instinctively, and immediately regretted her words.

SHE SPENT THE DAY trailing Richard from one nursing home to the next. The first was as dirty as a hospital, Richard said. The second too gloomy and full of old people. In the third, the receptionist asked Margaret if it was she who wanted a room, and Margaret politely said, No, it wasn't.

That was where Richard signed up Uncle Herbert. He was concerned because the place was run by the Salvation Army, and Uncle Herbert did like his little nip. But the room was quite nice. Some of the people there were still functioning rather well. It was clean and nearly cheerful. Richard remarked on all these things in a muted, sadly hopeful manner, as if he were trying to convince himself, or Uncle Herbert, or perhaps Margaret. But Margaret didn't need convincing. In fact, she had been particularly taken aback when the receptionist had asked if it was she who expected to move in, because just a moment before she had been thinking that she might be happy to settle there, that it might be pleasant to live in a place where people you barely knew made the meals, the beds, the conversation. The cool, pale anonymity seemed somehow restful. Edward's boundless vitality sometimes made her want to lie down.

"It's just that you must be over sixty-five to get in here," the receptionist had hastily explained after Richard began to roar with laughter.

"Well, Margaret, that *is* a disappointment," he said, wiping tears from his eyes.

Margaret was a little disappointed with Richard, actually. She had expected that this personal and emotional experience would cause some kind of bonding, but in fact she felt further from her editor than she ever had in the past. He seemed somehow less interesting outside of the office. There were all these distractions, all these other people and other responsibilities interfering, and she recalled a little wistfully the last time she had seen him, seated at his desk, fussing through several piles of paper until he found one particular pile, her pile. "Aha!" he had cried, with genuine enthusiasm, and she had to catch her breath, waiting as he prepared to turn his attention, pure and unencumbered, to her.

MARGARET THOUGHT about Richard a lot after the day they spent touring nursing homes, in ways that were new to her: he appeared to her from unfamiliar angles. The features she identified as Richard had receded and revealed a stranger. Attached to the prim, irritable, rich, and melodious voice had been added a body, a walk, a configuration of gestures. Richard was tall. This was something she had never recognized. He was broad. And in his lavender oxford shirt, his coarse tweed jacket, his pressed corduroy pants, loafers, and gray crew cut, he was oddly fey, instead of simply fey. This troubled her. She had never thought of him in this way, and she didn't want to. Whatever else he was in civilian life, Richard on duty had always been simply her editor, hers. He existed to the extent that he interacted with her, with Margaret Nathan. This other business, this crisply tailored homosexual with a brush cut and an uncle would not do.

જ્જ જ્જ જ્જ

I lay on the bed and contemplated Rameau's niece above me,
contemplated those regions of the world of thought which the
wise delight to contemplate. (Dare to know! is a proposition
we had begun, with considerable energy, to investigate the night
before and were continuing now to study in greater detail.) She,
too, pondered the situation before her with gentle but eager
attention.

SHE: Is this what our great thinkers mean when they speak of
man having already arrived at his highest point of improvement?
MYSELF: It requires little penetration to perceive how imper-
fect is still the development of man; how much farther the sphere
of his duties, including therein the influence of his actions upon
the welfare of his fellow creatures, may be extended —

Here my pupil, struck by perfect understanding of my carefully
chosen words, cried out in a way that did momentarily discon-
cert me, but I quickly recovered and continued my discourse.

MYSELF: How much farther the sphere of his duties may be
extended —

She cried out again, but I continued, undeterred.

MYSELF: . . . by a more fixed, a more profound and more
accurate . . .

At this moment, I admit, I finally broke off my lecture entirely,
overcome by my own argument for observing facts and precisely registering sensation.

In the quiet that followed, I heard her voice, joyful, close to
my ear.

SHE: I still learn! My instruction is not yet finished. When will
it be? When I shall no longer be sensible!
MYSELF: The true delight of virtue is the pleasure of having
performed a durable service.

જ્જ જ્જ જ્જ

MARGARET had eventually arranged another lunch date with Till, who was now waiting for her outside the narrow restaurant. It wasn't just narrow, it was short, too. There were only four small tables in it, all of them, as always, taken. The restaurant was called You Are Hungry.

"Do you want to go someplace else?" Till said. "I don't want to go someplace else, but I will if you do."

"It's freezing," Margaret said, but she did not move. She had already slipped into the mild, semiconscious state adopted during the early stages of waiting in line. Later on, she might explode into a rage. But in neither case did she, or anyone she knew, ever leave and go to another place. "What are you working on?" she said. Till was her friend, she was used to having her as a friend, but Margaret rarely had that much she wanted to say to her.

"Well, it's about the space shuttle, actually. What people on a space shuttle really talk about, you know? Divorce, childhood, their children's reading scores. There's some singing, too. You know, Margaret, one of the characters is a little like you." Till looked at her in that way she had — deeply and with a single-minded purposeful attention.

"Really?" Margaret said, embarrassed, but also intrigued. "What am I like?"

"I don't know, actually."

Margaret blew on her cold fingers. Till was adorned by fringes today, beaded with jet. Was it a blouse? A jacket? Below she wore a long, tight black silk skirt, and her arms, waist, and neck were encircled by bands of Navajo silver and turquoise.

"So, have you seen Lily?" Till said.

"Mm-hmm."

"Oh."

Margaret thought that she could now easily begin to talk about what she always talked to Till about, which was basically nothing, a pleasant, comfortable code of small talk that said, We're old friends. But Margaret thought, Is that enough? Shouldn't I try to raise the level of discourse, and so strengthen, heighten, and enrich this friendship?

When she was younger, she talked to her girlfriends about boys. Maybe Till was going out with a boy and they could talk about it. Or a man. Or an old goat. Of course, maybe she wasn't going out with a man of any age, in which case the question would either offend her or depress her. And even if she was going out with someone, she wouldn't admit it, would she, being happily married and all.

What should Margaret say now, Margaret? Margaret should talk about current events, Margaret. Cold and confused, she tried to reconstruct her morning conversation with Edward. "So now the, uh, Nicaraguans can advance to a premodern artisan culture," she said.

"Jimmy Carter makes a wonderful ex-president, doesn't he?"

Margaret, you will have to remember that. It's more, well, more *conversational* than what you said. Premodern artisan culture indeed. She shifted from foot to foot. What now? She looked at Till, who jingled pleasantly, like a pony pulling a sled. Margaret smiled. And then Margaret, to her relief, had an inspiration, a conversational idea.

"You look great, Till," she said. "Radiant." She smiled again, proudly, waiting for a response.

"So you saw Lily?"

"Yes. She said menus are a sign of male domination. I think."

"Oh," Till said. She tapped her little foot. "That's all?"

"Well, some stuff about the library."

"Oh. Okay. Um, Margaret, do you want to know a secret?"

Margaret leaned her head down closer to Till's.

Till said, "Do you promise not to tell?"

"Doo-Dah-Doo."

"No, I'm serious. Promise."

"I feel that if you trust someone enough to tell them a secret, you have to trust them enough to know they shouldn't tell anyone, and if you have to warn them not to spread it, you shouldn't tell them in the first place."

"Oh, never mind, I can tell you. You'll forget it right away anyway. I'm seeing someone new."

"Really?" Margaret was shocked, but also excited. "Really? Don't you feel, well, sort of odd and, don't take this the wrong way, you know what I mean, sort of old, rusty I guess would be a better description, at least it would be for me. Really? What's he like? Why are you doing this?"

"He's very shrewd, very understanding, and he talks. The other one never said a word. All those hours, all those years, and he just wouldn't speak to me. I felt crazier than when I took up with him. I couldn't take it anymore. What a relief to be rid of him."

"You left him?"

Till nodded and smiled.

Margaret put her hands in her pockets and thought this

over. Till's smarmy husband Art was gone! "I never much liked Art," Margaret said.

"Well, we're writers."

"Yes," Margaret said. "That's true." What is she talking about? Margaret thought. Why do I never follow the thread of even the simplest conversation? What does writing have to do with her unctuous husband?

"Art has become a commodity, anyway," Till said.

"I'm not sure I know what you're talking about. God, you're cold."

"I'm okay. We'll be inside soon."

"No, no. I meant ruthless. The way you talk about Art."

"Art," she said contemptuously. "Who cares about that?"

"Well, you used to care about Art."

"Well, sometimes we used to go to galleries, I guess. But not anymore."

"I should say not."

"Art holds no charms for you, Margaret. That's obvious."

"Well, he's so phenomenally vain. I know marriage is a compromise, but I've never understood how you could stand him day to day."

"Art? Art Turner?"

"I guess in the beginning he seemed interesting."

"I guess so," Till said in a tight, angry voice.

Margaret was very uncomfortable. The wind blew cold and Till's gaze was colder still, but in spite of all of that arctic atmosphere, Margaret began to blush and perspire. "I, I just meant you would probably be better off without him, that's all."

"That's all? Well, I think actually that's more than enough. You know, Margaret, I share your distaste for the ridiculous contemporary art market, but I fail to see what your opinion of my husband (such a well-kept secret for so long, now unaccountably shared with me), what your opinion, unfair and unkind, what your opinion of my husband, whom I rather like, the man who made your reputation, Margaret, what your thankless opinion of him has to do with it."

Margaret stared at her. "But the new guy you're seeing —"

"I fail to see what connection my new psychiatrist has with this, my new psychiatrist with whom I have an appointment in forty-five minutes, thank God, so that I can discuss the behavior of hostile, disloyal friends . . ." As she spoke, she turned from the restaurant and began walking away, her voice whipping back toward Margaret borne on the icy wind together with a coffee-stained paper napkin. "Does friendship mean nothing at all? This is the unkindest cut of all, at least one of them . . ."

Margaret stood in the cold for a while, no longer interested in lunch at You Are Hungry, but reluctant, nevertheless, to give up her place in line.

LILY DID LIKE Trollope, as it turned out. Rachmaninoff, Trollope, and Margaret, too. Whether that meant that Margaret was second-rate, Margaret was not sure, but she would be happy to consort with Rachmaninoff and Trollope any old day, and with Lily, too, which she did more and more frequently.

For Lily began showing up regularly at the Nathan-Ehren-werth establishment, stretching out on the couch as if it were a grassy hill and she a pink-cheeked country lass. Margaret would look at her and wonder how she managed to look so odd, in her absurd outfits, and yet so natural, so fitting. For Lily, just sitting was a kind of caress. Or was it that the chair or the couch seemed to caress her? The sofa's cushions appeared softer, as soft as flesh. The chair's slender, rounded wooden arms held her in a delicate embrace.

Margaret welcomed Lily's attentions. It was gratifying to be visited, to be telephoned so frequently, to be so openly enjoyed, so wanted, particularly since Till was no longer speaking to her. When Lily broke into her whispery jargon, Margaret would momentarily ask herself if she hadn't better forget the whole thing, but even that began to seem almost charming to her, the way a lover's crooked nose becomes first less noticeable, then somehow indispensable, then positively beautiful.

"You and Lily are fast friends," Edward said one day.

"Fast? Well, anyway, she has certainly grown on me. Do you like her, Edward?"

Edward of course liked her. He liked everyone, for one reason or another. Margaret knew that. What she meant was, What reason? What have you seen, what tawdry trinket of character, ignored by the rest of us, have you stooped to pick up, have you polished and discovered to be rich, luminous gold?

"Lily is very sincere," he said slowly. "Deeply sincere."

"Lily? Our Lily?"

"That's why she's attractive, too, I think. Do you? Sincerity makes her passionate."

After this conversation, Margaret watched Lily with even greater attention. Yes, she was sincere. And passionate. It was not what she said, certainly. It was the way she spoke, the way she carried herself, the way she moved as if the very air around her was around her of its own volition, of its own desire, and as if she, on her part, had yearned for the air, had sought its gentle, insistent touch.

LILY SENT Margaret and Edward a postcard with a picture of a motel shaped like a cowboy boot. She was lecturing in Oklahoma. The menus were wonderful there. When she came home, she dropped by for dinner, her long-faced protégé Pepe Pican in tow. They were wearing identical silver bolos, and Margaret was jealous.

Lily came a few days later alone and Margaret asked her about Till. "She's not speaking to me," Margaret said.

"Well, she doesn't speak *about* you either. Does that make you feel better or worse? Look, I don't want to get in the middle, okay? Till is a difficult person. Touchy."

"Is she? I've always thought she was remarkably forbearing."

Lily shrugged and lit a cigarette.

Margaret coughed and waited. But Lily said nothing more about Till. In the weeks that followed, Margaret tried once or twice to talk about Till. Lily would invariably shrug her shoulders and smoke silently so that after a while, Margaret stopped mentioning their friend at all.

∾ ∾ ∾

Seated on the bed, she opened a large volume on her lap, thus tugging at her silk dressing gown to reveal beneath the delicate fabric the contours of her graceful anatomy in a way that considerably aroused my scientific curiosity and compelled me to move the candle closer.

SHE: I still must argue, sir, in accordance with Helvétius, that there is no separate faculty of judging and comparing, no faculty distinct from sensation. This gown that I am wearing. Touch it. Yes, like that. Yes, just there. Now, touch it here. I am experiencing a richly agreeable sensation, and so too, I think, judging by your facial expression, are you. Now, this business of comparing is nothing else than rendering ourselves attentive to these different impressions excited in us, excited in us by those objects we sense. Objects actually before our eyes, for example.

She paused in order to allow herself to become properly attentive to the object that I, standing up now, revealed before her own eyes.

SHE: Exactly. Notice how we both study the different impressions suddenly excited in us by the exposure of this object and the attention rendered it.

MYSELF: Yes. To this extent I agree with you. For the impression excited in me is clearly demonstrated.

SHE: I am moved by your appraisal of my progress. But what I hope we may do now is simply to continue in our proof that all judgment is nothing more than pronouncing upon sensations experienced: the sensation I am experiencing now is one of shortness of breath, a rising warmth within, an inclination to faintness, and a flushed and overwhelming sense of unbearable longing.

She had, indeed, begun to take on a very agreeable high color and to breathe in that exaggerated manner I had learned to cherish, but this time to such a degree that she quickly began to loosen her own garment, not waiting for the gentle aid I was accustomed to offer.

She removed her garment entirely, revealing the noblest attributes of the most regular beauty. And I observed this sight with a strange and sudden emotion, a disorder in my heart that spread through all my senses.

I succumbed to this rush of impressions, of course. How could I do otherwise? The justness of the mind or judgment depends on the greater or lesser attention with which its observations are made, and I made my observations with the greatest attention I could.

The force of any union between human beings is always in proportion to the force of both habit and want. It is one of the peculiarities of the type of union I was accustomed to forming with my pupil that want often increased with habit, and so the force of habit and want were equally great, and the force of the union therefore overwhelming.

After a while, I closed my eyes, preparing to rest. But I found I could not, for still something was bothering me. Perhaps what I am about to reveal will be considered ungenerous of me. But I see it as not ungenerous. On the contrary, as a sign of the degree of esteem in which I hold human nature, and therefore my pupil. For this is what occurred to me then as I lay restlessly with closed eyes: that, I believed in the perfectibility of the human mind and human understanding. And that, therefore, the time had perhaps come to introduce my pupil to a different level of understanding.

MYSELF: The exchanges we have had on this subject have been vigorous, certainly, my dear, and enchanting, made so by all the radiant freshness and charm of your fair youthful mind. And your reasoning thus far has been full of felicity. But you have also shown, as indeed is fitting for these early stages of learning, an enthusiasm that would profit from further reflection.

Startled, she pulled her garment closer to her until it covered her again, draping over her body in a most delightful way, revealing nothing that was but suggestive of all that had been and that might be again.

SHE: I do not understand you.

MYSELF: To perceive is to feel. From the course of our studies, we have inferred this fact to our satisfaction time and again. You have mastered this proposition, haven't you?

SHE: As you can easily surmise from my actions, even at this moment, I have indeed mastered this agreeable proposition.

MYSELF: Yes, I find you are able to demonstrate the truth of your statement and the proof of your mastery in a stirring fashion. But let us pause here for a moment to reflect further.

I sat up and moved to the foot of the bed, where I found I could think with greater clarity, and I resumed speaking.

MYSELF: To perceive is to feel. But to compare is to judge. To judge and to feel are not the same. The time has come in your education, I believe, for us to turn our attention to comparison. Now, according to Rousseau, I may have at the same moment an idea of a big stick and a little stick without comparing them.

SHE: I will attempt to entertain such an idea [she closed her eyes].

MYSELF: I may have at the same moment an idea of a big stick and a little stick without judging that one is less than the other.

SHE: Does this really strike you as reasonable? I hold the ideas in my mind now. But I discover it is somewhat difficult to refrain from judgment, as I find myself quite partial to the big stick.

MYSELF: Yes. Indeed. But here is the point. Big, little — though my mind only produces these comparative ideas when sensations occur, these comparative ideas are not themselves sensations.

My pupil, and so the lesson, momentarily took a slightly different direction as she again sought to complement her contemplation of the big and little stick by seeking a more direct and empirical approach, and sensations did indeed begin to occur with remarkable rapidity and diversity.

But I, determined to continue the new portion of our lesson, insisted we move ahead.

MYSELF: If the judgment were merely a sensation, my judgment would never be mistaken, for it is never untrue that I feel what I feel.

SHE: And I feel what I feel.

MYSELF: But often my understanding, which judges of relations, mingles its own errors with the truth of sensations, which only reveal to me things.

SHE: I confess I am experiencing the truth of sensations. But, too, I understand that sensation is not judgment. And so, if judgment is comparison, then —

MYSELF: Then let us compare!

The rest of the lesson involved some refreshing experimentation with different objects, for the sake of comparison, and after a time my increasingly brilliant young student seemed to begin to comprehend my teachings in a way that allowed me to consider that this difficult lecture had been well worth my trouble.

෨ ෨ ෨

MARGARET HAD been sitting with the dust in the library examining this passage and comparing it to the sections of Rousseau's *Émile* and Helvétius's *A Treatise on Man* from which it had been concocted. As she read, she felt herself becoming increasingly uncomfortable. It's only eighteenth-century empiricism, she told herself. Discredited, limited, old empiricism. But somehow, these familiar ideas from the past loomed suddenly, strangely, large and threatening.

Margaret had carefully, and she thought rather deftly, made a life for herself which minimized the need for comparison and choice. Comparison meant confusion, chaos. One sought certainty in life. But now it seemed one was meant to seek certainty through comparison. Did that mean there was no certainty in her life? In her marriage to Edward? For if judgment was comparison, why did she think she was happy with Edward? How did she know? How could she judge?

SHE SAT ON the couch beside Lily. Edward sat on the chair. Pepe, who had come with Lily, as he often did, sat moodily atop the dining room table eating the last of the lettuce out of the large salad bowl, which he held on his lap.

"Dinner was so divinely ladies mag," said Lily.

"Edward made it," Margaret said. Ladies had nothing on him. Perhaps there should be Edward mags. *Body Electric* and *Ode* and *Edward's Home Journal*.

"Pepe, get down," Lily said. "You're spoiling the bourgeois ambiance."

Pepe impassively raised his eyebrows and stayed where he was.

Observe, Margaret told herself, turning away from Pepe, whom she instinctively sensed was best left unobserved. Listen and observe. Then you can compare. Then you can judge. Observe.

Edward's ankles are showing between his socks and his pants. They are white. Fish-belly white. Lily is dressed in a sixties-inspired outfit that includes high lace-up moccasins, patterned tights, a mini miniskirt of crushed purple velvet, and a transparent paisley blouse. Beneath the paisley blouse, her skin is white. Why is the white of her skin different, less fishy, than the white of Edward's ankles? Is it because a shoulder is intrinsically more appealing, less fishy, than an ankle? Or is it that her shoulder in particular is aesthetically superior to Edward's fishy ankle in particular? Is her shoulder really more beautiful than Edward's ankle, or am I trapped in layers of received, culturally determined lies, and it's really Edward's ankle that stands as a thing of beauty?

With some effort, Margaret attempted to listen to what Edward and Lily were saying.

"Our fleet entering the gulf? The gulf? The vaginal gulf!"

"I mean the Persian Gulf."

"So do I."

Never mind, Margaret thought. She wished Till were there. She missed Till, but she was too ashamed to call her. What would she say, anyway? I apologize? Oh, that's okay, Till would answer. Think nothing of it. You've secretly hated my husband, who gave you fame and fortune, for all these years? Why, I'm flattered that you've stayed friends with me when seeing us must have been such a trial for you.

Margaret returned to her musing on the nature of ankles, shoulders, beauty, and truth. Edward's ankles were white, fish-belly white, and so were suggestive of fish bellies. While Lily's shoulders, skimmed by the transparent paisley blouse, were indistinctly white and so were suggestive of — shoulders! The white, hidden and yet apparent, was therefore a conscious color, a decision, a decision made with a purpose, and the purpose was to make the viewer think about how hidden the shoulder was, and by extension to think of what else was hidden. Edward's ankle, on the other hand, was bared thoughtlessly, and so expressed no purpose, in fact expressed the very antithesis of purpose, a lack of interest in the ankle and by extension in his body as a whole.

So, Margaret thought, that is why Lily's shoulder is sexy and Edward's ankle is fishlike. Margaret was struck, suddenly, by how very sexy Lily was. She was a bit blowsy, or so Margaret had always thought. But perhaps it was just that she was voluptuous? Margaret had never had occasion to wonder whether a woman was voluptuous or not, and she was not sure how one judged. She continued to observe Lily carefully, the way she whispered and tucked her feet beneath her on the couch.

Lily caught her watching and looked at Margaret, long and earnestly. Margaret turned back to Edward's familiar ankle, which suddenly looked quite nice after all. Margaret blushed. Did Lily know? Could she tell? That Margaret, tilting her head, had been wondering if Lily was or was not voluptuous?

∽ ∾ ∽ ∾ ∽ ∾ ∽ ∾ ∽ ∾ ∽

ℐ Two

∽ ∾ ∽ ∾ ∽ ∾ ∽ ∾ ∽ ∾ ∽

SONG OF MYSELF
11

Twenty-eight young men bathe by the shore,
Twenty-eight young men and all so friendly;
Twenty-eight years of womanly life and all so lonesome.

She owns the fine house by the rise of the bank,
She hides, handsome and richly drest aft the blinds of
    the window.

Which of the young men does she like the best?
Ah the homeliest of them is beautiful to her.

Where are you off to, lady? for I see you,
You splash in the water there, yet stay stock still in your
    room.

Dancing and laughing along the beach came the twenty-
    ninth bather;
The rest did not see her, but she saw them and loved them.

The beards of the young men glisten'd with wet, it ran from
    their long hair:
Little streams pass'd all over their bodies.

An unseen hand also pass'd over their bodies,
It descended tremblingly from their temples and ribs.

The young men float on their backs, their white bellies bulge
 to the sun, they do not ask who seizes fast to them,
They do not know who puffs and declines with pendant and
 bending arch,
They do not think whom they souse with spray.

— WALT WHITMAN

AT THE AIRPORT, Margaret waited to have her bags x-rayed and thought that when she passed through the metal detector, she would be passing into a new world. She would be on her way to Prague, formerly part of the second world, now reborn. Perhaps she would be reborn.

A little boy ran up to her, grabbed her hand, looked up, realized she was not his mother, and ran away in horror.

"I'm here," she heard a woman call. "I'm right here."

Margaret stepped forward, passed through the metal detector, watched the x-ray of her bag as it rolled along on a conveyor belt. Overlapping round coins, her keys, and several indistinct lumps — she was setting forth naked and alone.

Once on the plane to Paris, where she would spend the night before continuing to Prague, Margaret thought again how sad it was that Edward could not accompany her. No marvelous, heroic Czech Philharmonic together, but Edward had given her a long article about the orchestra to read on the plane as a stand-in for his own attendance and instruction and conversation. Professor Ehrenwerth had to stay home and coddle his students. Which was just as well, Margaret decided, for it was demeaning to have become so dependent on another person, even one as interesting as Edward.

And so Margaret was by herself. With the exception of 150 or so passengers who provided international atmosphere by speaking French or Japanese or richly American dialects of English, she sat unaccompanied on the plane.

If Edward were here, she thought, he would already have discovered that the stewardess was studying in her spare time to be France's first female rabbi, that the 250 other passengers would consume forty-five liters of red wine during the journey, that the five-year-old Japanese girl across the aisle was a violinist who had performed at Carnegie Hall — twice.

But Edward is not here. I am alone. The stewardess probably belongs to Racially Pure Young Women for Le Pen. What if the 250 passengers, having consumed their forty-five liters of wine, become ill simultaneously? The Japanese girl is to be given to an infertile Parisian couple in exchange for a Manet painting.

I am alone.

Dinner came and went. She read about the Czech Philharmonic, on strike, performing *Má Vlast* in an unsanctioned concert to an audience that stood up, with the orchestra, to totalitarianism, literally rising to their feet. The Czech Philharmonic had helped to topple the Communist regime! And in East Germany, where orchestra conductors led marches and played his Ninth Symphony as protest music, Beethoven had taken to the streets. Truth and beauty to the people!

She thought of Edward with a sudden pang, for he seemed, from the distance of three hours and thirty-five thousand feet, extremely handsome, even more handsome than he seemed up close. "Should you take up with a young, French bisexual airplane attendant, still I shall welcome you with open arms on your return," he had said, and she wondered whether he meant a male bisexual or a female one, and whether he would, in fact, take her back if she were really to stray with one of the slender, smooth-skinned, rather unreal attendants in their blue uniforms. At this thought, the thought of straying, she shuddered, for the flight attendants looked so alien to her, and the touch of a stranger seemed impossible.

And how could Edward, making his little joke about infidelity, have known, how could either of them have guessed, how much she would enjoy her new solitude? She felt she should guard it, it seemed that precious. No one here knew who she was, no one cared. She was free. There was nothing to spoil the rich alienation she was enjoying!

IN THE MORNING in Paris, she went straight to her hotel in order to sleep. There, a small brass plaque informed her, Casanova had also slept, although with whom the plaque did not say. There was a suit of armor on the staircase, and red carpeting extended up the steps and into her tiny room, which was far taller than it was long. The wall that held the windows was hung with deep crimson velvet drapes, and Margaret felt like a trinket in a little padded box.

Let me out, she thought, sinking into a deep sleep.

She woke up in time for dinner, for she had plans to meet Juliette and Jean-Claude at the apartment of one of their friends, a composer whom Margaret knew slightly, an aging avant-gardist, small, nervous, generous. He had the habit of hopping from foot to foot (hoof to hoof, Margaret thought, for he looked rather like a goat). When Margaret arrived at his apartment in Passy, he was nearly butting his guests in his eagerness to admit and entertain them. From the windows, a whole wall of them, in his living room, Margaret stared out at the Eiffel Tower.

Seeing Juliette and Jean-Claude, Margaret grew almost painfully nostalgic for Edward and their first trip together, and she quickly drank several glasses of the composer's excellent wine in memory of that time.

Oh, Edward, she thought, smiling dreamily at the witty and increasingly blurry French intellectuals the composer had collected around him. The composer himself briefly interrupted his endless shuttle between the door and the table and stood beside Margaret. "You're not eating?" he asked, gesturing toward a table covered with baskets and bowls.

"No, I'm drinking." She refilled her glass and held it to her lips, savoring the wine. She realized her eyes were closed and that she was swaying with pleasure. She opened them and stood still.

"So," said the composer. "Prague. Though nothing is going on in Eastern Europe, isn't that so?"

Margaret stared at him, startled. Had she blacked out briefly, missed some crucial link in this conversation? She searched his face for some clue, but saw only a bony nose, long chin, and a rather long, upper lip, like a goat's.

"Musically," he added.

"I'm going to hear the Czech Philharmonic," she said.

"Czech Philharmonic. Yes, well, limited repertoire," he said over his shoulder as he headed toward some new arrivals.

Yes, well, when's the last time you toppled a government, you hideous silly *chèvre*? she thought.

Margaret noticed she was drinking a glass of wine. Still. Or again. Which was it? How many glasses had there been? Margaret, Margaret, calm yourself. And always remember, the aim of art is not to topple governments, Margaret, any more than it is to support them, so just go sit down over there, right on that alarmingly low leather armchair, you can make it, and drink your nice, tasty wine, close your weary eyes, lean your head a little to this side, where the cushion bulges comfortably. Just like that.

She had heard one of the composer's own works performed once, an opera. Drums thumped luridly. Corpses were strewn about the stage, which had been splattered with red paint. What was it about? Greed and capitalist corruption and redemption through revolution, certainly. But what was the plot? It was hard to recall, hard to recall even what period it was set in, partly because she was now, she realized, thoroughly drunk, but primarily because there had been so many soldiers in so many different uniforms — World War I Tommies in gas masks, Nazi storm troopers in boots, Napoleonic cuirassiers, Roman legionnaires with ten-foot spears.

She hadn't thought of the opera, whatever it was called, in many years, and was surprised she remembered as much of it as she did. It was on their first trip together that Edward and Margaret had gone to see this rousing, panhistorical bloodbath, which included several gang-rape scenes during which a chorus chanted, "U.S.A.! U.S.A.!" That was the trip on which we decided to get married, Margaret thought, and she opened her eyes and gazed at the composer, twitching toward the door now, with a little more warmth.

She and Edward had also gone to Versailles on that trip, for neither of them, in all their visits to France, had ever been there. And there they had marveled at a vulgarity so self-confident, so immense, and so ultimately frail. How could people with mirrors that big not realize how puny they themselves were?

Most of France survived in her memory as vivid fragments, moments immediately preceding or following meals. The meals themselves she remembered in detail. The steak with green peppercorns at a shabby inn famous for its steak with green peppercorns. The inn was of some historic importance, but Margaret could recall only the steak and on the other side of the steak, Edward watching her, and then, after the steak, the twisted rickety staircase to their closet-sized room and single single bed. A plate of shrimp at an outdoor seaside café, past which a bull ran frantically, chasing a few brave souls and followed by what seemed to be the entire population of the town. What town? That fact was lost forever in the happy scent of garlic and olive oil, the pink of shrimp, the pale dust cloud heralding the arrival of the bull, the thrilling clarity of the very blue sky.

Only Versailles stood its ground, bigger than any *gigot.* How conventional, Margaret thought. Why not marvel over the Eiffel Tower as well? But then, I am marveling over the Eiffel Tower, aren't I? There it is, that symbol not of Paris but of all those who come to Paris, not of romance but of one's desire for romance, one's need. Some French writer said he ate lunch at the Eiffel Tower every day because it was the only place in all of Paris from which he would not have to look at the Eiffel Tower. Gide? Maupassant? Roland Barthes? Crébillon *fils*?

"I love the Eiffel Tower," she murmured to Juliette, who had perched on the arm of Margaret's chair. "It's on the wallpaper in my aunt Eunice's bathroom."

Margaret smiled uncomprehendingly at the rest of the French people around her. Smoke filled the room. Juliette had begun deconstructing the Eiffel Tower with all the enthusiasm someone or other had put into constructing it.

"Who built the Eiffel Tower?" Margaret interrupted Juliette.

Juliette stared. "Eiffel," she said.

"Ah."

"You have read of course Barthes, the little essay? You know? Where he says that the tower has both sexes of sight, that is to say that the tower can both see and be seen."

"You mean it sticks up and you can also go inside it?" Margaret asked. "Yes, I read it."

The composer ushered in a new arrival, a young man, and Margaret noticed heads turn. There was a sudden buzz of whispered excitement.

"That's Henri de Goldbaumois," Juliette whispered. "He is the rising star of France."

"Movie star?"

Juliette looked at her pityingly.

"Rock star," said Margaret.

"Philosophy," Juliette said patiently. "Star of philosophy."

De Goldbaumois was surrounded by people, all listening intently.

"There is only standing room in his lectures," Juliette continued.

"Really? Meta-Heideggerian semaphorism?"

Juliette looked at her even more pityingly.

"You Americans!" she said.

"Us Americans."

"He teaches *The Federalist Papers,*" Juliette said with some excitement. "They are by Alexander Hamilton and James Madison and *Jean* Jay," she added helpfully.

In another corner, the conversation had become suddenly animated, and Margaret shifted her attention and listened. Real estate and summer homes! Oh! She missed New York, so near and yet so far.

And then, blotting out the Eiffel Tower and James Madison and the smoky room, a sudden, forceful wave of homesickness for Edward struck Margaret. When the wave receded, she stood weakened in the sand. When he smiles, she thought, his whole face lifts, and his eyes blaze, the lines around them radiating like baroque sunbursts. What a hideous image, she thought. My poor Edward and his beautiful smile reduced to such a hideous image. I am a terrible wife.

Absentmindedly, Margaret watched Juliette's dark red lips moving.

And yet they do look like Baroque sunbursts, don't they, those lines around Edward's eyes? she thought.

She looked at Juliette's smooth face, at her wide cheeks and high cheekbones, and back at her unsmiling rouge red lips. The red lips parted and came together. Margaret no longer noticed what, if anything, came from them. She wondered how long she had been watching them. Did Juliette know Margaret was staring at her lips? Juliette put a fat cigarette between the red lips. When she removed it, inside a swirl of smoke, Margaret could see the marks of the red lips on the cigarette like fingerprints, no, no, lip prints. She felt strangely moved by the garish smears on the cigarette. "My aunt Eunice used to work in the Empire State Building," she said softly, taking Juliette's hand in her own. "On the second floor." Tears came to Margaret's eyes. "The second floor," she repeated.

THE NEXT MORNING, she dozed, dozed seriously, on the plane to Prague, a sleek Air France craft that only emphasized to her how small and shabby she herself felt. One day away from Edward and she had become drunk, for the first time in years, and in public, too.

She tried to take a few notes when she woke up. Margaret had prepared a talk on eighteenth-century French philosophical works printed in Switzerland, then smuggled back across the Swiss border into France and sold by starving Parisian hacks who were then hounded by the police until they disappeared into exile, abject poverty, and utter obscurity. The discovery of *Rameau's Niece* had drawn her into this study of underground literature, which included not only works by philosophers like Voltaire and Helvétius and Locke, but also titles like *Venus, Wild in the Cloister* and *The Tender Guidance of Dom Bugger,* all of them referred to as "philosophical books."

For her talk in Prague, Margaret had prepared a short selection of anticlerical, antiaristocratic pornographic poems popular at the time, with lines like "Watch the scrofulous count / Upon his trembling sister mount." You see? she would say. Enlightenment philosophy, the search for scientific and moral truth, was as unsettling as incest and debauchery. Truth threatened an unjust and hypocritical rule. Truth was revolutionary. And always must be revolutionary.

Yeah. That sounded good. In Prague. Now. But then what, Margaret thought. Freedom of expression and freedom to make a living, those Enlightenment bequests, were revolutionary ideas, but once realized, those freedoms turned away from revolution, didn't they? Revolution, democratic revolution, fought to make itself obsolete.

Margaret stared at one of the translations she had made, a sort of porno-limerick-libel.

> *The king's weenie*
> *Is so royally teeny*
> *That the poor queenie*
> *Does not know where to turn.*

> *Says the cardinal, asked for succor,*
> *"Sooth! My vows do bid me fuck her.*
> *So, first this frontal liturgy,*
> *Then the sacrament of buggery!"*

Ah, freedom, Margaret thought. Freedom from debauchery. Freedom for debauchery. Confused, she leaned her head against the little oval window and faded back to sleep.

When she woke, Margaret read an essay by Havel she had brought along and felt sheepish and ashamed. For so far from living in truth herself, she lived in a fog, and liked it like that. In Czechoslovakia, where until a few months ago scholars had stoked boilers and writers washed windows, she would be just a gaping voyeur. But then, encouragingly, in Czechoslovakia, Frank Zappa was a major cultural figure. They landed, not too far from a large mound of hay. Margaret saw that the plane was being guided past other aircraft to its parking spot by a small car, its orange paint dull and chipped. There was a red light on the roof of the car and a large sign that said, in English, FOLLOW ME.

IN THE LITTLE airport, she stared in fascination at the big gold stars on the shoulders of the bored customs officers. She waited for her luggage, surrounded by French and German businessmen. In the taxi, as they drove past blocks of Stalinist housing developments, the Castle in the distance, she listened in inattentive confusion to the driver's tape of a choral group singing, "'Cause you've got personality! Smile! Personality! Charm! Personality . . ."

The hotel was a large, slightly run-down place built in the twenties. Her room was heavy in spirit in spite of its being both clean and nearly empty, the windows enormous and facing a building from the turn of the century, judging by the medallions of rather mournful Art Nouveau ladies who stared from the facade.

"Cheer up, girls," Margaret said to them, as she had no one else to talk to.

SHE HERSELF WAS almost giddy. Without Edward, she felt off-balance, as if one eye were covered. She walked carefully down the wide steps to the dining room, drunk with solitude.

Dinner alone in a restaurant was a novelty for Margaret. When she somberly spread her napkin on her lap, she noticed its size and how severely starched it was; when she held the large, heavy menu, she consciously experienced its proportions, the sensation of its weight. She wondered what Lily, the menu maven, would have made of Margaret's almost awed response to the leather-bound multilingual price list. But alone, one took nothing for granted, not even the feeling of a menu in one's hands. One sensed everything: for, after all, there was nothing else to do.

Cabbage and dumplings and goose! At her round table, sitting in her soft, padded chair, Margaret rejoiced. She flipped through her *Baedeker's Prague,* which she had brought to dinner with her as company, leaned back, and was comfortable and content. They would cook her goose, and she would eat it. Ah, to be on one's own and make such feeble jokes to oneself! It was good that Edward was home, titillating his students with dirty poetry by Walt Whitman, perhaps, but never mind, for she was an authentically isolated soul being served stale rolls by a man in tails in the shadow of a towering bronze statue of a nude woman, her arms flung out dramatically, as if she were taking a bow, Ethel Merman's bow, a bangle bracelet high on each arm emphasizing her nakedness.

After dinner I will take a walk, Margaret thought. A short walk to the Old Town Square. I am in Prague. I am free in a free city. I am on my own. No one knows I'm here. I can do as I like. No one cares about me. They're too busy being free. I can stare at people and dress badly, and no one will care, no one will even know, because no one knows me.

She gently nursed her solitude. The sparkle of the silverware occupied her attention for a considerable period of time. She drank mineral water and heard herself swallow. The other tables seemed far away, insignificant islands in the foggy distance, across an impassable sea.

And then from the shore came a mighty roar, a tidal wave of chatter and exclamations and peals of laughter, a foaming surge of petite elderly women and petite elderly men, a crash of Belgians.

"We may join you, please? The room is so full. We are from Brussels. You are American? My son is visiting America next week. And New York City. Your address, please? New York City! I will pass it to him! First he is in Paris. You have been in Paris? I am from Brussels, *un juge.*" The man, a trim little fellow in a cardigan sweater beneath his suit jacket, smiled serenely. "I put men in jail."

His wife nodded her head and said, "*Oui! Oui!*"

"My son goes to New York City for business, to Manhattan. This is near to you, Manhattan? We have never visited America —"

"*Oui! Oui!*"

Margaret smiled. The Belgians smiled. The Belgians sat down and smiled some more. At one end of the dining room, there was a podium on which stood a piano and a set of drums and a microphone. Margaret watched with foreboding as a man in a tuxedo sat down behind the drums, another behind the piano and, last, a third limped (his tuxedo seemed to contain at least one wooden leg) to the microphone. Was that a toupee? She had never seen one quite like it, combed down in front of the ears to create wide, flat black sideburns. He lifted a violin and began a whine of misery, bobbing and swaying with a resigned heartiness. Turn the pegs! Margaret thought desperately. Tune the instrument! The violinist grimaced in a kind of smile. The drummer too smiled unceasingly. Margaret was relieved she could not see the pianist.

"In America," said the *juge,* "many men are in jail, the black men and the poor men —"

"*Oui! Oui!*"

"Yes," Margaret said politely.

"Ah! You are so well informed about American criminal justice system!" said the man.

"You're American?" said another man excitedly, turning toward her from the next table. "This is very different from America. I know. I've been here two weeks." He paused dramatically, then said, "The people do not know how to make a profit."

The violinist was playing loudly, vibrantly, and quite out of tune. He is doing this on purpose, Margaret thought. He has tuned his violin to be out of tune. He hates us. Are they really playing *Eine kleine Nachtmusik* with a snare drum?

"I'm from L.A.," the man at the next table was saying. "Los Angeles," he explained to the Belgians.

He was a degenerate-looking man who could have been anywhere from forty to sixty-five, his skin leathery and drawn, an alarming, inhuman yellowish tan, and his eyes glowed from deep sockets, lifeless, meaningless, but shining bright, as if someone had gone out and forgotten to turn them off.

"Ah! Los Angeles! In Los Angeles, they put the Mexican people in jail, I think," said the *juge*.

The American had turned so far toward them that he was able to put his long tan fingers on their table. "I'm a photographer so I notice things," he said. "Take for example your table setting. Not being photographers, you probably haven't noticed, but I've been trained to notice. Now we're in a nice restaurant, in a classy hotel, right? We're being served by guys in monkey suits. They've got all this silver." He lifted Margaret's fork by the tines, as Margaret watched with stunned attention, held it up for all to see, then lifted her glass. "This is real crystal, I'll tell you," he said, pinging the glass, her glass, with the fork, her fork, then shaking his head. "You ever hear of Bohemian crystal? But what's missing? You don't notice, right? But I pick up on things, and these people don't know how to make a profit. Why? Because for all those years, their bosses said, Just fill your quotas, just fill your quotas. So they'd sell ten shirts, then quit for the day. They don't care that fifty more people are standing in a line waiting for shirts and that they have one hundred shirts left in the store. They don't care. They *filled their quotas*! See my point?" He had returned Margaret's glass, but still held her fork in one hand, thumping it on the white tablecloth. His voice had a thin, droning rhythm, not unlike water dripping from a faucet.

"So," he continued, "what is missing from the table in this elegant restaurant? The salt and pepper! With all their crystal and silver, they leave off the salt and pepper. Then you have to ask for it and then they have to go and fetch it, which keeps the waiter from doing something else, which means someone else has to sit around with no dinner, which means these people are inefficient. I mean no disrespect, of course, they're a decent people. We just have to teach them."

Margaret lifted her *Baedeker's* to reveal a small crystal salt shaker and a small crystal pepper shaker.

"Hey!" said the sinewy photographer with his dying, smoldering eyes, as if this discovery somehow proved his point. "We're in Eastern Europe."

"No, no," cried the small Belgian man.

"*Oui! Oui!*" said his small Belgian wife, in agreement with whom, Margaret was unsure.

"No, no," the Belgian man continued. "This is not Eastern Europe, you know, but central Europe. Historically, central Europe. Central, central. Here was the home of Kafka and Dvořák of course, but also Rilke and Smetana and, too, Kepler and Einstein and Alphonse Mucha! Central, you see?"

The violinist was clumping painfully among the tables now, asking for requests. Haven't you filled your quota yet? Margaret wondered. A large table of Germans waited while most of the waiters in the restaurant assisted in preparing a preposterously large brandy glass, holding it over a flame, then pouring a thimbleful of brandy in, lighting it, and blowing it out. Why it took so many waiters to perform this ritual, as only one was active at a time — the thimble pourer waited for the glass heater to finish, then passed the glass in turn to the brandy lighter, who gave it to the brandy blower-outer, who passed it on to various servers — was not immediately clear.

"See what I mean?" the American photographer said, nodding his head toward the waiters. "Inefficient."

But no one in the restaurant seemed to mind, everyone watching the procedure in fascination.

"*Oui! Oui!*" said the Belgian man and the Belgian lady together, cheerfully observing the blue flames.

"Nice people," the American said, shaking his head. "Nice little country."

Margaret looked at him, twisted in his chair in his determination to speak to them, and she hoped that suddenly, like a wound-up rubber band when it is at last released, he would spin back to face the other way. But of course he didn't, he simply continued chatting. He had a terrible cold, which he referred to as the Prague Plague, and he sniffed a great deal.

"In Prague," said the Belgian wistfully, "I think only political dissidents are put in jail. That is, they used to be, have been, were put in jail. Who now is being put in the jail? Who now?"

AFTER DINNER, Margaret and her guidebook went on a walk. She could hear her footsteps. In the middle of a city. She noticed how few cars were on the road. One, and then none. A few minutes later, one. And then none. Just the clip of her footsteps.

The Civic Forum building at the bottom of Wenceslaus Square looked smaller than it had on television. What a good-natured headquarters for a revolution, Margaret thought. A white banner flew with the initials O.F., a happy face drawn inside the O. There was a café on the ground floor.

"Change money? *Cambia? Changer?*" a man asked her.

She shook her head and followed a narrow street, from which cars were banned, past darkened shops, until an irregular square of pastel buildings opened before her, so delicate in the lamplight that she stood still in wonder.

Kafka, you're crazy, she thought. Well, of course, that's not a very original observation, but look! This city is light and airy and elegant and kind. I've been here nine hours, so I know.

Tourists filled the square. Folksingers with stringy hair strummed guitars. A man in a plumed helmet played the tuba. Margaret walked along the edges, looking up at the surrounding buildings. There were little narrow houses and large rococo palaces, all painted lime green or lemon yellow or shell pink or robin's-egg blue, covered with statues and curls, the decorations white and luminous in the night.

Margaret had almost forgotten the pleasure of being a tourist. No responsibility, except to look. I like to look, she thought. With my guidebook to tell me what it is I'm looking at. She waited with the other tourists for the elaborate cuckoo clock on the medieval Old Town Hall to chime ten. Finally, two windows in the tower above opened, behind which the twelve apostles could be seen parading by. A skeleton rang a bell, his bone arm moving up and down, pulling a string, his head shaking eerily. A golden cock crowed in a harsh squawk.

THE BREAKFAST buffet table offered yogurt with a dozen bowls of powdery toppings in different pastel confetti colors, as well as sliced cucumbers, meat soup, and cold brussels sprouts. The musical trio was absent, but Margaret saw the Belgians, who waved, and the photographer, who sneezed extravagantly, then winked at her. She gratefully followed the waitress to a table far from her acquaintances, a table directly beneath the bronze statuess, her arms spread above Margaret like the fronds of a sheltering palm.

Late that morning Margaret met with a white-haired professor of philosophy who spoke so quietly she had to lean very close to hear him. He had studied with members of the Vienna Circle in his youth, established himself as a distinguished university professor in Prague, then become an important dissident, a teacher with no post, an underground writer and translator, a man who chose not to emigrate, a political prisoner off and on for years. Margaret wondered if that was why he spoke softly, out of habit, the habit of not wanting to be overheard. She leaned toward him, grateful to listen to this gentlemanly figure, cultivated and generous. Frail and ancient physically, he was so robust spiritually that his hushed, weak voice was irresistible. He did not blame the Allies for giving Czechoslovakia to Hitler. Why didn't Beneš fight? Beneš had one of the best-equipped armies in the world! Margaret, in her entire life, had never heard anyone say such a thing, not any Democrat, not any Republican, not anyone. He loved "The Star-Spangled Banner," calling it "almost as nice as 'The Marseillaise.'" Margaret had never heard anyone say he liked "The Star-Spangled Banner." He quoted from Shakespeare, from *Henry VI,* a play Margaret had barely heard of, much less read. He quoted from Henry James and Jane Austen and Balzac and Auden and Wittgenstein. He was funny in a way that forgave the victims of his wit, and easily, comfortably learned, as if these books and these ideas were his chums (hers, too!). He drank his coffee and murmured gorgeously. She wanted to reach out and take hold of his hand. If Americans were tolerant, unaffected, sensible — if Americans were really American, Margaret thought — they would be like him.

Instead of discussing the revolution itself, he seemed to be enjoying the freedom to chat afforded him by his revolution. "Look," he said at one point, pointing to an empty bracket on the wall. "That's where they used to keep their cameras." Then he went back to discussing the state of Czech theater in the seventies. Margaret had spent so many late nights with so many graduate-student revolutionaries that this real revolutionary seemed almost impossible to her. He told stories about a Czech surrealist poet and remarked on Slav theorists between the world wars and their influence on French structuralist thought and then taught her a limerick by Edward Lear.

There was an Old Lady of Prague, whose language was
  horribly vague;
When they said, 'Are these caps?' she answered, 'Perhaps!'
That oracular Lady of Prague.

This somehow led to a quotation from Karl Popper, an unfashionable philosopher of science, so far out of the circuit that, just for a moment, Margaret thought her new friend was referring to a children's book about penguins. "Popper once wrote that the greatest scandal of philosophy is that, while all around us the world of nature perishes, philosophers continue to talk, sometimes cleverly and sometimes not, about the question of whether this world exists." His voice wavered. His complexion was pink and white, as delicate as a girl's. He smiled and patted her hand reassuringly.

"It is the human condition," he said, "to theorize and criticize theory. It is our mechanism of adaptation to the world. Like flippers. Or a sharp beak. Like a giraffe's long neck!" He laughed, almost inaudibly. He coughed for some time. Margaret leaned closer, afraid the old man would die, his lovely white hair tipped forward into the dark espresso.

"To see is not to believe," he said finally, smiling again. "To see is to philosophize."

Margaret was supposed to speak at the Charles University, not under the auspices of the history department (still staffed by professors who had learned their stuff under the Communist regime, while more independent-minded professors swept floors), but by an independent group of students and intellectuals who had organized a series of talks by visiting scholars.

Margaret was shown around by one of the students, a small, earnest girl named Anna, who took her on a streetcar to see "the real Prague," apartment blocks from the twenties, black with coal dust.

"These buildings could be beautiful, very beautiful, if they were restored," said Anna. "But the Communists would rather tear down and build a new, ugly building."

"How capitalistic of them," said Margaret.

Anna looked at her in disbelief. "But why?"

Margaret was silent. How did one answer such a question? It was like asking why people breathe. Why *do* people breathe? Margaret thought.

Then Anna took out some photos she had in her purse. "This is the trip my boyfriend and I took to Paris," she said.

Margaret smiled as she remembered her first trip to Paris. There would be snapshots of the Eiffel Tower, the Tuileries, the Seine.

"This is Jim Morrison's grave," Anna was saying. "This is another view of it, and here's the back, and this graffiti we liked very much . . ."

Jim Morrison was buried in Paris? Well, he would be, wouldn't he? Maybe she, Margaret, could contrive to be buried in Prague. No, no, that was Kafka territory. She'd have to find her own city. Bridgeport, perhaps.

She looked at Anna, to whom Jim Morrison meant something. In Prague, rock still meant something. Not just nostalgia or marketing spin-offs or pretentious videos, but something.

That night Anna took her to the Stalin Monument high on a hill overlooking the Vltava. The monument itself, a statue of Stalin almost as large as the Statue of Liberty, had been torn down in the early sixties. Underneath it, a warren of tunnels and concrete reinforced bunkers had been discovered: a bomb shelter and command center built in the fifties as a home for the elite after Armageddon. The new Czech government had turned it over to a group of students who had turned it into an art gallery and rock club called Totalitarian Zone.

Margaret stood rather uncomfortably in the cold cave of a place. Tomorrow she would deliver her talk. She was supposed to inform a roomful of people who had recently risked their lives in pursuit of the ideals of the Enlightenment about the Enlightenment. To tell a group of Czech students about an erotic bastardization of Locke when they were in the midst of an authentic realization of Locke's ideas — this was absurd, this was preposterous, this was chutzpah!

Water dripped from the concrete beams onto the dirt floor. Papier-mâché grotesques, huge murals, metal sculptures, and mobiles of standard SoHo design sprawled through these dark catacombs, lit by bare, hanging bulbs. Whether the works were interesting or not, Margaret could not tell because there, underground in Stalin's abandoned legacy of a bunker, they were more than interesting — they were inspired. This was a celebration. The kids lounged against piles of cement rubble, and in spite of being dressed in generic European semipunk style, they did not look like German or French youth, angry and disgusted, posturing self-consciously. They weren't angry or disgusted. They were delighted.

Margaret stood beside a sculpture — boots and catsup bottles hanging from ribbons and wires. She began to feel more comfortable, that she somehow belonged here, that there existed a certain affinity, not so much between her and the students as between her and their exhibits. With a flood of relief, Margaret realized that she was expected not so much to instruct her betters as to be another colorful part of the celebration. Her talk, which she had worried would be irrelevant and trivial, an offense to the real business of democratic revolution that was taking place, was important simply because it was possible for it to be given. Oh, thank God, Margaret thought. I'm just part of the fun, an example of Western culture to be freely displayed. *Ich bin eine* catsup bottle.

She was an American abroad, and no one minded. In Prague, people liked Americans. Intellectuals liked Americans. Intellectuals in America didn't like Americans. And there was Anna, an authentically revolutionary student, carrying in the pocket of her black leather jacket a Penguin edition of *The Princess Casamassima*. Margaret gazed at the sculptures and listened to the crude Euro-rock coming from the stage. The Enlightenment lived.

THE LECTURE went smoothly. She talked, they listened, and Margaret was relieved. She read from *Rameau's Niece,* then spoke, carefully reading her notecards, on which she had written every single word she would say, underlining those she ought to stress.

Was *Rameau's Niece* a libertine novel? she asked them. Or was it a philosophical tract exploring empiricism? Or was it both? In the eighteenth century the desire to know was wedded to desire itself. In order to fool customs officials, smugglers placed pages of *Beneath the Naughty Nun's Nightgown* between pages of geography books or the Gospels. This interlarding was called "marrying," an amusing and rather suggestive name, Margaret said.

Pornography was used to discredit the clergy and aristocracy as decadent, perverted, impotent, and scrofulous. Philosophical, political, and pornographic works were lumped together by the book trade, which called them all "philosophical books." Why? Because empiricism and philosophy itself are both sensuous and sensual. The desire to know is desire.

Her audience, about fifty students and writers, seemed satisfied but rushed immediately off to a reading by Allen Ginsberg which had been inadvertently scheduled to overlap with Margaret's talk. Margaret sighed with relief that her performance was over. What nice, well-mannered revolutionary young people, she thought, watching the students file out. And she went alone to lunch in a kosher restaurant, the only one in Prague, located in what was once a synagogue. Above the doorway was a framed photograph of Barbra Streisand.

MARGARET SAT AT breakfast and consulted her *Baedeker's* and planned her day of sightseeing. She loved guidebooks. Even the idea of a guidebook appealed to her: a vade mecum, so sure of itself, so accommodating and considerate. Come with me and I will reveal to you the house that Jack built, the house that Jack slept in, the house from which Jack was expelled by a rival political faction, the house where Jack died a violent and untimely death. I will tell you the architectural significance of the house of Jack's mistress. I will tell you where you are, and I will tell you why you are there.

It was her last day in Prague, and she planned to use it wisely. First she would go to the Castle, which lay on the other side of the Vltava, then back again across the Charles Bridge to the Old Town. Margaret had not been sightseeing like this in years, and she thought again what a strange and strangely satisfying activity it was, superficial yet intense. She turned down corners of the guidebook's pages; she marked different buildings with a red pen. She studied maps in anticipation of studying the city. It was true that information never lingered for long in her mind, but every fact, all knowledge, was welcome for a visit. Sightseeing was a pure, sensual encounter, a subtle, deeply moving flirtation with a stranger.

She got into a taxi, which backed up at dizzying speed for two blocks, then shot off down a side street in what seemed to be the wrong direction, twisted and turned past beautiful, run-down buildings, baroque palaces, and turn-of-the-century apartment houses, then across the river to a wooded park and up a long hill toward the Gothic spires of St. Vitus's, the huge cathedral within the Castle walls. In the square, she got out, paid, and stood looking around her at the palaces, large and damp in the gray morning.

"Excuse me," said a man, coming up beside her. "I noticed your guidebook there. Are you American? Can you tell me what this is? Sorry to bother you, but I'm from New Jersey."

He was balding and wore a round-collared raincoat. He shivered and smiled, and even though he was from New Jersey and was, in all probability, a terrible driver, Margaret handed him the guidebook.

"That's the Schwarzenberg Palace?" he said, pointing. "Thanks, thanks so much. I should have brought one of these. You certainly can't get one in Prague. I'm here on business," he said, and Margaret feared he would begin a lecture on how the Czechs didn't know the first thing about making a profit. "But I snuck away this morning. I couldn't help myself. I've never seen a city like this."

"Neither have I," Margaret said.

Then they parted, he heading toward the Castle gate, she to the art museum in a cold, drafty palace staffed by stern, glaring Slavic matrons.

Margaret leaned forward to stare at one painting that struck her as curiously chaotic. A naked, expressionless Mary Magdalene, tresses trailing luxuriously over her breasts, was swarmed by cherubs, winged naked babies perched on her back, straddling her shoulders, fat cherub feet planted on her head. On their identical faces were identical expressions — disappointed, doubtful, tiny mouths all turning down on one side in an odd, halfhearted frown. One cherub pointed up, but toward what, it was not clear.

A thickset museum matron appeared suddenly, from nowhere, waving her heavy arms at Margaret, charging, a round, female, uniformed bull. Her face was closer, close, her nose red from the cold. Fine red veins crisscrossed her cheeks. She will arrest me, Margaret thought. Who now do they put in the jail? the little Belgian judge had asked. Why, tourists!

The matron said something, gesturing toward the painting, then began making noises like an alarm, then melted back into the shadows, where a folding chair draped with a sheepskin awaited her.

Margaret moved on past a Rubens portrait of a mountain of female flesh wrapped in a green snake, to which she was careful not to draw too close; past more matrons glaring dutifully from folding chairs; through large wooden doors and chilly echoing corridors. She bought some postcards from a woman downstairs and walked past a pile of coal, up the steep, narrow alley to the square.

Margaret heard the bleat of a trumpet. Around the gates to the Castle stood a large crowd, many of them schoolchildren. A group of five or six boys, about thirteen years old, their cheeks and the tips of their noses pink in the cold, were laughing and pushing each other. They began to move their arms, their hands, their fingers. They were deaf, Margaret realized, and were speaking to each other in sign language with the speed and exuberance of adolescence, shrieking with laughter, covering their faces in mock embarrassment, punching, shoving, and laughing again.

Margaret reached into the large pocket of her parka for her *Baedeker's*. But her *Baedeker's* was not in her pocket, nor was it in her other pocket. It was not in her bag. It was not in her hand. It was in the hand of the man from New Jersey. He had forgotten to give it back. Margaret stood miserably in the cold, her day of sightseeing ruined. By an act of off-hand generosity, her *Baedeker's,* its pages elaborately marked and turned back, was in the possession of another. She had been forgetful, as usual. Now she would be ignorant, as usual.

She looked up at the gate. Huge pillars stood on either side. On top of the left one rose an enormous statue of a naked man pushing another naked man to the ground, about to plunge a dagger into his throat. On the right, an even larger, stronger-looking man stood poised to club to death his fallen enemy. Who were these nude, sinewy bullies, and why were they guarding the Castle? Who made them? Who ordered them put there? She would never know, and the statues, unexplained, writhed above her in an insinuating, eerie mystery. The violence and heft of the tangled limbs, the sparkle of the gilded dagger and club against the coal-darkened bodies, all looked wildly incongruous against the rather subdued, refined building within.

Who would tell her now from what window the defenestration of Prague took place? Margaret walked reluctantly through the gate, past a stiff, ruddy-faced young guard, into the unknown.

In a cold gray fog, Margaret wandered from unidentified courtyard to unidentified courtyard; through large rooms, empty except for a throne or a metal folding chair; past fountains held aloft by contorted bulging bodies. Sometimes there were signs in English, but often there were not. In St. Vitus Cathedral, an endless, ice-cold barn, an impossibly gaudy silver casket stood on a pedestal surrounded with thick, bulging silver babies and garlands — an imperial tomb, obviously, only whose? Margaret had no one, and no book, to tell her.

She glanced at it sadly, longingly, a soul robbed of certainty.

Heaven help me, Margaret thought. There is no truth, no objectivity, no disinterested knowledge. Prague, sweet Prague, has been unwittingly deconstructed by a careless man from New Jersey. Barely registering the tomb's truly magnificent ugliness in her despair, she moved on.

Edward's silly, girlish students could have lived without him for a week. And Edward would have known who was buried in the silver bauble, who built the Eiffel Tower, who was buried in Grant's tomb. Edward would have memorized the guidebook, or at least not lost it, or he wouldn't have needed it in the first place, devouring the sights raw. Margaret missed him terribly; she missed his loud voice.

GLOOMY, BENIGHTED, and cold, Margaret sat in a taxi and passed all the buildings she could not identify, through the wood the name of which she no longer remembered, to the bank of the River Whatever.

Before her stretched the Charles Bridge, its cobblestone path not at all straight, but curving slightly this way, then that, leading eventually to slender Gothic towers, to Renaissance domes, to tilted red-tiled roofs. In the dark gray sky, gulls shot by, screeching, floating upward, then coasting down again, graceful and swift. Statues, dozens of dignified figures in flowing, stony robes, stood at intervals, rising on either side of the bridge. Margaret leaned over the side and saw the grim, slate water turn suddenly golden with a shaft of sunlight. Swans plunged upside down to feed, their tails pointing up comically. Above the harsh strumming of a guitar, an American voice sang, "Git out of my room, girl. You're as crazy as the moon, girl. Oh! The world is full of garbage. Don't throw me away!"

Margaret turned and saw, perched at the foot of a statue, a long-haired boy in jeans and a fringed leather jacket. Several teenage boys, clearly not Americans, stood around him, nod-ding their heads in approval. The sun was pouring through the clouds now, and the boys and the statues and the red rooftops and the golden spires of the Castle glowed, warm and vibrant.

Margaret watched the sun light up the city. Each build-ing it shined on, she thought, had some name, some promi-nent place in the history of Western culture, a name and a place she would never know. The sun and the gleaming city mocked her.

I am a failure as a sightseer, Margaret thought. Why didn't Edward take off some time and come here with me? But her husband was home seducing shapely but intellectually un-formed girls with dramatic readings of poetry, and this city was sparkling and beckoning, a coy temptress, forever be-yond her reach.

Beside her, a young man was setting Soviet officer caps and belt buckles on the stone railing. A cardboard sign in English said CLEARANCE ON TOTALITARIANISM!!

"So!" said an American tourist, pointing his miniature video camera at the man selling the Red Army castoffs. "May I ask you a few questions, sir?"

His voice had the tone of a father at a birthday party for three-year-olds. Margaret felt ashamed.

"First, sir, could you tell me, what do you think of the Russians?"

"I don't like," said the man, facing the camera, then grin-ning and looking down.

"You don't like them. I see. And why is that?"

"They are Communists."

"And why are you selling these things, sir? Would you say it was because you prefer capitalism?"

"I would say, yes."

"Thank you, sir, for your candor," said the officious tourist, turning suddenly to Margaret, aiming his little machine at her. "And you?"

"I would say, yes," Margaret said.

"You're an entrepreneur," said the tourist, turning back to the Czech. "Do you understand? En-tre-pre-neur." With his free hand, he patted the man's arm. "You will do well."

Margaret, in penance for her people, bought a pin from the entrepreneur, a red star with a white enameled portrait of Lenin, in shoulder-length curls at the age of five, in the center.

What a horrible man, Margaret thought, watching the tourist, who was now interviewing the folksinger. And yet I am no better. A voyeur. Not even a voyeur. I'm too inept to be a voyeur unless I have a narrator, a book of instructions, a *Baedeker's*. I'm too insensitive to sightsee.

But the city glowed delicately all around her. The river was wide beneath the bridge. The gulls laughed above in the new sunlit sky. Oh well, fuck *Baedeker's*, she thought. What do I care who built what? I'll only forget it tomorrow. What do I care who lived where? They're all dead now, anyway.

She gazed around her with new determination. She, Margaret Nathan, pedant, scholar, seeker of truth, was in Prague, city of truth. Observe! Experience! Know! Dare to know? said Kant. Dare to sightsee! says Margaret.

The quick little gulls were oddly stubby, their heads black, their black beaks as straight as needles. Chilly, pallid vendors in thin parkas sold glasses painted with red flowers. A skinny man offered elongated tin soldiers in World War I uniforms, painted by his mother. There were thirty statues along the bridge — she counted — all black with coal dust. Above the American folksinger, the statue was of an anguished Christ on the cross, a woman facing him, her hand gently pressing his leg. Around them fluttered a mountain of curly-haired cherubs, lips parted. The woman's face lifted toward his.

Carefully Margaret observed the statue, the woman's up-turned face and parted lips, the gentle insistence of her fingers resting on his leg, her thumb reaching almost to his thigh. His head sank toward hers. His muscles strained.

She's trying to kiss him, Margaret thought. He's trying to kiss her. They long to embark on the pursuit of pleasure. What I am observing is a highly charged, erotic moment. This is a religious statue depicting desire. The woman's hand pressed against the flesh of his leg, an insistent caress. Their faces reached, hopelessly, toward each other.

I am going insane, Margaret thought.

But her observations continued to yield the same sort of data: on every side of her, statues rose up, statues of bodies, the curves of their legs and shoulders outlined by the clinging drapery of their long garments. Men lifted their hands imploringly to women standing magnificent atop cherubs piled up in fleshy heaps. These are *saints*, Margaret reminded herself. Saints praying to the Virgin. If Jesus looks like his muscles are straining toward a woman below him, perhaps it's because he's *dangling from a cross*.

Their robes flowed, sweeping across their limbs, across their stomachs. The sun was shining on the city, lighting up the thirty statues of men and women entangled in their clothing and their passions.

Margaret hurried from the sunny bridge, from the Red Army caps and the singing hippie, from the swans upside down in the sparkling waters of the River Whatever. She hurried into the refuge in the dark and crooked streets of the Old Town. Children waited in line at an ice cream shop. The windows of a rare book store displayed eighteenth-century manuscripts and three fairly recent issues of *The New York Review of Books*.

She walked on as if she knew where she were going. She followed the curves and dodges of the little street. The statues had been left behind on the bridge, but here were more figures, mounted on the walls, over the doorways, great arched doorways opening along a street so narrow it was almost an alley. Neoclassical men flanked one doorway, baring their perfect chests, every muscle just visible beneath the skin, their arms lifted in graceful, balletic poses. What are their legs like? Margaret wondered, for the statues ended just above the groin, below each lovely manly man a decorative pedestal.

Margaret stopped and tried to gain control of herself, for surely one did not come to Prague to ogle nude architectural decoration. These were the streets where, only a year ago, people walked in fear of Soviet tanks, and now they crowded around vendors selling copies of *Ameriký Sen,* by Norman Mailer, on the sidewalks. This was where Kafka walked, where the story of the Golem was invented. This was where *Don Giovanni* premiered. This was central Europe!

Above, art deco maidens, broad and bland in an oddly alluring way, giants of women, stared down at her from a rooftop. Their breasts, circular emblems of breasts, stood out above their Egyptian skirts, stood out above the central European city.

Margaret turned and turned again, up one street and down another, again and again, each turn bringing her face to face with yet another man of stone, another woman. Before her, their massive feet nearly at the level of Margaret's eyes, stood two titans, two Herculean males groaning beneath the weight of the building they strained to hold on their bulging shoulders, lion skins flung carelessly across their magnificent nakedness. On the other side of the street, an impassive woman in bas-relief fanned her own flat breasts and taut, flat stomach. Two giantesses in Edwardian hairdos framed a doorway, their arms outstretched, each having only a belt with a round medallion just above the navel to clothe them; an awful owl, its wings spread threateningly, stood between them. Their feet were big masculine feet, with prominent toes.

Margaret scurried guiltily beneath the breasts and buttocks and feet. She could not take her eyes off them, and stumbled stupidly against the mere mortals on the street. She passed a butcher shop and looked in horror and fascination at a display of sausages — long white ropes coiled thickly; pale pink wieners hanging in bunches; skinny, wrinkled sausages drooping white and sad; a burst of fat, greasy, stubby ones; others mottled red and white, protruding from their pile in grand eighteen-inch curves. Blushing, Margaret continued on, through the Old Town Square again, this time past what seemed to be a wedding party with cars decorated in garlands, a doll in a top hat on one, a doll in a white dress strapped to the fender of the other, a clownish man leering and playing the accordion.

She came at last to a large baroque church squeezed incongruously into a small area not even large enough to be called a square. Three doors opened into the church, each topped by a hill of tangled naked bodies — cherubs with round, open mouths, youthful angels smiling flirtatiously, men reaching out toward one another, their bodies turned and twisted impossibly, a great, writhing monument to flesh.

Margaret rushed on, past a fountain of three thick-lipped fish, their tails fat and entwined. Was this the way back to the hotel? Was there a way back to the hotel? What hotel was it, anyway?

Her footsteps clattered in the cramped street. She had no idea where she was, where she was going. Just visible, peeking out around the corner of an art nouveau building, were a pair of round plaster knees and slender calves and gently, slightly curled white feet.

Margaret stared helplessly at them, disoriented and tired

and defeated. She heard a violin, and then noticed against the wall a young man playing, Mozart maybe, and playing beautifully. A few people had gathered around, including some rather tough looking teenage boys and a bent old woman carrying a mop handle as a cane. The violinist finished. There was clapping. The woman began to sing suddenly in a high-pitched, wheezing voice. The teenage boys were looking at each other, smirking. As the woman sang, on and on, tapping her mop-cane on the ground for rhythm, and the boys nudged each other and whispered and smirked, Margaret felt suddenly afraid. What kind of boys were they? Thugs? What did Czech thugs do? Were they like American thugs? Would they knock down a cracked old lady? Kafka crazy? Kafka was a realist.

Margaret felt ill. She'd been going for hours, through the streets, the twisted streets beneath the flesh of statues. It was getting dark. She would be lost forever in the alleys of this horrible, narrow, dark, obscene little city.

She took a few steps backward. She bumped into someone. "Oh!" cried Margaret.

"*Mon Dieu!*" cried the someone.

"Excuse me," Margaret said as she turned around.

"It is you!" cried the someone, who was the Belgian judge.

"*Oui! Oui!*" said his wife.

"*Oui!*" said Margaret.

The old lady stopped singing.

The thuggish boys looked at each other.

Margaret bit her lip and looked away.

The boys began clapping politely.

LED TO THE HOTEL by the little Belgian judge and his little Belgian wife, Margaret wearily walked up the steps to her room. On the landing, she stopped to look at a large painting, so dark that in the daytime it appeared to be all black. But now, in the evening, it was lit up to reveal itself as a scene of an Edwardian man at a table. Beyond the French doors was a pink sunset.

That's nice, Margaret thought as she passed it. A nice, conventional turn-of-the-century bourgeois scene. She smiled and then noticed something under the table in the painting, something large and bluish white, soft and voluptuous, female and naked — a big, curvaceous gal, stashed beneath the table as if an afterthought, no allusion to it anywhere else in the painting, the man above looking out the window, unperturbed, oblivious, beneath him a drift of snowy flesh.

MARGARET DREW herself a bath. The bathtub was long enough for her to stretch out in, and only her head and feet protruded from the water. In the steamy tub, Margaret closed her eyes. Edward, Edward, she thought. The tub was big enough for two. But her husband was home. Twenty-four young men bathe by the shore. Or was it twenty-eight? "Twenty-eight young men bathe by the shore," he was reading, reading Whitman to the students who watched him with slightly parted lips and half-closed eyes. And Margaret bathes alone.

She opened her eyes. Her feet stuck up from the water like plaster feet, large, white plaster feet. Plaster feet hung from the ledges of doorways, doorways of pale lemon–colored buildings. Margaret closed her eyes to rid herself of these images. Feet begone. But what now? What were these? Thighs? Thighs, startlingly clear, white plaster thighs of large and impressive proportions.

Is corporeal sensibility the sole mover of man? The sole mover of Prague? The sole mover of Margaret?

Edward is not here. He is home with his girls. You never

heard the Czech Philharmonic. They are in New York. With Edward. You are in Prague. You are alone. Your search for knowledge has led you here, to this bath, to this revelation: alone, you see a perfectly respectable city as a throbbing, eroticized house o' weenies.

God, she thought. I was right all along. The desire to know really *is* desire.

AFTER A TWO-HOUR WAIT in Paris, Margaret boarded the connecting flight to New York. There were men on either side of her, probably businessmen, one beside her by the window, the other across the aisle, and as they both appeared to be asleep, she felt she could study them without inviting conversation.

The American businessman across the aisle wore the blue pinstripe suit (the jacket off and folded carefully in the overhead compartment) and red foulard tie of one still dressing for success even as success had lost its cachet, the newsmagazines having recently announced the death of the Greed Decade that had made success so successful to begin with. The Frenchman (she had not heard him speak, but he was a Frenchman — they knew how to get that across somehow) was dressed in dove-colored trousers of so fine a material that she longed to touch them and in a pale green-and-white-striped shirt that stretched somehow elegantly over his large belly, as if bellies — good, classic, fashionable bellies — were meant to protrude *comme ça*.

Margaret leaned with some difficulty over her seat belt and examined their shoes. The American wore loafers with tassels as small and useless as a whale's internal ankle bone. Smaller, actually, Margaret thought. Whales are quite large, leviathan, aren't they, and even their miniaturized evolutionary detritus must be gigantic. She suddenly, involuntarily, saw before her an image of several dolphins whipping gracefully round and round a deep concrete pool, a memory of Flipper's Sea World, an aquarium she had once visited. Round and round went the dolphins, faster and faster, exposing large, oddly pink extrusions on their pale gray undersides. "Look!" a child had cried. "Dolphin dicks!"

Our cousins from the deep, Margaret thought. She turned and surveyed the Frenchman's crepe-soled, soft leather oxfords. Our cousin from another land. For a moment she felt that she hated this man. From his thick crepe soles to his light brown hair. Why did she hate him? His elbow was not on her armrest. He neither snored nor carried with him the stale odor of cigar smoke. He had not insulted her. She liked his pants. Why did she hate him?

She decided she must hate him because he was French. She had never hated the French before, but these things can grow on you. After all, their food was so good, their books were so good, their paintings so good, they dressed so well. Those were reasons enough, surely, to hate them. And then they were smug, they had beautiful cities, they were intellectual Stalinists, they revered bad American movies but had a history of making good movies themselves. They cheated on their wives.

My, aren't we the cultural-stereotype wallah, Margaret thought. Since really you would die to be French and have those small French female feet that fit into those small shoes they wear. Well, we did have a better revolution.

She was staring at the Frenchman's face now, a comfortable face just gone the slightest bit fleshy, an extremely French face with thin but sensuously protruding lips that always looked moist, she was quite sure. He has daughters, nymphets, little blossoming girls that he watches with more than paternal interest, Margaret thought. That's what they do there. They're so civilized.

The man stirred, opened his eyes, put on his glasses, big thick-framed unexpectedly shaped glasses. He had gray eyes, and they looked into hers in such a direct way that Margaret thought she was being appraised, like a stone. Gem quality, but flawed, mister. Try down the block.

Soon he would speak to her. Then she would have to answer. Perhaps she didn't hate the French, she thought. Perhaps she didn't hate this man, either. Perhaps what she hated was the inevitability of social relations with him.

He would speak to her. And she would be required to answer. Edward was not there to do it for her, or even to support her in her own efforts, to remind her of the name of the book of Czech essays she had just finished reading, of the opera she had just seen.

She'd been in the last row of the tiny gilded opera house. Row thirteen. The opera, by Dvořák or Janáček, it was a little muddled already, had been beautiful and moving, although she was not certain what had taken place. There was a young woman who ran off to meet a young man. An old woman in black (her mother? grandmother? stepmother? mother-in-law?) mistreated her and bossed around a man with some close connection to the young woman (father? husband?). The young woman sank to her knees regularly. The young man she was in love with went away. And in the end, after a thunderstorm, she threw herself in the river.

Margaret had had a coughing fit in the beginning of the first act and had to climb over a blind man to get out, but after buying some mints at the bar, she had returned to the grandly intimate little golden theater and felt great sympathy for the suffering soprano, whatever the problem might have been.

Edward would have remembered the name of the opera. He would have known what it was about. Maybe this Frenchman would know. Why do all people from France have those lips, she wondered. It must be from the way they speak. Over the years, their mouths take on that provocative little pout. Oh, how to quash the inevitable, unsolicited bid for an exchange of pleasantries? I don't want to talk. Leave me alone, to fester in unhealthful isolation.

She felt how close she was to him, the two of them pressed against each other in the narrow airplane seats. He shifted in his seat, and his beautiful shirt, smooth Egyptian cotton, brushed against her bare arm. She guessed he was in his late forties and looked slightly older, owing to French indulgences like insatiable mistresses and cream sauces.

Oh shut up, Margaret. Edward likes strangers. Be like Edward. He speaks to foreigners. Of course, he *is* a foreigner. The Frenchman smiled at her, then pushed his glasses up until they rested on top of his head.

She had always considered cynicism a particularly sour form of provincialism, and it was now clear to her that she had become a sour provincial. But that's what happened when you went off by yourself — you discovered your true self. And her true self, she now knew, was a sexually hysterical, xenophobic, middle-aged midwesterner from the 1930s.

The Frenchman had gone back to sleep, a thin camel-colored blanket pulled up to his chin. His reading light was on, shining down like a spotlight, illuminating him in his innocent, childlike slumber. One arm was tucked under the blanket, the other hugging the blanket to his chest, his Rolex sparkling in the white glare.

Without thinking, Margaret reached up and turned off his little light. As she was still leaning over him, the Frenchman opened his eyes. They looked at each other, he in soft, sleepy confusion, she in the awareness that she was looking down at a complete stranger with moist, pouty lips from a distance of six inches.

"Sorry," she muttered, pulling away from him, from the intimate image of his face and sleepy eyes. Oh, that's why I hate him, she thought. I want to sleep with him.

He moved his head back and forth slightly, as Europeans do when they mean any number of completely contradictory things, and, clutching his blanket closer, closed his eyes once again.

I want, I want, I want, Margaret thought. I want to sleep with him. I want to forget I am married and drown myself in an affair with a stranger. No. I want, I want, I want to forget this stranger and drown myself in marriage. No, no, that's not right either. *No drowning.* I want to observe, to experience, to know! I am in search of truth and beauty. I am a scholar! That's why I want to fuck the French fellow.

Margaret watched him as he slept. Here was beauty, anyway. A beauty of sorts. If debauched Frenchmen were to your taste. He breathed softly but audibly. Edward, she thought, Why aren't you here? You are my husband. You're meant to protect me, to shelter me, to surround me, to make me forget everything and everyone else.

Edward engulfed the world; he held out his arms in an irresistible embrace, a gesture of supreme self-love and supreme largess. Margaret admired this ability to co-opt existence, to make it his. She loved Edward for that embrace. She had married him in anticipation of it; then, soothed and warm, she had lived among Edward's enthusiasms, swept up in the wave, the nirvanic swoon of living someone else's life.

Hey! Drowning again, Margaret, she thought. Waves indeed. Wake up. Smell the flowers. Fuck the Frenchman.

Adultery, Margaret thought, is an epistemological necessity. Rameau's niece found that out. To know is to fool around. She wasn't married of course. But still. Fuck the Frenchman.

Margaret got up and made her way to the bathroom. The Frenchman had long eyelashes, she thought. And his eyes, opened so suddenly, had looked at her with such easy amusement. She had expected him to launch his offensive then, having been given an opening, to surge ahead into the unavoidable friendly chat. Why hadn't he?

As she returned, walking slowly down the long aisle, looking for her seat in the darkened plane, she saw and recognized the top of his head and, it being the only head she recognized, the only object in the entire plane that had any personal relationship to her at all, and because it signified that there beside it was her own place, the crown of light brown hair looked reassuring, familiar.

Margaret sat down and took out a few sheets of her manuscript of *Rameau's Niece* and read: "MYSELF: Simple ideas enter into the mind through the senses pure and unmixed."

She looked up from the page at the Frenchman. My idea regarding you is simple enough, she thought. She watched him sleep for a while. He was awfully good-looking, in a prosperous, *bon vivant* sort of way. The more she looked at him, with his pursed lips and his pretty pants, the more oddly alluring she found him.

"MYSELF: When the understanding is once stored with these simple ideas, it has the power to repeat, compare, and unite them, even to an almost infinite variety, and so can make, at its own pleasure, new complex ideas."

It had been so long since she had flirted with anybody, she thought. A century, a decade, anyway. She turned back to her reading: "The coldness and hardness which a man feels in a piece of ice are ideas as distinct in the mind as the smell and whiteness of a lily or as the taste of sugar and the smell of a rose."

The Frenchman stirred slightly.

His head fell onto her shoulder.

His temple was pressed against her lips. The coldness and hardness of his glasses was perceived by her chin, and she sensed the smell and whiteness of his skin, as pale and sweet as a lily.

Oh God, Margaret thought. She could almost taste him, the taste of sugar.

Go away, she thought, terrified. I was only joking. Daydreaming. It was a secret.

He would wake up eventually, and then he would be bound to notice that their relationship had assumed a rather intimate physical nature, which he would undoubtedly attribute to her, for how could she possibly say, Look, your face fell onto my lips? She stared into his hair. The pleasant scent of his shampoo, the smell of a rose, filled her nostrils.

Well, Margaret thought. At least he's not trying to talk to me.

The rhythm of his breathing made her aware of his whole body, pressing closely onto her own. She shifted, just a bit, and her lips moved across his skin, an experience Margaret found pleasant, too pleasant. In fact, the entire experience of this unfamiliar male body against hers was too pleasant.

This is not a statue, Margaret told herself. I am not sightseeing. Just move your head away and we'll forget the whole thing ever happened. Your handsome, noble head with its clear gray eyes and long, feminine lashes and thin, moist lips, your head like a lily, a rose, like sugar and ice.

Each time she tried to move away, he seemed to move with her, snuggling in closer, his head heavier and more intimate. Margaret closed her eyes. But he was still with her. I am very attracted to a strange man sleeping on my shoulder, she thought. What does this mean?

I am a happily married woman. That is a synthetic proposition, one based on observation, with no inherent, necessary logic. But does observation really support this proposition?

Well, I am happy. Yes. Satisfied? Yes, that too. But then if I'm so happily married, why didn't Edward come to Prague to be happy with me? Because of his students? Fuck his students! Oh lord, what if he did fuck his students?

Margaret suddenly thought of the small university offices where she used to stalk her own professors. The invariable cramped rectangle with its bookshelves, battered desk, worn wooden chairs, and black linoleum floor came back to her, or she returned to it, and to that moment of fear bordering on joy when she would knock on the door.

Knock, knock.

Yes, I certainly got my money's worth of higher education, she thought.

Hello, Mr. So-and-So, I just came by to ask you about Kant's critique of Hume, I want to ask you about Hume and Kant, I have come by for you, I want you. I have waited for weeks but could wait no more. I see you in my dreams, the arrangement of your pens in your pocket in my dreams. The place in the back where your belt misses the belt loop in my dreams. Your scornful interpretation of your colleagues' interpretations of the works of long-dead Germans in my dreams. I dream of these things because they are part of you, professor. I have read your books. But now I want to stop dreaming, stop reading. I have come for you, and I will get you, too. Never mind that I have forgotten all the clever things I thought up last night in bed to impress you so that now I sit before you frowning in concentration on whatever it is you are saying, reduced to hoping you'll find me young enough and adoring enough and willing enough to make up for being stupid and tongue-tied, because that is exactly what will happen, and we both know it, knew it after the first class. There's one every semester, you're thinking. That's what I'm thinking, too.

Why not? she had always asked herself. There was something so alluring about them. No real evaluation of these men was necessary because these affairs could not lead anywhere. What difference did it make if they turned out to be as smoothly pompous as balloons, swollen with self-love and self-importance, floating with garish indirection above their fellow men? She wasn't stuck with them, was she? That was the wife's problem, wasn't it?

Oh lord, Margaret thought. I am the wife. I am the wife.

The Frenchman sighed and burrowed deeper, until his head was resting on her breast. Oh God, just go away, mister. *Monsieur*. I am a happily married woman. But if I'm a happily married woman, why am I sitting here with this man's head on my breast? Oh, Edward, I'm sorry. What am I doing? I'm not doing anything, actually, but I'm thinking. And why shouldn't I think, anyway, when you're home fucking twenty-eight girls in the bathtub?

I am a happily married woman. I lust after another man. Happily married women do not lust after other men. Therefore, even though I think I'm happily married, I am not happily married. Or am I?

The Frenchman opened his pale, seductive eyes and sat up. He ran his hand through his hair, the hair she had just felt against her face, and looked at her with some surprise.

"Well," she said, feeling herself redden. Well, indeed.

For a long time, Margaret pretended the Frenchman was not there. He seemed equally embarrassed, for he was silent. Margaret stared in front of her at the blue seat back. Out of the seat back's pocket stuck a laminated drawing of a plane, perfectly intact, which had supposedly just made a crash landing on the Atlantic Ocean. Happy survivors whisked down colorful inflated rubber slides.

The silence and embarrassment were becoming oppressive. She hadn't done anything wrong. Why should she sit there, tormented and ashamed? Anything would be better than this guilty, confused silence. Even conversation. In fact she longed to talk, to launch into one of those droning exchanges of banalities that would occupy her mind as thoroughly as an army occupies a town, as visiting relatives occupy a living room; it would prevent her from thinking, overwhelming and clouding all sensation in a fog of boredom and convention.

"So," she said. She looked over at the Frenchman. "Long trip," she said.

The Frenchman nodded.

"Longer on the way back. On my way back, that is. On your way back it will be shorter. It always seems shorter on the way back, doesn't it? But in your case it will actually be shorter. For me, it's just a subjective illusion."

She continued to talk, warming up now, for the Frenchman, to her surprise, was a wonderful listener, nodding, smiling, laughing once in a while, never interrupting to add his own self-involved anecdotes to compete with her self-involved anecdotes. I'm pretty good at this conversation business, Margaret thought. I just needed the proper partner. She began to talk about Prague, about the opera there, about her talk, about the manuscript she had translated.

"The way ideas are disseminated is interesting, yes. That's what I write about — the history of ideas. But what is really marvelous is the human being's appetite for ideas. We're gourmands, indiscriminate, lustful idea hogs," she said. "Even though sometimes ideas, sometimes philosophy itself, are, is, just stupid. Stupid. Do you know what I mean? For example, for centuries there has been an argument about subjectivity versus objectivity. I mean in one form or another that's what they're always going on about. But that is stupid. Finally, it's just stupid. Obviously what we think or say or notice has to be subjective. But we wouldn't be able to think it, say it, or notice it if there weren't an 'it' to think, say, or notice, would we? And we wouldn't have any subjective information to project onto it if we hadn't already received that information from objective impressions before. But then again, it's not the 'it' that does the thinking, it's me. This is all so obvious, isn't it? I mean, these people have no common sense. Of course common sense is out of fashion now, anyway — it's an ideological construction of the bourgeois social formation. And there's no subjectivity either anymore, is there, because there's no subject. Because any attempt to act or perceive as a subject suggests that you are trying to conquer the object, and that's bad because it's impossible. You see, meaning is impossible to obtain, so any search for it is false and oppressive. And anyway, the subject is now the object, because we are trapped by language, which determines what we say and what we do. So the object — the world — is now really the subject, because it holds all the cards. Of course, you already know all this, being French. But finally it seems to me that this just brings us back to what I was saying in the first place: subjectivity is rooted in objectivity and objectivity can't really exist without subjectivity. Big deal."

The Frenchman looked at her with furrowed brows, with his pale gray eyes, and then without showing his teeth, his lips pouting just a bit more, turning up slightly at the corners, he smiled.

I've made a friend, Margaret thought. Is this really the kind of friend I meant to make, though? she wondered. The kind I kind of want to sleep with?

"You're awfully quiet," she said after a while.

He reached into his briefcase, took out a slender leather case with a gold pen and a pad of paper inside.

"*Laryngite*," he wrote. He pointed to his throat.

Margaret stared at her new friend. *Laryngite?* She took the pad from him, and the little pen.

"Sorry," she wrote irritably.

They sat silently for a while.

"Was there a dead baby?" the Frenchman suddenly wrote.

She started to write "Huh?" on the leather-bound pad. Why am I writing? she thought then, and shoved the pad rather ungraciously back to the Frenchman.

"Huh?" she said.

"A dead baby in the opera?" he wrote.

"No. Just a dead girl."

"*Katya Kabanova,*" he wrote.

"Oh yeah," Margaret said. "*Katya Kabanova.*"

IN HER DREAM, the Frenchman on the airplane stared at her as if she were a jewel he was appraising. His green-and-white-striped shirt rubbed suggestively against her bare arm. He examined her as if she were a jewel, with a jeweler's glass, while she lay naked on the hotel bed and his green-and-white-striped shirt stretched alluringly across his stomach.

"Enlightenment," said the Frenchman, "is man's emergence from his self-imposed nonage."

I know, she thought.

"Nonage," he said, "is the inability to use one's own understanding without another's guidance."

I know.

"Kant."

Kant.

"Kant said, 'Dare to know,'" said the Frenchman, handing her the jeweler's glass, but keeping hold of her hand once the jeweler's glass was in it. "Dare to know."

"Okay."

"FOLLOW ME!" he said, and pulled her into a little orange car with peeling paint.

Three

Because of a short journey I was obliged to take, to Geneva to attend to some matters regarding the publication of an edition of my *Treatise on Sense and Sociability,* I was forced to abandon temporarily my instruction of Rameau's niece. Separated from my pupil for over a month, I found myself bound to her more and more in imagination. I could not concentrate. I tried to write but could not. I tried to find something to do and began one task and gave it up for another, and that for yet another; my hands stopped of their own accord. I had never experienced anything like it.

At last, my business was successfully completed, much to my advantage, I might add, and yet I had so regretted the necessity for a trip that interrupted the education of my remarkable pupil that I returned with the greatest alacrity at my command.

Immediately upon reaching the house of the marquise, I inquired as to the whereabouts of Rameau's niece and, hearing that my student was walking alone in the garden, without stopping even to change my clothing, I followed in order to search her out.

My trip had afforded me many new experiences and given me much time for contemplation of new ideas, as well as the ideas my pupil and I had explored so diligently together, and I longed to impart to my student the fruits of my discoveries and of the many evenings spent in lonely contemplation, as soon as was feasible.

Walking through the garden, I recalled with rising spirits our first meeting, for memory can produce the most delicious state in a sensitive soul. I recalled how the affection we had conceived for our studies had grown from day to day. I rapturously recounted the observations I had made during our mutual pursuit of enlightenment: her sweet breath; her forehead, white and smooth and beautifully shaped; her eyes, sparkling with curiosity and intelligence; her tiny, dimpled hands; her bosom, firm as a statue and admirably formed; her rounded arms; her neck, exquisitely unusual in its beauty.

I walked on, thinking of how, after a night of the give and take of rigorous philosophical discussion, of delving unrelentingly for knowledge and for truth, my pupil would wrap her figure, which was of perfect proportions, in a muslin nightgown and leave my room, turning back at the door, running back to me to thank me for my efforts on her behalf, throwing her arms around my neck and covering me with kisses of gratitude. Truly, there is nothing so rewarding as the instruction of the young.

Ꙭ Ꙭ Ꙭ

WHEN MARGARET married Edward, she felt as if she'd walked in through a door and closed it gently behind her. Now that door had somehow opened. She'd looked through it, and it would no longer stay shut. It rattled with every breeze.

I have become an adulteress, she thought. An adulteress in the head. Many people are adulteresses. But until now I was not one of them and could not imagine becoming one of them. Now it is all I imagine.

She, Margaret Nathan, was one of those hateful people — the doctors who let their wives support them through medical school, then messed around with someone younger. She was the father of three who decided to find himself with his daughter's best friend. She was a restless housewife who became a campaign volunteer only to run off with a losing senatorial candidate. She was a philanderer, a liar, and a cheat, the villain of every pop song ever written.

In New York, away from statues and mute Frenchmen, Margaret waited for her intemperate, wanton mood to disperse. But it did not. I am obsessed, she realized. I think of nothing else. A visit to the fish market has become a bawdy escapade during which I look at young men in their running tights. I look at the man in Apartment 3E across the hall and I wonder if I will sleep with him. I look at Edward and wonder when I will betray him.

She had always told Edward everything, but she certainly could not tell him this. He would laugh at first, then, when he understood, he would be disgusted and hurt. Margaret ate with him and slept with him, but she did not really talk to him. The only thing she had to say she could not say to him.

It seemed impossible, to feel so distant from the man she loved. She had gone to Prague, seen some marble feet, and felt desire. So what? But her adventure played itself out in her imagination, over and over again. The man in the plane, asleep on her breast, burrowed deeper and deeper in her dreams.

"LOOK," Edward cried, pulling her to the window. "Look outside." He showed her proudly, as if the deep blue sky, its clarity, its quick white clouds, were his, or at least his doing. "Now out you go. A nice brisk walk. Do you good, darling."

"I walked in Prague. In New York I sit."

"Margaret, I'm worried about you. You're so glum and remote. You require cheering up. Shall we go out tonight? Do you want me to buy you a puppy?"

Margaret sighed.

"A mink coat? Just like Mummy's?"

Margaret thought of how they electrocute minks. One of Edward's students, the boy who had grown up on a mink farm, had described it to Margaret at dinner as one of Edward's other students, the adoring girl from the Boston suburb, had listened with a hurt, sad expression.

"Why are you being so nice to me?" Margaret asked Edward now.

"Yes, well, perhaps it was misguided. But I felt your absence deeply, Margaret. It's a relief to have you back with me."

Felt her absence deeply? How deeply? Deeply enough to seek solace elsewhere? A relief to have her back? What did that mean? Why a relief?

"Didn't you have your students to keep you company, to occupy you?" Margaret said.

"Well, I suppose."

Aha! Margaret thought.

"But it's not really the same thing, is it?"

Aha!

SHE THOUGHT about Prague constantly, confused and simply embarrassed by what had happened there. Which was precisely nothing, she reminded herself. Yet that nothing filled her with shame.

Then again, she thought, if I felt that way, if I felt overwhelmed by desire like that, then my marriage must be lacking. If my marriage is lacking, Edward is lacking. If Edward is lacking, I need something else, someone else. That certainly is sound, logical, circular reasoning. And anyway, who knows what Edward does with those adoring students of his? And if Edward thinks Walt Whitman is so great, then a little overwhelming sensuality and indulgence will strike him as healthful and grand, won't it? Not that he ever has to know.

For weeks, she went over the same ground, becoming more and more resentful. She had been sexually attracted to a stranger on a plane! How could Edward do this to her?

I am a fallen woman, she would think, and she would feel sick with a sense of her own dishonor. Edward, she would continue, the be-all and end-all of my existence, is not all, after all. He has failed me. And then she would become angry.

One afternoon, as she walked toward the bus stop, seething with regret and fury, she saw a man drop a candy wrapper on the ground. Don't do that, you fool, she thought, outraged. There is a garbage can not two feet from you. Don't litter. And then she laughed at herself, a sinner worried about a litterbug. And then she laughed again out loud and felt a sudden sense of power. She was a sinner! She had already transgressed, just by thinking of it, just by wanting to. Now she had nothing to lose. She was free.

The force of her attraction to another man, to other men, was exhilarating, an almost kinetic intensity carrying her along with it. Adultery, the failure of loyalty and honesty, was really an act of sublime Romantic rebellion. She had been given a chance at self-fulfillment. That door she'd let click behind her when she married Edward was now wide open, and it opened onto a pilgrim's path, the path to truth and philosophical awakening — to Enlightenment.

Reason fueled by Romanticism. Or vice versa. She felt herself overcome by an analytical fascination with her own desires. She luxuriated in a cold, cold passion.

THE MARATHON editing sessions with Richard became oddly charged now. They worked in Richard's office until the days became a week and then almost two. When Margaret left the office each day it was night. Once, fat wet snowflakes fell, silhouetted by the yellow of the streetlamps. Margaret bumped home in a taxi through the unearthly flurry. Had she eaten? Edward asked her. No, she didn't think so, she said. And she went to bed. Richard's voice, caressing, followed her, murmuring in her dreams.

"You're never home," Edward said one night, bending over her to kiss her before she fell asleep. "You've left me for an overrefined homosexual pedant." He sometimes referred to Richard as her other husband.

Each morning she rode to the office on the subway. She could think of three times when she had felt this same tremulous anticipation. When Richard had edited her first book. When she'd gone to a psychiatrist for a year. And her first trip with Edward. Courtship, psychotherapy, editing, Margaret thought. For the true egotist, they are all one.

She watched Richard as he hung up his jacket, rolled up his sleeves, then furiously slapped through piles of papers on his desk, found something, handed it to his assistant, and sarcastically inquired if he could manage to make three Xeroxed copies. They were where they belonged now, side by side at Richard's desk in Richard's office. No more shapeless world, infinite and buzzing with aimless attention-sucking uncles and nurses and taxi drivers.

To Margaret's delight, the phone rang, and Richard spluttered, stomped, and finally yanked the receiver toward him, then murmured his silvery "Hello?" At the sound of his voice, Margaret found herself unaccountably happy.

Perhaps she was in love. Perhaps it was Richard she desired. With gratitude and tenderness, she watched Richard speak into the phone and did not hear what he said. With his close-cropped hair and pink, close-shaven face, he looked very, very clean — radiant, Margaret thought — and she was overcome by a desire to touch that cleanliness, as if some of it, shining and uncomplicated, would rub off on her. To touch Richard, Margaret thought. What an astonishing idea.

"Margaret," he said, when he'd hung up, "your eyes are glittering and your cheeks are flushed."

"What?"

"Do you have the flu?"

"What? No."

"You're not contagious, are you?"

"No."

"I don't want to catch anything."

She studied him, so sturdy and well groomed, a refined Ivy League wrestling coach sort of a style. He leaned back in his chair and returned her stare. Richard, she thought. There you are. She smiled at him, excited by her secret thoughts.

"Germs are airborne," he said gravely.

Well, it felt like being in love, very much like being in love. She couldn't bear to be away from him. She forgot what to say when they were together. She thought everything he did was wonderful, even the things she knew very well were not wonderful at all but petty and unpleasant. He was her editor, her teacher. She felt indistinct, barely recognizable stirrings of physical desire. Yes, that all sounded right.

"Richard, I think I'm falling in love with you."

"You may admire me from afar if you like."

HER LUST for Richard was irritating and short-lived, like a mosquito. Puzzled, though somewhat relieved, Margaret considered possible reasons for this. Richard was not interested in women? Yes, but that made him something of a challenge, and it had not stopped her initial infatuation. She was no longer interested in other men? No. She was still cruising dads pushing strollers in the supermarket.

We've finished editing! That's all, Margaret realized. And so, didactic lust has bit the dust.

She turned toward Edward, who was lying beside her in bed, correcting papers, and watched him carefully. He had been unusually quiet this evening. His hair stuck up in tufts so defiant they seemed political. Had he read his students the poem about the boys bathing? The twenty-eight young men? And the one woman watching them? He had, she knew. He had read the poem, and twenty-eight young women had been watching him. He should be reading Whitman to her, not to twenty-eight girls trembling at their desks.

"How many in your Whitman seminar?" she asked.

"Nine. That's the cutoff. Nine spotty children who want to know if attendance counts."

"Does it?"

"No. They come to class anyway, they arrive early, they stay late, they dog my steps, loyal, adoring little pups jostling one another in their eagerness to approach their master. You know, I can't wait to see them either. Each Tuesday, each Thursday! Completely ignorant, this litter. They stare up at me, hushed. Whitman is astonishing the first time round."

They stared up at him, hushed. It was part of his magnanimous sense of his own glory, teaching. He rose before a class and presented himself and all he knew, and facing him, in the cloudless morning sunlight of his presence, his students basked, warmed themselves, and grew.

Which is all very nice, unless you happen to be the wife, Margaret thought. I am the wife.

∽ ∽ ∽

I dwelled on happy thoughts of Rameau's niece and our imminent reunion. Barely registering my surroundings, I realized I was headed directly toward a secluded spot to which my pupil and I had often come, a lovely corner of the garden little frequented by anyone but us.

I heard a rustling, perhaps of skirts, and my heart leapt. Could it be she? Here, in our own corner of the garden, our own private place of study? Had she sensed I would return that day? Had she gone there to await my arrival, knowing I would repair there directly in search of her?

I reached the place and, oh! that I had lengthened my trip, or that the horse had thrown a shoe, or that I had rested, a long and sound sleep, or changed my clothes, dressing slowly and meticulously, before seeking Rameau's niece. For indeed she was there, my pupil, in that spot where I expected her. The skirts that rustled were hers. But she was not alone, and her skirts rustled not from the breeze, nor as they brushed against a shrub, but as they were lifted and arranged by her companion, pushed here and there as her companion sought their most expeditious disposal.

Her companion was clearly a man of low birth. He was in fact, the gardener, and I at first assumed this meeting was not of my pupil's choosing; but one look at her face, her gentle, untroubled expression, convinced me otherwise. She was sighing, breathing heavily. Through her half-open eyes she saw me then, and with an effort, she sat up, her clothes draped in disarray, and pushed the gardener from her. A robust young lad with an appealing aspect, he had caught my eye more than once as he toiled in the kitchen garden. But now I looked at him not with admiration, although what I saw of him now was robust indeed as he stood stupidly before me, his breeches below his thighs, his shirt rolled up under his vest. Then, in an instant, he was gone, running, as well he should have, pulling up his breeches as he went.

I turned to my pupil, now rearranging her skirts, smoothing her bodice. I waited, expecting her to hurl herself at my feet, to beg my forgiveness, trembling, with downcast eyes. Instead, she looked at me, evenly and without embarrassment. And, to my further astonishment, she smiled.

ᘒᘒ ᘒᘒ ᘒᘒ

MARGARET WOKE UP each morning in a groggy panic. Often she had been dreaming of the Frenchman, and as she opened her eyes she wondered where she was. Then, as the feel of his skin against hers receded further, she would see the Venetian blinds and hear Edward humming in the bathroom. What time was it? What was she forgetting? she wondered. What had she neglected while dreaming of a man she didn't even know? What meeting? What phone call? What bill to be paid? What was she working on? What brilliant ideas had slipped her mind while she slept?

Restless and disgusted, Margaret tried to console herself with this romantic formulation: To forget is to live in a world of shadows, of unreality. A forgetful person was the only authentic person, for life made no sense and so confusion was the only truth!

No cigar, Margaret. Try again?

Forgetfulness is an absence of humanity, of concern for one's fellow man. To forget is to negate. Forgetfulness is nihilism.

Or perhaps forgetfulness was escapism? Or a sign of purity, an inability to be tainted by the worldly horrors of existence?

Forgetfulness was insensitivity! Forgetfulness was sensitivity, openness to anything new! Forgetfulness was antipathy! Forgetfulness was sympathy, an embrace of life unencumbered by prejudices!

Was forgetfulness discretion, the ability to filter out what didn't matter?

No. Margaret knew the real answer. Forgetfulness was never knowing what mattered. To judge was to compare? Then forgetfulness was an inability to make judgments based on information because of an absence of information. Forgetfulness was stupidity. Margaret shuddered.

Edward was singing now, and listening to him crow splendidly, Margaret felt anger and disappointment wash over her. I am angry at Edward. Therefore, she thought in an attempt to meet this difficulty in a useful and rational way, Edward must be doing something to make me angry at him. What, though?

It was true that Edward was going to be forty in a few months. Perhaps that was it. Everyone knew what that meant, every American anyway. Forty meant mid-life. And mid-life meant mid-life crisis. Husbands chased young girls in order to deny their own mortality. They moved to faraway places with warm climates. They quit their jobs. They chased more young girls to deny their own mortality even more in faraway places with warm climates, where, without jobs, they had plenty of leisure time in which to chase young girls. In the sun. It was almost inconceivable that this was happening to her husband, her Edward, who didn't much care for young girls or tropical vacations, whom she had trusted so completely — but not inconceivable enough.

Margaret was going to be thirty. In two years, anyway. Being so much younger than Edward had always seemed such a good idea, a deterrent to this absurd phenomenon. But thirty, while still two years away and ten years younger than forty, no longer struck her as being all that young. Edward was going to be forty and have a mid-life crisis. It said so in every pop psychology book in every rack in every airport gift shop. No wonder she was angry at him, Margaret thought.

"IT'S BLOODY AWFUL out there," Edward said one day, his eyes red and teary from the sub-zero wind.

"What do you mean? It's March. What do you expect. The seasons are very important. It's boring to live in an unchanging climate, day after day, sunny, sunny, sunny. It's enervating and debilitating. The British Empire wasn't built by beachcombers."

"The British Empire has collapsed, and I'm thinking of joining it. What a ghastly day."

"I think it's lovely outside. Invigorating," Margaret said.

"Yes. You are young and foolhardy. But now you have inspired me. What is a little cold to an Englishman? Even an aging Englishman like me? Come, Margaret. A stroll!"

"I suppose you want to move to Tahiti. You want to retire, don't you?" she said.

"The women there are far too voluptuous for my taste," Edward said. "But it's a thought."

Margaret watched him drink a cup of tea and remembered when they had been married only a few weeks, how she would wake up and wonder where she was and look at him with a sudden, powerful recognition and wonder how this had happened to her, how she had wound up beside someone she loved so much that she wanted to wake up beside him forever.

MARGARET poured her coffee and turned on the TV in the kitchen. Seated in an armchair by a coffee table, a woman in a navy blue dress and pearls sat demurely reciting obscene rap lyrics. Was she the wife of a senator? An enraged mother moved to unaccustomed political action? A new, white female rap singer with an ironically understated style?

"Face down, ass up, that's the way we like to" — she paused, gave a small smile, and said in a quiet, refined voice — "F-curse." Her hands were folded in her lap. "Now, does the first amendment require that we expose our children to violence and demeaning sexual rhetoric?" She shook her head slightly. "I don't think so."

She smiled pleasantly, then lifted up a magazine and began waving it. The magazine looked familiar to Margaret.

"I would like to refer you to the work of the distinguished historian of ideas, Margaret Nathan, who has shown that pornography has served as a destructive, revolutionary force, leading directly to an epidemic of bloody excess during the French Revolution, to mob violence, to oppression and the destruction of the very freedom these irresponsible young people use as a shield for their unsavory music . . ."

Edward laughed. He was just back from running, his sweat-shirt hood still up. "Margaret Nathan, public enemy of Public Enemy."

Margaret turned the set off. This was the final humiliation.

"Rapping, the root of eighteenth-century chaos, cause of the Terror," Edward went on. With his long red face and tight hood he looked like an emaciated baby. "I always suspected something of the sort. Disc master Robespierre. I wish people would misquote *me* on television."

"What do they want from me?" Margaret said, not because it related directly to the immediate situation, but because it was what her grandfather had always said when anything was wrong in any situation. "What do they want from me?"

Edward said, "Whatever it is, they certainly can't have it. You're mine, mine, mine."

Margaret wondered what he wanted with her, what he wanted with what was his, his, his. She had been cold and unpleasant to him for weeks. She no longer laughed at his stupid jokes or bothered to ask who he was quoting or told him about her work that day or asked him how to spell a word.

"I've been very unpleasant," Margaret said. "I'm sorry." She was sorry. But she knew she would continue to be unpleasant. She was angry at Edward. Couldn't he see that? Didn't he notice what a bitch she was? Why did he continue to be nice to her when she was behaving so badly?

"Yes, well, I think of marriage as being quite like the weather, you know, in that it changes frequently, it's unpredictable, and I just happen to live in a particularly stormy climate. But then I rather like storms. Beautiful, exciting. And then the sun comes out."

Margaret stared at him, moved and infuriated. Storms indeed. He should only know from storms. The fire next time, pal.

"Did I ever tell you of my theory of adultery?" Edward continued.

Margaret sat rigidly in her chair. She stared at her coffee cup. It was a lovely coffee cup, part of a set given to them as a wedding gift by Edward's mother, a professor of anthropology at York University who made her own jewelry and avant-garde furniture. Did Edward's mother know he had a theory of adultery? She probably taught it to him, the old reprobate. But why was she calling Edward's mother an old reprobate? Edward's mother was old. But it was she, Margaret, who was the reprobate. Nearly. And Edward himself, of course.

"My theory is this: that with monogamy came the end of evolution for the human species. For if a male has only one mate, then the superior male cannot plant his seed hither and thither —"

"Thither?"

"Thither. And so, he cannot perpetuate his superiority in lavish numbers, if you see what I mean. As for the female, the superior monogamous female who is capable of enticing all the superior males sniffing about cannot mate with all of them, and so cannot improve the gene pool to any significant extent. Natural selection requires selection. But monogamy precludes that. Swans mate for life. We could all end up like swans, with those absurdly long necks. Enter adultery! The savior of evolution, the hero of the race!"

"My gene pool's not good enough for you? You're going to fuck around to save the world? Fuck you, Edward. That's a terrible theory. Go back to weather."

Edward looked at her, alarmed. "I didn't mean you and me, Margaret. That was my point, that we are irresponsible, you and I, thinking only of ourselves instead of the greater good. Monogamy is an indulgence. But perhaps the human race can take care of itself," he added. "And long necks are very pretty, I think. Audrey Hepburn has a lovely long neck."

"Why don't you go plant your precious seed there?"

"In her neck?"

Margaret looked at him. His eyes were almost frightening when she looked at them head on, a pale but piercing blue, unyielding, intense. They took in everything and gave nothing back, not even a clue.

"You have a lovely long neck, too," Edward said softly. "A splendid neck."

"Well," she said, "I think I feel a storm coming on." And she walked out of the room.

Edward didn't argue, he didn't scold her. But she did notice that in spite of a large reservoir of Romantic poetry on the subject of meteorological excess, she left him silent behind her, quoting nothing.

MARGARET SAT in the library gazing at the dancing dust, golden and airy, all around her, from the lofty ceiling to the scuffed wooden floor. Perhaps Jove lurked in this flurry of sunlit particles, cruising for an undergraduate Io.

She was reading Hobbes, and she thought of Art Turner. "To have received from one, to whom we think ourselves equal, greater benefits than there is hope to requite," wrote Hobbes, "disposeth to counterfeit love; but really secret hatred; and puts a man into the estate of a desperate debtor. For benefits oblige, and obligation is thralldom." You can say that again, Margaret thought.

She got up to go, glancing around the room again. *Adieu,* Jove, *adieu.* And, look, there is a girl reading *Leaves of Grass.* An exquisite little girl with long brown hair, as smooth as silk, and that complexion that girls with silken hair always have. Was this the one? Yes, it was the girl who had come to dinner. Stick to your books, that's a good girl. But what if this *was* the one? Margaret stared at her, disgusted that Edward could be drawn in by such earnest innocence. Edward is a fool, she thought. *Adieu* to you both.

She took an empty but overheated bus home, and her anger rose until she heard a humming in her ears. This is my karma, she thought. As ye sow as a student, so shall ye reap as a faculty wife.

"YOU GOT HOME awfully late last night," Margaret said.

"Yes, you were asleep. I like you when you're asleep."

"I wasn't asleep."

"Ah. I like you when you pretend you're asleep."

Margaret noticed that he had changed the subject. The subject was that he had come home late. Why had he come home late? Why had he changed the subject? She thought she knew why, and she didn't like it.

"You didn't answer my question," she said.

Edward, cooking his horrible tomatoes and mushrooms for breakfast, looked at her in irritation. "You didn't ask a question," he said.

"It was implied."

"How subtle of you, Margaret. I'm so bloody literal-minded, though. I was in the library until it closed, then I went to have a drink with some students. I was home at midnight, wasn't I? What on earth are you sulking about?"

Margaret's coffee was cold, which seemed typical, symptomatic, symbolic, and Edward's fault for drawing her into this absurd situation. "My coffee is cold. Perhaps you spend too much time at your work," she said.

"Sunny von Bulow uttered just those very words to Claus. Tread carefully, Margaret."

Why did he think of Claus von Bulow? Margaret wondered. Von Bulow had been seeing another woman, hadn't he?

"Yes," Margaret said. "I will. I will tread carefully."

MARGARET LIKED watching Lily puff on cigarettes and rollick verbally through the iniquities of society as if they were fields of wildflowers and she a little lamb.

"Cappuccino?" asked the waitress in the coffee shop. "We just got a machine. New machine."

"Now take the word *machine,*" Lily said. She tilted her head just a bit. "Why not 'da-chine'? Why ma-chine? I'll tell you why not da-chine. Because it is woman, ma, ma-ma, who has been objectified, turned into a ma-chine, a sexual apparatus." Lily smiled contentedly.

"No cappuccino, I guess," Margaret said to the waitress. Lily, I don't see what I see in you sometimes, except perhaps what you see in me, she thought. You are the pool to my Narcissus.

As Lily rambled on, Margaret silently admired the color of her eyes, which were almost lavender, and daydreamed. Lily, in her breathless desire to spot the world's linguistic traps, was like a child opening a book, trying to find drawings of animals hidden in pictures of living rooms and shoe stores. Instead of the sour, jaded intellectual that Lily meant to be, she seemed young and open and charmingly naive.

Lily noticed Margaret staring at her, and she blushed, quiet for a moment. But her blush seemed a sign of comfort. Her very presence was a sigh of contentment and belonging. I belong here, said the sigh. I belong to you and only you — every one of you.

The essence of charm, Margaret thought, was the ability to see others in their best light, to perceive them honestly in the way they would like to be seen, to present to them an interesting, a marvelous, version of themselves. Lily saw Margaret as a happy, well-rounded bourgeoise, a liberal humanist who was perfectly socialized. Bless you, Margaret thought.

"Lily," she said, "I have a feeling 'machine' derives from a Greek word, don't you? Did they say 'mama' in Greece?"

"Oh, well, you — you're in denial, Margaret," Lily said. She held her water glass to her lips but didn't drink, rolling the rim back and forth instead, rather suggestively.

ONE OF LILY'S most appealing peculiarities was her passion for shopping. A reformed suburban princess in so many ways, she still clung to this one bit of unreconstructed behavior, altered considerably by where she shopped and for what but still easily recognizable nevertheless to the trained eye. Lily operated primarily in thrift shops, but she could also be found in SoHo or on Madison Avenue. She viewed clothes as costumes and enjoyed herself immensely on these outings.

Margaret, who remembered the monotony of her private school uniforms with longing, nevertheless would watch Lily with attentive amusement as she slipped in and out of dressing rooms. It was like playing dolls. Try the poodle skirt and the sweater with pom-poms, then the shimmering cranberry tuxedo jacket or the flowered housedress. Sometimes Margaret would sit in the dressing room with Lily, lazily watching her wriggle into a black cocktail dress or step out, with dainty feet, of short shorts decorated with salt and pepper shakers.

There was something exclusively feminine about these expeditions, even those on which Pepe Pican tagged along. The piles of rumpled clothing, the lacy flash of bras and underwear, the intimate presence of pale, rounded, slightly scented limbs, intoxicated Margaret with its alluring, somehow exotic familiarity, while outside the dressing room Pepe moodily examined old neckties, which he collected.

Once Margaret asked Pepe what he was working on.

"My diction," he said.

"DO YOU HAVE a lot of friends?" she asked Lily one day.

"No. Well, enough. But what I really need is a lover."

A lover, Margaret thought. Why not? Maybe that really was the way to go. Sordid, perhaps. Disloyal. Or was it her duty to herself? "Maybe that's what I need, too," she said.

Lily laughed at such a preposterous idea.

"Well, marriage is not perfect, you know," Margaret said.

"No. But neither is anything else."

"You're supposed to say that marriage is an enslavement of my soul."

"Your soul craves enslavement, Margaret. That's what gives you a sense of security and perpetuates the bourgeois myth of happiness."

"Oh, yeah. That's right," Margaret said.

"Stability, happiness, loyalty — these are artificial constructs, disguising themselves as 'the nature of things' in order to prop up the tottering status quo. There is no happiness. Happiness is just another narrative, a net in which we're caught."

"Just so it doesn't drop me," said Margaret.

∽ ∽ ∽

MYSELF: You are my pupil! How can you have done this thing?

SHE: Sir, the passions can do all things, is that not so?

MYSELF: Passions! Nonsense!

SHE: A man, or a woman, without passions is incapable of that degree of attention to which a superior judgment is annexed.

MYSELF: I hope I do not understand you to question my own attention?

SHE: Certainly not. You are a teacher of genius.

MYSELF: Ah.

SHE: And yet I have read, regarding genius, that a genius is an adventurous leader who penetrates the region of discoveries.

MYSELF: I find nothing to argue with there.

SHE: I have read that truths yet unknown wander in the regions of discoveries, waiting for someone to seize them.

MYSELF: As I have seized?

SHE: As you have seized, yes, seized the truths that were wandering, waiting for someone to seize them and transport them to this terrestrial sphere. But I have read that once these truths have descended to earth and been perceived by superior minds, they become what might be called common property.

MYSELF: Common property? What absurdity! What are you saying?

SHE: A genius lays open the road. As, for example, you have laid open a road, my road. A genius lays open the road so that men of a more common capacity may rush in crowds after him.

MYSELF: I have done no such thing!

SHE: For we must remember that common man does have the force necessary to follow the genius, otherwise genius would there penetrate alone.

MYSELF: And what is wrong with that? Why should not genius there penetrate alone?

SHE: But you yourself have taught me that the end of the social art is to secure and extend for all the enjoyment of the common rights which impartial nature has bequeathed to us all. The only privilege of genius is to make the first track.

My pupil (or was she now my teacher?) had remained seated upon her shawl as it lay spread on the grass. Could this really be she, this philosopher of her own pleasure? Is this what I had taught her? Her search for knowledge had led her away from me, her teacher. I turned from her and made my way back to the house, disconsolate and miserable.

☙ ☙ ☙

THERE WAS an unexpected message on the answering machine. "Margaret," said a female voice. "I know you haven't seen me in almost ten fucking years, but I'm having a book party. For the book I started when I knew you. So would you come? You better!"

It was Jessica. Margaret recognized the voice, and she had seen a review of the book, pretty favorable, in the *Times* last week. It was a mystery set at a local TV station called *Murder in Media Res*.

The party was on Tuesday at an East Side grill. Margaret had a terrible toothache, a toothache that rattled her head, but she went, of course. Jessica also had been a reader at the same small publishing house where Margaret had worked one summer. Rhodes Press, now defunct, had published highbrow radical works and Edwardian pornography. There had been several young editors and readers who hung out together that summer.

Margaret spotted Jessica easily. Her face was ridiculously familiar. She was now a TV journalist who had achieved some notoriety by giving the soundman the finger while still on camera. "I have a kid now," she said. "Can you believe it? I'm married to a lawyer. Can you fucking believe it? Do you still smoke pot? Oh, you never did, did you? I don't anymore. I mean I would if anybody ever had any, which nobody ever does."

Edward had to leave the party early to give a lecture somewhere. Margaret, who found herself daily more angry at and less tolerant of Edward, had not even bothered to ask what about or to whom, and after he was gone, she stood surrounded by her old friends. The icy cold of her demure glass of mineral water, with its bright, slender wedge of lime, rolled across her bad tooth in shattering pain. She considered having some wine to numb things a bit, but then remembered her bibulous evening in Paris, and so, uncomfortable and sober, she observed with fascinated nostalgia the four men standing with her and Jessica. She realized that she had slept with all four. Teddy, who had become a tenured professor of comp. lit. specializing in narratology, now had long stylish hair and was wearing a sharkskin suit and delicate Italian loafers that looked like pumps or bedroom slippers, in spite of which he still had a lugubrious physical charm.

"I can't smoke pot now," he said. "Fucking cocaine fucked me. I said to my students, 'What do Sherlock Holmes and Freud have in common?' And this girl says, 'Drug addiction?' I said, 'Why do you put it that way? Not drug addiction, you idiot. Cocaine.' Margaret, it's fucking amazing, but you look just the same. We all look the fucking same to each other, because we're all ten years older. You know, you taught me to speak like this, Jessica. I grew up in a nice home, then I met you. I never say 'fuck' to my students."

"Girlfriend?" Jessica said.

"Two years. New apartment, thirtieth floor. Great view. So now I've got vertigo and go to a fucking shrink twice a week."

"I thought narratology was passé," Margaret said, annoyed somehow that he had a steady girlfriend. He had a hangdog

Russian Jewish face that she had always found irresistible. "In France they're reading James Madison."

"The fucking French."

The rhythms and patterns of the past came back to them, crept back, stealthily. They had talked like this in the exhilarating late-night boredom of people whose jobs meant nothing to them, on and on into the morning, at restaurants, on street corners. Had they done anything else? Yes, there had been those vague sexual encounters, less the products of desire than of opportunity.

One of these former flames standing around Margaret was now a gay activist who was occasionally quoted in the *New York Times*. Another was a Marxist film professor at a community college. Margaret had argued with him into the wee hours of many a morning, but she couldn't remember his name. She'd see him on cable TV once in a while over the years. (Thin enough to be a drug addict, she thought, but certainly not one. Perhaps he jogged. No, Marxists didn't jog.) The last in this group of past follies was now a very hot editor of lurid minimalist novels. His picture appeared regularly in the tabloids with club celebrities. He nodded at Margaret, then left the party with a thuggish young man in a large suit.

Margaret sat down at a little table and closed her eyes and tried to remember. What had they looked like, these lovers, as lovers? Had she liked them? The spin of statues in Prague came back to her. The man on the plane, breathing, human and close, came back to her.

She opened her eyes. Desire is a state of uneasiness. She had read that in *Rameau's Niece*. She was uneasy and stood up to go home.

"Margaret!"

It was Till. Margaret had forgotten that Till might be here.

Now she watched Till approach. Please don't yell at me in front of all these people, she thought. Please don't tell them I hate Art Turner, the man who discovered me. Please go away.

"Margaret! I'm so glad to see you! I was hoping you'd be here."

Why? Margaret wondered. She put her hand to her cheek, where the tooth throbbed. Had Margaret been forgiven? Had time healed Till's wound? Or had Till been storing her anger and resentment for lo, these many months, and now, with a really well stocked larder of the stuff, she was sliding through the crowd to share some of it with Margaret?

"Hi," Margaret said.

With a jangle of bracelets, Till threw her arms around Margaret's neck, kissed her on both cheeks, and said, "Margaret, I want you to know I've written the most wonderful play. It's about egotism. And selfishness and insensitivity, of course, and it's all based on you, and I'm really so grateful to you, you really are a wonderful friend, this is clearly my best work, commercial but serious —"

"You're not mad at me? You forgive me?"

"Forgive you? I want to thank you! This play is inspired, and inspired by you."

"What about Art?" Margaret said, looking around for him, for the smile, the teeth set perfectly, like traps.

"That's what I'm trying to say — this is art!"

"No, no, your husband."

"Art?" Till said. "Why, we split up last month. I'm living with my therapist. Didn't I tell you? I think I have you to thank for that, too, Margaret. You're loyal and honest in your way, aren't you? The truth shall set you free. Free at last, free at last, thank God almighty, free at last. Do you and Edward want to come for dinner? Willibald and I are having a little dinner party. Friday . . ."

*

IN THE WEEK following Jessica's party, Margaret's tooth continued to hurt, not all the time, but on and off throughout the day. Each time it hurt, she thought first of Till and Art, a couple who had uncoupled, and she felt instead of the triumph that she expected to feel, a nervous uncertainty. Then the tooth would throb again, and, like a dog in an experiment, she would think of her friends at Jessica's party.

One morning she lay on her bed after a shower, closed her eyes, and for a moment she remembered lying back in her narrow bed in a high-ceilinged room in Florence. It was a summer session of her college in a villa surrounded by hills blooming with lavender and olive trees. When she finished her classes each evening, she would stand and look across the hills and think of taking a long, solitary walk. But she hated to be solitary, she was tired, it was beastly hot, and so she would go to flirt with one of the professors, a young, fresh-faced midwesterner. At night, when the heat was unbearable, the two of them would plunge into the small swimming pool. In the dark they could not see the thick green algae. In the dark they could not see each other. But they sensed each other as they floated on their backs. They never spoke in the pool.

After staring at the stars and soaking in the cool, green brine, Margaret would silently leave the pool and go to her room to lie there, wet, to feel the water evaporating in the heavy heat.

She lay back on her bed now, wet, and cursed her throbbing tooth and cursed Edward's students more.

They never slept together, not that summer, not in Florence. They never even acknowledged it as a possibility. He was married, and Margaret liked his wife. She liked his wife more than she liked him, actually. He was blustery, assertive, boyish. His wife was capable and witty in a surprisingly straightforward way. They never slept together that summer.

But Margaret visited them in Chicago the following winter. Then they slept together. It had seemed inevitable. Awful, sneaky, dishonest, exciting, and inevitable. Margaret was sickened whenever she thought of it, pleasant as the actual encounter had been. It was the worst thing she had ever done.

Edward came into the room.

"Why do you look so miserable?" he said. "Your tooth again?"

"No. I'm thinking of the worst thing I ever did."

"And what's that? Raped all those students in Gainesville?"

"I can't tell you. I can't tell anyone."

Edward looked intrigued. "Margaret! What can it be?"

For a moment, the new strangeness between them forgot itself, forgot to assert itself, and Margaret kissed Edward's hand as he stroked her cheek. He lifted a lock of wet hair, dropped it, and made a face. "What can it be?" he said again, then stood up and walked away, his mind already on something else.

Margaret sat up and brushed her hair and tried to forget the worst thing she ever did.

She decided to call Richard. "Do you have a good dentist?" she asked.

"Yes. He takes dentistry awfully seriously. I receive regular correspondence from him keeping me up to date on late-breaking developments in the field of teeth. Extremely expensive. Handsome —"

"I'm almost done with the book," she told him. "And it's just as well. I'm turning into a libertine. I think I used to be a libertine, actually. I sometimes think I'd like to be a libertine again."

"How athletic of you even to be able to contemplate such a thing, Margaret."

IN THE WAITING ROOM, she wondered what Richard's dentist would look like. Perhaps he would look like her last dentist, who retired at the age of fifty, a trim, tennis-playing, Jewish, art-collecting man with a slightly receding hairline. She had been to several dentists in her life, and all of them had looked like that, so perhaps he would, too. She sat on the modular couch in the sunken well in the gray-carpeted waiting room (there was carpeting on the walls, as well as the floor) and put her hand to her cheek where the tooth throbbed.

She took some photocopied sheets of Rousseau's *Émile* from her briefcase. She had traced several sections of *Rameau's Niece* to *Émile*. The strategy of the anonymous hack author of *Rameau's Niece* had been to lift lines, paragraphs, a phrase, whatever he chose from whomever he chose, and use them in whatever ways he chose. The result may have been incoherent at times, but it always maintained an unmistakably libertine sensibility, a sense of a world order as tangled as bed sheets.

"I am aware of my soul," she read from *Émile*. "It is known to me in feeling and in thought; I know what it is without knowing its essence; I cannot reason about ideas which are unknown to me. What I do know is this, that my personal identity depends upon memory, and that to be indeed the same self I must remember that I have existed. Now after death I could not recall what I was when alive unless I also remembered what I felt and therefore what I did; and I have no doubt that this remembrance will one day form the happiness of the good and the torment of the bad."

That leaves me out, Margaret thought as she imagined herself floating in some confusion through the heavens. I forget, she would say to the celestial gatekeeper. I forget, and so I am not.

She closed her eyes, listened to the woman across the room turn the pages of a magazine, opened her eyes, looked briefly and enviously at the woman, who had white hair and a short mohair jacket and a sensible skirt and sensible shoes and probably sense as well. What a good idea, Margaret thought, to be sensible.

"Just put it on the right line. Don't screw me up," said another waiting patient, a woman in late middle age sitting beside a man filling out insurance forms. Margaret assumed he was her husband, but then he said, "You're treating me like my wife. You're getting to be like my wife." Maybe she was his mother.

"She's a pain, but she's beautiful. My wife is beautiful," he was saying. "Her skin —"

"Dream," said the woman sharply.

"What-ya mean, 'dream'?"

"Like a dream," she said. "Skin like a dream."

Margaret turned from the pages of *Émile* to some pages from *Rameau's Niece*. "MYSELF: What I do know is this, that my personal identity depends upon memory. For the body will be worn out and destroyed by the division of its parts. But does the promise of storms stop our enjoyment of today's beautiful sun?

"After death, I would not be able to recall what I was when alive unless I also remembered what I felt and therefore what I did. Let us, therefore, dear pupil, feel and do and so create memories worthy of eternity."

THE RECEPTIONIST opened the door that led to the little rooms and their low-slung medical-modernist chairs. She motioned Margaret to follow her, and Margaret obeyed, stung by the sudden scent of cloves.

She stretched herself out on the dentist's chair and closed her eyes. The room was cool and she was tired. Muzak burbled gently from a loudspeaker somewhere above her. She wondered what Edward was doing at that moment. Waving his arms at his students, reciting to them. Who were his students this term, anyway? Had he mentioned any?

No. He hasn't mentioned any, has he? she thought. She lay in the dentist's chair in the dim and frigid pearl gray room. Sprawled there, she suddenly felt the cold.

Why hasn't he? He always talks about his students, especially the one or two bright ones who frequent his office after class to talk, but mostly, Margaret suspected, to listen. And to flirt.

"Margaret?" An oddly textured hand touched her cheek. She opened her eyes and saw him. His black hair was slicked back like a TV drug dealer's. Beneath his starched white doctor's coat, a white polo shirt clung to a slender but startling, articulated, muscular torso. Around his neck, he wore a thin gold chain with two small gold charms. His watch, which touched her cheek, beeped in little shrill, computerized gasps. His face was covered by a large transparent blue plastic shield. The hand that had touched her was covered by a milky yellow rubber glove, the color and texture of a condom. Margaret was in love.

*

MARGARET KNEW that since coming home from Prague she'd felt increasingly guilty and increasingly suspicious, that the sight of Edward had become distressing, almost an accusation, a reminder of her flirtation with faithlessness, of his own probable faithlessness, and worst of all, of her failure to be faithless in the face of his presumably successful faithlessness.

But did that mean she had to fall in love with the first thing that crossed her path, as if she were a duckling that hatched from its shell to follow a bespectacled naturalist, quacking the duckling's equivalent for "Mama!" because it knew it was due for a mama, and the man in the hiking shorts was there first?

Dr. Lipi had put his rubber-gloved hand on hers, and said, "What is your relationship to your teeth?" She lay in bed at home, dizzy from codeine. What is my relationship to my teeth? she wondered. Close? Estranged? Frosty? Neurotic?

And with a sigh of pleasure she again felt his hands brushing her shoulders as he unhooked the cool metal chain that held the wrinkled square bib of sea green paper. He had lifted his mask to reveal a face oddly balanced between absurd sensuality and stony severity. His cheekbones were high and angular, his eyes lurking narrowly above them. But beneath, the soft landscape of his full lips curved seductively. He stared at her blankly, his eyes, deep and remote, seeming to focus only when he trained them on her teeth. He was horribly handsome, a puzzle of exaggerated features. Margaret had not been able to take her eyes off him. His very indifference excited her.

Margaret lay in bed and thought longingly of the dentist's chest and the dentist's lips and the dentist's latex-clad finger along her tender gums. She saw the dentist's narrow eyes neutrally moving toward their goal, her diseased molar, then brightening with excitement. She saw this, in her mind, and her pulse quickened. "Mama!" cried the duckling.

And she thought she had caught something in his manner when he told her she would have to come back, something in the way he swung the blue protective mask he was holding to and fro, his nervous throat-clearing, the extra moment, the pause, as he accidentally caught sight of himself in the small round mirror he set down on the table — something, anyway, that suggested he would be pleased if she returned, that he wanted to see her again.

"There will be a bruise," he had said, with particular tenderness, she thought.

AFTER THE SECOND VISIT, Dr. Lipi asked her to come into his office and sit across from him, his large mahogany desk between them, just like a regular doctor. In England, Margaret thought, you'd be Mr. Lipi, so what is all this about? You're just a dentist, after all.

"I am a dentist," Mr. Lipi said with an almost solemn excitement, and then he paused.

"I hope so," Margaret said, putting her hand to her cheek.

"Now please pay attention," he said. His eyes had a zealous, discomfiting sparkle. In fact, there was something generally sparkling about him, an electricity, a static, a charge with no place to go, a light with no bulb to contain it, a radio wave with no receiver.

He pulled several photographs from his desk drawer. "The movement of the human mandible is forward and downward," he said.

Mandible, she thought. Renamed the desmoulins, after Camille Desmoulins, a lawyer who placed leaves in his hat, calling for all patriots to arm themselves and don a similar green cockade.

Dr. Lipi had moved on to explain the anatomical correspondence between the forms and the arrangement of teeth, in particular the form of the condyle of the inferior maxilla. Individuals who have teeth with long cusps have the head of the bone much rounded, he said, and he paused dramatically, staring at her, waiting for a response.

She looked away, embarrassed by his intensity, until he began to speak again.

"There is a preponderance of the direct over the oblique muscles of mastication," he said loudly, almost angrily, and he thumped the desk with a clenched fist. Then he smiled, and in an ordinary, genial voice, said, "But of course that's not an issue with you, Ms. Nathan," handed her a new toothbrush, and dismissed her.

Whew, she thought, when she'd left the office. Someone has not been taking his lithium.

MARGARET LOOKED forward to another of these meetings, to sitting before the immense, glossy desk, waiting restlessly for the room to fill with the edgy vanity, the urgent, heroic sense of importance of Dr. Lipi the dentist. And Dr. Lipi did call her in, several times. He tenderly handed her samples of dental floss, as if they were the Host and he a prophet of a particularly mighty God. He scolded her for past transgressions against her teeth and, worse, her gums. He encouraged her with the possibility of redemption through quarterly curettage.

But mostly he discussed the way things worked — the mechanical operations of the jaw, the chemical composition of enamel. He considered it part of being a dentist, teaching his patients, alerting them to the wonders of their own mouths. She found herself caught up in his need to explain, feeling a corresponding need to understand.

"I know it seems silly," he said softly, after showing her a series of drawings depicting the evolutionary relationship between the ape jaw and the human jaw. "But the mouth does so much! It's miraculous, and, without teeth, what are we?" He showed her a drawing of the vertical section of the tooth *in situ*. "Toothless."

Margaret lusted after Dr. Lipi, Dr. Lipi the beautifully proportioned, proselytizing tooth scholar. Once he projected onto a screen slides of bacteria he had scraped from her teeth. Margaret sat attracted, repelled, transfixed. They discussed the anatomy of teeth, Margaret wondering at his unquenchable fascination with the bits and pieces of the mouth, looking at his own mouth, his sensuous lips, his teeth, listening and watching, occasionally offering one of the new names created by Madame de Montigny, to Dr. Lipi's obvious delight. He was an extraordinarily handsome man, muscular but without bulk, his face half soft and sensuous, half craggy and almost unnaturally alert. He stood often in a pose so suggestive and so familiar and yet so unusual that Margaret felt her breathing lose its rhythm and the blood thump crazily in her ears. His wide shoulders and slim torso tilted languorously back, his flat stomach curved in gently, one leg bent at the knee, one arm curled up in front of him until his cupped hand rested in the crook of his neck, as though he were holding something slung over his shoulder, and sometimes he did hold something like that, a manila folder or his blue plastic mask. Margaret stared and stared until she realized that he stood as Michelangelo's David stood, a perfect, magnificent copy, like the one in the square by the Uffizi, the one covered with pigeons. Pigeons would have gathered with pride on Dr. Lipi, so elegantly did he stand, Margaret the pigeon delirious among them.

Dr. Lipi had a cable dentistry show called "Eye on Your Teeth." He had a tooth spa at Elizabeth Arden. He traveled in private jets to attend to the teeth of the rich and famous. He chatted on about osteoblasts and cement corpuscles, Hertwig's epithelial sheath, and the interglobular spaces of Czermak. And sometimes he wondered if perhaps he didn't owe it to the world to minister to those less fortunate as well.

"You could have a truck," Margaret suggested. "Like the Lubavitchers."

As Dr. Lipi gravely considered this suggestion, Margaret considered his lovely, shapely, sinewy arms as they emerged from his short-sleeved shirt, and she thought, He's mad as a hatter, isn't he?

But the spark of fanaticism was itself a draw. Excitement burned within Dr. Sammy Lipi, glowing embers of proselytizing passion, and excitement excites those around it, like a preacher howling in the stifling shade of a southern tent.

I believe, Margaret thought. I can floss, oh, Lord! I can floss!

JUST AS Richard predicted, Margaret began receiving newsletters from Dr. Lipi. They touched on dental implants, the controversy over fluoridated water, adhesion techniques, base and noble metals, acrylic and porcelain, treatable anatomical deformities, as well as total etch, "wet field" dentin bonding, and intra-oral plating. She kept the letters in her dresser drawer among her socks, taking one out and perusing it occasionally as if it were a billet-doux. But her favorite remained the first, a letter sent routinely to all new patients, an introduction of sorts, entitled "Enlightened Dentistry."

NEWSLETTER #101

Dear Patient:

I am a dentist, it is my job. But in the United States, at the dawning of a new decade, "to dentist" is more than an occupation. With the most recent technological and scientific progress in oral health care, Americans, indeed all of modern mankind, have the opportunity to reach higher than ever before toward dental achievement. Perfection is no longer an unattainable myth, but a real possibility. Dentistry, for me, is a search for that perfection for *my* patients, for patients everywhere.

A natural contract exists between each of us and his or her teeth. Each has a responsibility to the other. Man was born with an innate ability to care for his teeth — saliva. Saliva is nature's own cleansing solution. But it is through observation and education that we build on nature's gifts. Observe, keep in touch with your teeth. Listen to what they have to tell you. If you were to pay half as much attention to your teeth as I do, thousands of teeth could be saved each year. A tooth is a terrible thing to waste. Visit your dentist, periodontist, or oral-maxillofacial surgeon for regular checkups.

And remember, I am here for you twenty-four hours a day, seven days a week. Your teeth don't take vacations. Neither do I.

As patients, all of us can play a role in the realization of universal dental health.

> Your dentist and fellow patient,
> Dr. Samuel Lipi

❧ ❧ ❧

The person who is completely deprived of a good memory feels;
but he does not judge: judgment implies the comparison of two
ideas.

❧ ❧ ❧

AT LUNCH WITH Lily, this time in the park, Margaret sat
on the bench trying not to lose control of her tuna fish sandwich and wondered if love would improve her memory. Could
she recall Dr. Lipi's voice? His words? The curve of his neck,
the hue of his skin? Perhaps. She wasn't sure, so overwhelmed
were all her thoughts of him by simple desire, her own desire.

"I'm in love with my dentist," she said.

Lily looked at her attentively. Her mouth was full.

"I think I got married too young. I showed a lack of judgment. Judgment requires comparison."

"Margaret, you can hardly claim a dearth of experience,"
Lily said.

"Yes, but a person completely deprived of a good memory

feels but cannot judge. I am completely deprived of a good memory."

"Judgment is tyranny, Margaret. Anyway, Edward is so sexy."

"Yeah," Margaret said. She ate her sandwich and silently admired the green of the new grass, the warm air, the pink flush of Lily's cheeks, the highly intellectual nicotine stains on her fingers, the rough whisper of her starlet voice.

"I like you, Lily," she said, embarrassed by her earlier confession. "You listen to any old crap I feel the need to say." And I to you, she added silently, as Lily happily wondered if the homeless men camped in the tunnel over there had chosen it because of its vaginal resonance.

DR. LIPI WAS in her thoughts. Margaret daydreamed like a teenager. They would go to the beach and walk, the way teenagers went to the beach and walked. They would ride in a car and talk, earnestly, with the radio playing. They would hold hands in the park. In all of these fantasies, Dr. Lipi wore a white dentist's shirt, suggestively unbuttoned, then abruptly removed.

"Richard," she said to her editor on the phone, "I'm in love with your dentist. Our dentist."

"Oh, yes, so was I. You'll get over it."

"No I won't. Will I? Why will I?"

"When the bill comes."

"Richard, I'm not joking. I have a burning crush on Dr. Lipi the dentist," Margaret said. She meant to seem as if she were joking, or could be joking, but there must have been something in her voice that betrayed her.

"What does Edward think of your new interest in dentistry? Planning caps, dear? Laminates, perhaps. Margaret, behave yourself."

"Why?"

"Open wide!" Richard said, laughing.

Dream on, Margaret thought, but she couldn't quite bring herself to say it.

"Margaret, finish your dirty book, for God's sake," Richard was saying. "Is your husband neglecting you?"

"No. Edward doesn't neglect anyone. Not even me."

"MARGARET, what ails you these days?" Edward said when she came home from the library and walked past him without saying a word. "It's spring!" He spread his arms dramatically and spoke in his deep, booming teaching voice. "But you come in the door like a blast of winter. The sun pales; gray winds howl; leaves shrivel on their branches." He stopped and then added in an ironic, gently mocking tone, "What is going on, Margaret?"

Problems were delicate, mysterious objects to him, to be handled gingerly, with a mixture of self-deprecation and awe, as a new father handles a new baby. So few things were problems for Edward that when he encountered one, he slowed down the great roar of his being to a soft purr.

"What's the matter, Margaret?" he said again, and he put one hand on her shoulder and stroked her cheek with the other. "What have I done?"

"I don't know," Margaret said.

"But I've done something?"

"Have you?"

"Well, it appears so," he said.

"Aha!" she said, and turned to walk away.

"Margaret," Edward called after her. "Margaret, you know I am a man of unlimited patience. But even unlimited patience has a limit." And his voice was no longer ironic, or gently mocking.

∾∾ ∾∾ ∾∾

That desire is a state of uneasiness, everyone who reflects on himself will quickly find. Like hope deferred, desire deferred makes the heart grow sick.

My desire and my hope had both been deferred at the sight of my pupil lying in the green grove, there bestowing in so liberal a fashion the favors of her understanding on another. And my underlying desire was of so high a pitch that it now raised my uneasiness to such a level that the heart within me cried out, "Give me the thing desired, give it me or I die!" Life itself and all its enjoyments became such a burden that it could not be borne under the lasting and unremoved pressure of such an uneasiness.

After leaving my student still sitting, with no sign of remorse, upon the shaded green grass, I walked through the grounds of the estate of the Marquise de——, heedless as to my surroundings. I could have been walking in the shade of coconut palms, banana trees, and lemon trees in flower, on the slope of a mountain on a little island in the southern ocean. For all I could see before me was Rameau's niece.

Anyone reflecting upon the thought he has of the delight which any present or absent thing is apt to produce in him has the idea we call love. I reflected upon the thought of the delight my pupil had produced in me in the past. I reflected upon it helplessly and without end.

When a man declares in autumn when he is eating them, or in spring when there are none, that he loves grapes, it is no more but that the taste of the grapes delights him. Certainly, I thought, the taste of Rameau's niece had delighted me when she was there to be tasted. And when she was absent, then the recollection of that delight had followed me for hundreds of miles, accompanying me deliciously for days, for week after week, on my trip to Geneva. I had loved her.

But let an alteration of health or constitution destroy the delight of the taste of grapes, and a man can be said to love grapes no longer. On the contrary, the thought of the pain which anything present or absent is apt to produce in us is what we call hatred.

When I thought of my pupil, I thought of the pain she had produced in me, and the thought of that pain did indeed produce in me what we call hatred. I hated Rameau's niece.

ฅ๓ ฅ๓ ฅ๓

THE DAYS WERE getting longer, a little longer, and Margaret waded through swarms of elderly women at the fruit market out into a silvery dusk and an unaccustomed wash of clean, windy air which made her remember many other places and other times, albeit not very specifically. A mountain somewhere in northern Europe or maybe Colorado, a spring walk to school in Massachusetts, a beach, some beach.

This was it, she realized. In New York, this was spring. She had just experienced it, a moment that recalled other moments, that suggested other places where trees and flowers blossomed, rodents awoke, insects hatched, and birds showed off. And now it was over. Springtime in New York. It had come and gone on that one fresh breeze. A bus roared past. A man stood on the corner holding an empty picture frame to his face, hollering, "I been framed!"

At home, she threw herself down in the armchair in the living room and looked out at the sky as it grew darker. Was there milk in the grocery bag, or yogurt or chicken or fish? Something she ought to put away? She didn't care. She thought about Dr. Lipi, the way he stared with his sharp eyes. The man on the plane had such soft gray eyes. She'd seen a teenage boy in the lobby with fresh pink cheeks and the slack, greedy face of youth. Margaret leaned her head back. She liked this time of day, when everything faded so softly.

When the doorbell rang, she jumped and shuddered and realized she must have fallen asleep. The apartment was quite dark now. She stumbled to the door. Edward must have forgotten his keys. Good. Everyone should forget something sometimes. And she would somehow not have wanted him to find her asleep, for when she slept she dreamed. She no longer wanted Edward to know what it was she dreamed about.

"Hello," she said, blinking at the glare from the hall lights as she opened the door.

" 'Allo," replied the figure in the door. "But look who it is! It is you, the pretty girl from the airplane. *Bonjour!* 'Allo, 'allo!"

No, not Edward.

Margaret looked closer. Those thin lips, moist and pouting. The gray eyes. And the shirt. The green-and-white-striped shirt. It was the man from the plane, the man she dreamed about, the man who fell asleep on her face. But what was he doing here when he was awake, when she was awake? How had he found her? She hadn't told him her address, not even her name. And didn't he have any other shirts? She said nothing in her excitement. Nothing at all.

"You are astonished to see me."

Margaret nodded.

"And I am astonished to see you!"

But I live here, Margaret thought.

"I look for Marguerite Nathan."

"You find her," said Marguerite.

"Yes? So pleasant that she is you!"

"Yes. So pleasant." Margaret stared down at the bag of groceries she'd left on the floor by the door. The smell of scallions and overripe strawberries drifted up.

"You are acquainted with my father. I am Martin Court, son of Jules Court, of Brussels. You have met him in Prague, yes? He gives me your name and location and says I am to meet you. But we meet already!"

"Yes, we do."

"That is really something!"

Margaret looked at the shirt and the blue cashmere blazer and the unself-consciously protruding belly. I'm looking at him too long, she thought.

"Follow me!" she said.

In some confusion, she switched on lights, a lot of lights, every light she passed. The apartment glared. Margaret led Martin Court to the living room. She was not looking at him at all now, careful not to look at him. She turned to motion him to take a seat. Martin grasped her hand.

I will swoon, she thought. She felt ill, and the bright lights burned her sleepy eyes. He had come for her. She was meant to take a lover, and now her lover was here, here for her to take. His hand closed around hers, large and warm around her suddenly icy fingers, tighter and tighter, drawing her toward him. His long fingers, curled around hers, pressed harder and harder, drawing her hand up slightly, but urgently, then down again. Martin Court was shaking her hand.

"That is really something!" he said again. "Really, really something!"

Margaret coughed, nodded, and sat down.

Martin Court was an engineer of absurdly expensive hi-fi equipment whose company was hoping to break into the American market. He had been to New York twice since his father had rescued Margaret from the dangers of Prague's suggestively beautiful architecture, but only now had he found the time to look up the beneficiary of his father's excellent sense of direction.

Margaret did not want to offer him coffee because he was French and would judge her coffee harshly, until she remembered he was Belgian. "Would you like a cup of coffee?" she said. Her voice sounded sharp to her, the squawk of an unpleasant night bird as it pounced on its prey.

"Tea."

In the kitchen, Margaret stood over the kettle and watched it not boil. He was here, in her house. His name was Martin, a name impossible to pronounce properly in French without sounding as if one's sinuses were blocked. His hair fell over his eyes, onto his big, oddly shaped glasses. What did she say to him now? She had already given him her life's history on the plane, told him her secret philistine theories of epistemology. Perhaps she should tell him Edward's Theory of Monogamy and the End of Evolution, a.k.a. Adultery, the Ultimate Self-Sacrifice.

Margaret heard the front door open.

"Oh, hello," she heard Edward say.

" 'Allo. I am Martin Court, a friend of Marguerite. You are a friend of Marguerite, too?"

The kettle whistled shrilly.

Margaret made a cup of tea for Martin Court and sat down and drank it. She hated tea.

I will never go out there, she thought. I will stay here, by the stove. I will sleep on the stove like a Russian house serf. It's nice and warm in here by the stove. Out there, it's too hot.

She heard them laughing, talking about Wagner and George Bernard Shaw, the advantages of tube amplifiers and the necessity for something called Monster Cable.

"Margaret," Edward said, coming into the kitchen. "How funny that you met your new chum on the plane. Have you asked him to dinner? He'll keep you company. I can't stay, I'm afraid."

Margaret looked up at him, torn between suspicion and relief.

"Department meeting," he said. "Multiculturalism in Literature — Too Little Too Late? I shouldn't think so, but then I have been wrong before. Ah well, the more the merrier. Bring on the cultures, let graduate students at 'em, a new supply of obscure works to grind into obscure theses, the new dry dust of new classics, sprinkled pitilessly upon innocent undergraduates. Perhaps my poets can survive. I can pass them off as homosexuals, or closet homosexuals, or proto-homosexuals. Parahomosexuals!"

"Don't be bitter."

"No. You're right. It's ludicrous, what goes on, and I quite enjoy it. 'Me imperturbe . . . aplomb in the midst of irrational things.' Did you offer the man a drink, darling?"

He pulled two beers from the refrigerator and walked out.

"Tea," Margaret said to his back. "I offered him coffee, and he wanted tea."

But Edward didn't hear. He was already back in the living room with his new pal. Margaret listened to them. Her husband talking to her lover. Well, her lover in theory. Her husband in fact. She would sleep on the stove. In perpetuity.

MARGARET and Martin Court ended up going out to dinner. Margaret took him to the least romantic, noisiest restaurant she could think of, a sports bar with six large-screen television sets. Here I can think, she said to herself, and decide what I must do. Without any music or soft lights to cloud my judgment. Just flashing scoreboards and the din of an angry mob.

Martin drank a beer, and Margaret watched.

"I am happy to get to know you," he said.

He ran his hand through his hair, and Margaret remembered the smell of it and the feel of it against her face.

"My father and mother like you so much. My father say you are so knowledgeable about prison reform in the United States."

His hands rested on the polyurethane-coated table. His fingers were long and all nearly the same length, his nails rounded and regular. He wore no wedding ring.

"Your husband has a good taste in music," he said.

"Are you married?"

"Divorced."

Martin had a polished, elegant manner that occasionally burst into boyishness. Through the cheers, boos, grunts, and squeaks of large sneakers on the televised basketball courts that surrounded them, he remarked that the sports bar was "really something!" He mentioned ways the establishment could upgrade both the video equipment and the audio equipment. He told her he had thought about her many times since their meeting on the plane.

"Your laryngitis is better," she said.

Martin stared around him at the young lawyers and stockbrokers and smiled. "America!" he said.

Several times he refilled her glass of mineral water with as much courtly solicitude as if she had been drinking champagne. At her coronation.

When her hamburger came, Margaret looked at it with distaste. She was too nervous to eat. Martin watched her with concern.

"Marguerite, you are not well."

"I don't look well?"

"You look very well! Very, very well."

"Oh."

"But you look as though you don't feel well, you see?"

Margaret saw. She saw a beautifully dressed, beautifully mannered, beautiful-faced man with a sexy belly and a kind disposition. No wonder I look as though I feel sick, she thought.

"My daughter loves New York," Martin was saying. "We have been here together." His daughter was twenty-four.

"Why, she's almost my age!" Margaret said. The dirty old man. No, no, that didn't fit him at all. The lecherous *roué*.

That didn't fit him either, but it suited Margaret's sense of romantic propriety much better.

"Yes," he said. "She's very much like you."

He kissed her good night on both cheeks. Margaret put her hand on his arm, on his cashmere-covered arm.

"You have the softest clothes," she said.

He looked at her quizzically. A lock of hair had fallen between his glasses and his left eye. Margaret thought to push it away, but he did it himself first.

"Good-bye, my friend, my old friend," Martin said. He raised his hand for a taxi.

Margaret panicked. Was he going? Just like that? Would she never see him again, never again see Martin Court, the man obviously fated to become her lover?

"I have something for your father," she said quickly. Good thinking, Margaret! "A gift. A book. I'm so grateful. Are you free tomorrow? I'll give it to you then. I'll take you sightseeing. If I don't get lost. I won't get lost. That was a joke."

"Yes, I know," he said.

Her hand was still on his sleeve. She pulled it away.

He reached in his pocket for a datebook. "Friday," he said. "That is good?"

"That is good."

"You're very kind, Marguerite," he said as he got into a cab. "Kind to foreigners."

Margaret walked home thinking that the cheers of sports fans would never be the same for her. The lock of hair that had fallen over Martin's left eye remained, tantalizing, in her mind, a veil she must push aside. Martin. Divorced. One twenty-four-year-old daughter. Forty-nine himself. Mathematics and music, he said, are the same; they are the laws of the universe. Would she care to listen to his electronics sometime? She would be astounded. They were really something!

Oh yes! she had wanted to say. I'll listen to your electronics. Just plug them in.

Across the table, bathed in the flickering light of the six TVs, he was irresistible, his face undeniably, obviously, foreign, his voice high-pitched and glamorously out of context.

Edward was already home. I've been hypnotized, she thought. Don't break my spell. Tall and familiar as a tree in the dark hallway, he put his arms around her, but Margaret thought again of Martin, the man on the plane, in the sports bar, on the sidewalk, a face in a cab.

"'Not to be in love with you,'" said Edward. "'I can't remember what it was like. It must've been lousy.'" He kissed the top of her head. "Schuyler," he said.

Guilty, and angry that she felt guilty — for absolutely nothing!—she said, "Why do you always quote other people? Don't you ever have anything to say for yourself?"

Edward jumped, he was so startled. He looked at her questioningly, then walked away, silent, into the study and closed the door behind him.

Margaret thought, He will never forgive me. He quotes things out of love and excitement, like a boy rattling a box of shiny pebbles, opening and closing it, then opening it again. I've insulted his pretty stones. I threw them in the river.

And Margaret had the feeling she had just crossed a line, a line of civility that was required for love. When in love, one felt free and safe to reveal the deepest, most secret truths about oneself. But there were truths about the other person that one never revealed, not because of fear or shame, but out of acceptance — out of love.

I have been capricious and thoughtless, she realized. Like a child who calls a fat man fat. But she couldn't apologize. Her mouth refused to form the words. She formed so few words for him these days.

Edward was too courteous to stop speaking to her altogether. But it seemed to her that after this he stopped taking any pleasure in his words. Margaret sometimes waited for him to try to speak to her about their not really speaking, but their silence only grew in authority, a strict and overbearing mother. It never quite let the two of them out of its sight. Edward, the booming Walt Whitman scholar, singing of "Life immense in passion, pulse, and power," lived his life with vigor and joy. It was the only way he knew how. But Margaret had withdrawn vigor and joy, leaving a vacuum, an absence, and he backed away from her uncertainly, like a cat from a puddle. They existed cautiously, new neighbors in their old life.

LILY SAT ON the grass in the park, where they now met quite regularly for lunch. She had taken off her shoes, black pointy pumps that lurked, stark and sinister, beside her bare feet on the bright spring grass. She had small, even toes (to match her teeth) dabbed with pearly nail polish.

Edward was with them, and Margaret was annoyed. She wanted to talk to Lily about Martin. She wanted Lily to herself. Disgruntled, she lay back in the grass, ignoring both of them. They ate their sandwiches and chatted about gardening. Gardening! Well, Edward was to be forgiven, being English and all. But Lily had no excuse. Lily was a garden, didn't she realize that? She tended to herself with such care. What interest could she have left for a patch of dirt with some plant life that required constant nursing and had names impossible to remember, and then, after months of being coddled, died?

"Gardens are depressing," Margaret said. "Everything dies. Right in front of your eyes."

"Margaret, you are an absolutist," Edward said.

"Just don't quote Whitman at me."

"Oh, Margaret," Lily said.

Margaret sat up. Lily was looking at Edward with her lavender eyes.

"Anyway, I like Whitman," Lily said. "He took on the bourgeoisie."

"He *was* the bourgeoisie," Margaret said.

THAT NIGHT, as Margaret watched Edward load the dishwasher and wondered if Dr. Lipi had a girlfriend, Martin called.

"Marguerite? You are ready? You still wish to be my guide?"

The thought of her being someone else's guide was appalling. She was the guided. She was very good at being the guided.

"Yes," she said. What would she show him? What did people do in New York, anyway? "Is there anything in particular you want to do?"

"Already I have visited to Harlem. On the bus, the touring bus. Ah, that was really something! I saw United Nations and SoHo and East Village and World Trade Center and Brooklyn."

"Really?"

"And Statue of Liberty from Staten Island ferry."

"Well. I don't know. The Empire State Building? My aunt used to work on the second floor."

"No longer? I love this building. I have been there three years."

"Three years ago."

"*Oui.*"

"*Oui.*"

Margaret pondered. Zabar's?

"Where are you staying?" she said.

"Hotel Elysée. You will meet me here, perhaps? Friday. We will have lunch downtown. Then perhaps a museum? I hope to see the Frick Collection. You will join me, yes?"

Well, Margaret thought, if this is what it entails — following Martin around — perhaps I can be his guide.

EDWARD HAD GONE out for the evening with a professor from Princeton whom his department was hopelessly wooing, so Margaret called Lily. They decided to do what it seemed to Margaret one always did when one required something to do — go to a restaurant. Lily expressed regret at the absence of Edward, but Margaret assured her she need not be so polite.

"I mean, how much life-affirming quotation can a person stand?" Margaret said. "Let him go show off to undergraduates. He's getting on my nerves."

Lily looked at her closely. "Margaret," she said, "Edward is not one of your schmucky college boyfriends."

"No. I didn't know him in college, that's true."

Margaret wondered if she would tell Lily about Martin, now that she finally had the chance. She observed her own actions these days with great curiosity, as if they were someone else's. I don't seem to be telling her, she noted. I want to, but somehow, given this opportunity at last, I am finding it difficult. I can't after all just announce it: The man on the plane! He's here! He's come for me!

They decided to go downtown to a restaurant owned by some friends. One of the friends was one of Margaret's college boyfriends, not schmucky at all, except that he had stubbornly preferred boys and came home from a summer in Rome with one who looked almost exactly like him. They had recently opened a restaurant in TriBeCa called Il Conto, and to their dismay, it had been discovered and approved by those people in New York who spend each evening discovering and approving new restaurants. Il Conto was a success. The two startled owners were now required to run it. To take reservations over the phone was easy enough, but then they had to honor them. They had to buy sufficient *finocchio*. The restaurant was not the toy they had expected, but a business crowded with artists and actors and agents all dressed in black and waiting, beaks gaping, to be fed.

Whenever Margaret went there, the room, undulating with black-clad figures, roaring with conversation, appeared to her as a massive, many-headed beast, the monstrous offspring of a funeral and a bar mitzvah.

Their friends were there, bookends in rumpled white shirts and Italian pants.

"Go away," Jimmy said desperately after he'd kissed them hello. "There's no room. There's no food."

"Stupid," said Carlo. "There's always room. There's always food."

They waited at the bar. It was early, so they would not have to wait too long.

"Maybe I'm not meant to be married," Margaret said, watching Jimmy fondly as he stood miserably at the door greeting patrons. She remembered waiting in the hall of his dorm so that she could accidentally run into him when he came out of his room. I'm going to tell her about Martin now, she thought. "There's this guy I met on the plane —"

"Margaret, adultery is such a middle-class indulgence."

"Edward thinks it's one's civic duty."

Lily frowned. "Edward?" she said thoughtfully.

Edward. Margaret sat on a barstool and sighed.

"What is it?" Lily said, responding to the sigh, tilting her head with both playful mock tenderness and with real tenderness.

"Nothing."

It was as if, once the idea of adultery had come into her head, it was the only idea there. She continued to notice men everywhere, all the time: men in suits, men in jeans; she noticed the bulge running diagonally across the frayed fly of every pair of faded 501s. Just like an old queen, checking out the merchandise. She watched young men in khaki pants filling out deposit slips at the bank; she watched their wrists, showing from their blue oxford cuffs, the way Victorian men had once strained to catch a glimpse of a well-turned ankle. She assessed delivery boys in their rippling bicycle pants. She had become an absurd receptor of sensory stimulation, undiscriminating, insatiable, a monster of empiricism.

Lily put her hand on Margaret's shoulder and said, again, "What?"

"Hi!" said a man who had silently — it seemed silent to Margaret anyway — crept up beside them. "You're waiting, too, huh? Like orphans in an orphanage! What a city. My friend is meeting me here. I read about this place."

He was not bad-looking, a little chunky, a little short, a little weak-chinned, but not bad. Suit a little too expensive. His main flaw in Margaret's eyes — in Margaret's nose, really — was that he was lavishly covered in perfume, or cologne, or whatever men called it. Margaret wrinkled her nose and pulled back. It was a physical reaction. He was dense with spicy fumes. Lily noticed her pull back. She looked at Margaret, then at the man.

Margaret suddenly realized the man was flirting with them. She realized it when Lily looked at her. She wasn't sure how she knew it from Lily's eyes, but she just suddenly did. He was trying to pick them up.

Sickened by his scent, Margaret felt dizzy. Flirting with her, with Margaret? She realized she was shocked. Couldn't a person go out to dinner without some creep sidling up to her and stinking up the joint? In a panic of embarrassment, she helplessly listened to him describe his health club, the condo he rented in the Hamptons, and whatever else he thought might induce the ladies to take an interest in him.

Margaret looked at the floor. Lily's shoes were blue suede and almost square, lifted high up on black rubber platform soles. Margaret tried to think of something to say to drive this impertinent man away. He had not even stopped to take a breather. Should he get a borzoi or a chow, or was a dog too much trouble for someone who took as many vacations as he did?

"A dog is a problem for someone as independent as me . . ."

How dare he, Margaret thought again. I'm a married woman! A married woman? Why, that was an idea. Margaret raised her glass with her left hand, hopefully waving her wedding ring in front of his face. Surely that would do it, would act upon him as a cross on Dracula.

Some of her drink spilled. The man kept talking.

"Now my accountant said, 'In your bracket? Move to Connecticut!' But, you know, I'm such a city person . . ."

Suddenly, Margaret felt two hands around her waist, Lily's hands. Lily, on the other barstool, pulled Margaret over onto her lap. Her hands were clasped, her arms around Margaret's waist.

"We're lesbians," Lily said in her alluring voice. She pressed her cheek gently against Margaret's. "We're lovers."

There was silence then, blessed silence. Margaret felt Lily's body, warm and soft, pressed against her back, beneath her thighs. Lily smiled: Margaret could feel the smile on her own cheek.

The man, annoyed and embarrassed, turned and walked to the other end of the bar.

Lily began to laugh. "Asshole," she said.

Lily moved her head, and Margaret felt her breath on her neck.

A lesbian? she thought. Lily's lover?

A lesbian! Lily's lover!

Margaret found it difficult to breathe. She didn't move from Lily's lap. She couldn't. She didn't want to. This was amazing. She was a lesbian. It had never occurred to her before, but it was undeniable. She was sitting on a sexy girl's lap thinking about sex. What kind of sex? She found that difficult to visualize, in spite of a Chantal Akerman movie she had once seen, but surely that could all be negotiated later. Oh, Lily, Lily, what a discovery I have made on your lap.

Lily gently pushed her off and Margaret stared at her, nearly speechless, for the remainder of the evening.

IT'S ALL VERY well to be Lily's lover, but what about Lily? Margaret thought as she lay in bed awake. She couldn't be Lily's lesbian lover unless Lily, too, was a lesbian. Lily, Lily, Lily. Margaret felt again the heat of Lily's breath on her neck. She tried to picture Lily at school, walking across the lawn with Till. She remembered visiting their apartment, watching Lily and Till stroke their old, snoring cat.

And then Margaret had a realization. It wasn't that she learned anything new, only that all the old scattered fragments of information suddenly made a pattern, a big bold unmistakable pattern that only I could have missed, Margaret thought — exchanges of glances, bitter arguments, an estrangement after Till's marriage to the odious Art, an awkward attentiveness to each other now, a way of speaking about each other, of not speaking about each other. Lily and Till. Of course. For years. The roommates. The best of friends. The couple. The lovers.

Affairs with other women were fashionable at school, Margaret thought. So I'm a late bloomer. Lily, the feel of her and the whisper of her absurd words, Lily, the insinuating Lily, has become irresistible. So who am I to resist?

Margaret lay in bed beside Edward, listening to his breathing, light and even. You're my husband, she thought. My wonderful husband. And she tenderly touched his head. There's been a terrible misunderstanding. Then she remembered Lily, the heat of Lily's body beneath her own on a barstool at a fashionable restaurant. She hadn't misunderstood that. She laughed and shook her head and said out loud, "This is ridiculous."

Edward continued his airy breathing undisturbed.

I am in love with three people and married to another, Margaret thought. But what is love? How do I know I'm in love? To "know" what love, or anything else, is, first I must ask, What is knowledge? Okay: "What is knowledge?" I don't know.

And then there are the three propositions. That is, (1) I'm in love with my dentist, (2) I want to sleep with a Belgian hi-fi manufacturer, (3) I am a lesbian. How can I be sure of their validity? Do they correspond to facts? Are they internally logical? Does certainty exist? Why can't I fall asleep? What is sleep? Does sleep exist? Not for me. I must demonstrate the validity of these three propositions. I must demonstrate the validity of sleep. I must verify the three propositions, but first the proposition of sleep. On the other hand, maybe I am asleep, and my inability to fall asleep is a dream.

This last idea relaxed her, and Margaret thought no more about it, or about anything at all, drifting peacefully into unconsciousness.

MARTIN was the kind of man who floated up stairs in spite of his bulk. He was noiseless, except for the occasional rustle of his elegant clothes. He possessed a calm, radiant satisfaction, almost paternal it was so comforting. There was something effortless about him, as if he were his own daydream.

He called Margaret "a little barbarian" and had insisted on eating at a barbecue restaurant in the West Village. He was, like Edward, intoxicated with America. He slid through the squalid streets of the city, an apparition of taste and polish.

"You have so many opinion, Marguerite," he said. "Opinion on everything. You have opinion on traffic lights!"

"I don't want to have opinion," she said. "I want to have judgment."

"Judgment of traffic lights! Yes, yes!" He laughed. "You remind of my daughter, Marguerite."

Do I, indeed? Margaret thought. It was not the first time he had brought up this daughter who was almost Margaret's age. To Margaret, he didn't seem quite old enough to have such a daughter, but if he needed a little Oedipal spark to his flirtations, by all means, let him dwell on his daughter, his Claudette.

"I am happy to have such a companion," he said, as they sat down at the pink Formica counter. "I have traveled with Claudette sometimes when she was younger, but now she is busy with her own life. Often I am so alone in a foreign city. It makes me dizzy to be so alone." He laughed again and looked embarrassed.

"It makes me dizzy, too," she said.

Oy, does it make me dizzy. She thought of Prague. And she felt his arm against hers on the counter, just as it had been touching hers on the plane. She glanced at him, but he was engrossed in the menu. She felt his arm pressed against hers, a meeting of arms, of minds, of plans and desires, and dared not move her arm away to open her menu.

As it turned out, she had no need to open her menu. Martin, a gentleman and a connoisseur of southern American cooking, ordered for her.

As she ate her pork chops all up, like a good girl, she watched Martin's every move, fascinated by the fact of her own attraction to him. Lily and Dr. Lipi receded for the moment before this large, garrulous man in his beautiful clothes. There was something smooth and rich about him, luxurious, like an expensive piece of luggage, the kind one runs one's hand over lovingly, longingly, as it sits, smooth, glistening leather, on a store shelf.

He was wearing a fine, gray cardigan sweater instead of the cashmere blazer, and a blue-and-white-striped shirt.

"You changed your shirt," she said.

He looked at her for a moment, then said, "So did you."

THE FRICK WAS almost unbearably tantalizing, tasteful but odd and idiosyncratic, a jewel of a museum, an ornament, a fantasy to try on with the tap of one's footsteps in the mansion's hallways. No children were allowed, and there were few adults that afternoon. In the hush of old wealth and art, Martin stood.

I must work this out, Margaret thought. Here is my problem. I want this man. At least I think I do. I think I want this man, therefore I want this man. Yes. That sounded right. It was a beginning anyway, a foundation from which to start.

Now, what is it I want about him? Do I want to stand beside him and look at a painting by Fragonard in which a pastel woman with smooth, rounded arms and blue bows on her tiny white shoes looks away, startled, holding her arm out toward a man, holding it out to push him away and to draw him closer as he climbs over a wall to find her, while behind them a statue of a naked mother turns from the outstretched arms of her gigantic baby, who seems to be falling to the ground as rambling roses spill over a stone wall and birch trees explode into leafy clouds in the background?

Martin put his arm around her shoulders and said, "This is really something, yes?"

"Yes," Margaret said. "It is really something." Yes, she thought. It is. And I want this, I do, I want to stand with Martin and a Fragonard. Then I want Martin to climb over a wall, too, crushing cascades of roses beneath his rubber-soled shoes as he rushes toward me —

"You have something, Marguerite, for me?" Martin said in a quiet voice.

"What?" Margaret was startled.

"I know that you want to give to me."

Well, Margaret thought, I wouldn't put it that way exactly. She frowned, unsure what to say.

"I'm sorry," he said. His hand squeezed her shoulder. "I have embarrassed you."

"No, no." She leaned against him, unsteady, nearly giddy

with the sensation of his arm, of his body. No, no, not embarrassed. On the contrary.

"You have forgotten the memento," he said. "The book, for my father. Do not be ashamed. We will meet again. Then you will remember. And now I will carry to him your very good wishes."

Now, yes, you have embarrassed me, she thought.

Martin parted from her outside the Frick. He had business to attend to. He shook her hand, he kissed her cheeks. Margaret stuttered good-bye. She walked home through the park, in a strong wind, the trees exploding into leafy clouds above her.

SOMETIMES SHE would gaze in fascination at one of her mind's eye's lovers, at Dr. Lipi, or the pursed, moist lips of Martin, or Lily sighing seductively, her big, bright eyes shaded by dark lashes, and then Margaret would suddenly see before her what was before her, and she would realize where she was, on the toilet facing the green tropical birds of the shower curtain; crossing the street against the light; accepting change from the square-faced butcher. She wandered from vision to vision, and from these daydreams of bodies to secret, minute observations of bodies, real bodies, strangers, the bodies of strangers.

I'm out of control, she thought. But she felt strangely in control, powerful. If she was at the mercy of her desires, those desires were *hers,* and they swept away all obstacles before them, slashing and burning and building their own fantastical cities.

I thought the cogito was just a myth. The subject is supposed to be dead. But I am doing this. I, the subject, the cogito. And Margaret felt like beating her chest and giving a Tarzan call of triumph.

*

ONE AFTERNOON, in Lily's funny, cramped studio apartment, filled (satiated) with brightly painted antique dressers and tables hailing from Holland to Argentina, Margaret sat on the enormous platform bed around which the painted dressers seemed to have gathered of their own free will, like birds waiting for seed, and she looked at Lily sitting close beside her. And then she felt herself blush, felt the horrible heat, the wash of sudden soundlessness.

She said to herself, Look. She's there before you.

She forced herself to look. She forced herself to hear through the silence roaring in her ears. "Yes," she said in response to something, and she said it nonchalantly and smiled, laughed, then looked more, helplessly now, wanting to look, but unsure of what she saw as she looked at Lily through the warmth and fog of her blush.

I don't care if you know, she thought. I want you to know. Do you know?

"So," Lily was saying, "I bought it. Why not?"

"Why not?" Margaret answered. "Why not?"

Margaret said good-bye, left the apartment, and stood on the street. When she tried to remember what Lily had bought, she could not. When she tried to remember what Lily had been wearing, she could not. All she could remember was the tilt of Lily's face through the heated blur of her own blush.

༄ ༄ ༄

Weary from my wanderings, I stopped beneath a tree, the very tree beneath which I had first stumbled upon Rameau's niece. In her company this garden had seemed a paradise, an Eden from which I was now expelled. There were trees and hedges and glades and flowers still, but sitting among them I sat in a lonely, windswept wilderness.

The uneasiness a man finds himself in upon the absence of

anything whose present enjoyment carries the idea of delight
with it is what we call desire, which is greater or less, as that
uneasiness is more or less vehement. Rameau's niece was absent
from me. The present enjoyment of her would have carried the
idea of delight with it. I was filled with uneasiness, overwhelmed
with desire, vehement desire.

It is said that desire is stopped or abated by the opinion of
the impossibility or unattainableness of the good proposed. The
good I had proposed for myself was quite impossible, but desire, far from being stopped or abated, increased within me, a
fire out of control.

My pupil had been seized perhaps with too quick and lively
a passion to be excusable, and yet I found myself trying to excuse her. I turned various ideas over in my mind. I knew I was
wrong to do so. But though good and evil work upon the mind,
that which immediately determines the will to every voluntary
action is the uneasiness of desire.

At last, confused and weary with the struggle of my mind
and my emotions, I wondered if perhaps it was true, after all,
that human blindness and weakness is the result of all philosophy, and meets us, at every turn, in spite of our endeavors to
elude or avoid it. And so until evening I walked along the garden paths, unseeing; and so until evening and beyond, I thought
and thought, without understanding.

∞ ∞ ∞

DESIRE IS A curious thing, Margaret thought. I want Lily
and Dr. Lipi and Martin. Or do I just want? I want to know.
I want to know what I want.

I am sitting reading Aristotle and looking out the window
at a high school wrestling team on their way to work out in
the park, staring at beautiful bare-chested teenagers in their
running shorts. If *Rameau's Niece* is a philosophical novel,
this must be philosophy. Philosophy has a nice hot, dreamy
feeling to it, doesn't it?

For some weeks Margaret had been sitting at her desk staring at the wrestling team as they passed, and devouring books of philosophy. It was a feast, a binge, an uncontrollable, necessary carousing debauch. It was an orgy. Forgetting, said Plato, is the departure of knowledge. We are never the same, always changing, as knowledge departs and we study in order to replace what we have lost. Forgetting allows for constant renewal, and so for immortality.

Margaret smiled. The *Symposium,* a book about drunken, married homosexuals sprawled three-deep on couches, telling stories of round creatures sliced in half, their genitals on backward, running about, trying to reunite. Ah, philosophy! The rising stairs toward the mystery of love, of beauty, of the ideal form. Clump, clump, clump, up we go, "from one body to two and from two to all beautiful bodies." Margaret stared out the window at the beautiful bodies. Ten, twelve of them. At the end, says Socrates, we arrive at beauty "through loving boys correctly." Fourteen, fifteen, eighteen, boys.

Margaret watched them pass beneath her window. The only thing we can be certain about, she thought, is what we want. Was that Rorty? It couldn't be Bertrand Russell. Duns Scotus maybe? It had all become a tantalizing muddle in her head. Surely it was Rorty. The only things that are really evident to us are our own desires.

I wish mine were evident to me. The only thing that's evident to me is desire itself, great, galloping desire.

℘ "AND HOW are the ivories this morning?"
"Fine, thank you."

Margaret watched as Dr. Lipi pulled the clear yellow rubber gloves on, watched his fingers pushing, sliding, first the left hand, then the right, watched the gloves snap on, pressing onto the hairs that showed through like decorative engraved swirls.

His white shirt, not a dentist's shirt, was opened, unbuttoned quite a ways down. She didn't blame him. One must always present one's good features to their best advantage. But was it hygienic? she wondered.

She put her head back and opened her mouth as he adorned it with this and that — wedges, sheets of rubber, gurgling hoses. Jingle, jingle, went the gold charms on his necklace. She looked at them carefully. They were teeth, gold teeth. His rubber hands approached. She closed her eyes, ecstatic.

AS MARGARET paid her bill (by credit card; Dr. Lipi was so up-to-date), she thought of Richard's warning: You will fall out of love when the bill comes. Yes, nine hundred and fifty dollars did take the bloom off things.

Dr. Lipi came up and stood at the reception desk beside

her. He smiled and patted her shoulder. "Ms. Nathan," he said, "I'm going to miss talking to you."

Well! Margaret thought, as his hand rested on her shoulder. Nine hundred and fifty dollars or no nine hundred and fifty dollars, I must determine what I really feel. Why, it's one of the primary concerns of a human being, a requirement of the human condition. I must sort out what is real from what is simple metaphysical daydreaming; I must discriminate between facts and nonsense. I must establish certainty with regard to my desire to be humped by my dentist.

"You know," she mumbled, suddenly inspired, through her novocaine-heavy mouth. "I'm thinking of writing a book about the history of the image of the dentist."

His eyebrows, beautiful, silky, dark eyebrows, lifted with interest.

"Dr. Lipi, may I interview you?"

MARTIN WAS GONE, to return in a few weeks. Lily, on the contrary, was in constant attendance, showing up at the apartment without warning, sometimes arriving when Margaret was out and then staying, chatting with Edward while she waited. Margaret would walk in, her head full of lascivious thoughts about Martin or Dr. Lipi or Lily herself. Disoriented, almost dizzy at this tableau depicting her own moral failing, Margaret would stare morosely and wonder how Edward, her all-powerful Edward, could have let this happen to her. Edward, she thought, has failed as a husband. All those years together, all those mornings lounging in bed as the light cut through the gaps in the curtains and lay in strips across the floor, as Margaret watched Edward come out of the bathroom, freshly showered, his hair flat, irresistible, not to be resisted, not resisting, either. After all those mornings, Margaret still had contemplated other men, other women!, as if Edward had never existed, as if she hadn't been happy and smoothly languorous in the big, comfortable bed. How, she thought, could he do this to me? How could he fail to protect me from this? If he cared for me at all, this would never have happened.

All those years just assuming I was happy. How naive. One must assume nothing. One must know. Years spent in libraries so that I could know something, just one thing, well, no, lots of things, well, actually so that I could know everything without forgetting it. Then, poof, it's gone and one must begin again, there's more to know, always more, and whatever one knows it's somehow not enough. And after all those years seeking knowledge, I actually thought one could settle down and Be Married. As if the search, that search at least, could just stop, as if Edward were truth, the goal of all desire. She daydreamed then about Edward and those days when the search had stopped.

Well, she thought, pulling herself together. Now I am free of illusions, the scales have fallen from my eyes, I must see life for what it is, starting with Dr. Lipi. He is a pure love object. There exists no emotion to cloud my vision. There is only objective analysis, a logical and scientific pursuit of a muscular piece of ass.

ONE DAY, during a long, aimless conversation with Lily on the phone, Margaret heard herself say, "I'm leaving Edward."

You're what, Margaret? Margaret thought. But, then again, Margaret, Margaret reasoned, I *must* leave Edward. I know I must. It's sordid to live with Edward and plot the seduction of others. I am engaged in an activity of clarification. How can I clarify with my husband always around? Edward clouds the issue. I must leave. Of course I must leave.

Nervously (leave Edward? really leave him?), she continued, "We're not getting along, and I think it would be best if we . . ." She paused. "If we separated for a while."

There. Maybe she should say it again, just to confirm her commitment to this plan. Perhaps it was indiscreet, relaying this information to Lily. But perhaps she wanted to be indiscreet. Now, there was no going back.

She knew it was the correct move — to leave Edward. Objectivity was impossible while Edward loped through the halls looking depressed, a force of nature sputtering, sputtering. That's all he did these days. It got worse and worse with each passing week. Guilt, perhaps. Fooling around with all those girls. Or just fatigue, enervated from enslaving his classes with the sheer force of his glorious self. He was glorious, wasn't he? Once, anyway. Now he was miserably depleted, silent, looking at her, then looking away, saying nothing for days at a time. Edward, saying nothing! The earth was square, the sun refused to rise, words no longer danced for Mr. E., dancing-word ballet master, retired.

Margaret felt sad and weary with guilt instead of relieved, instead of free at last, free at last. Why really was she telling Lily this? Did she want Lily to feel sorry for her? To comfort her? To jump in and take up the slack? I wonder what I am doing, she thought.

"Yes," she said. "That's what we must do. Separate."

"Margaret, come off it."

I wonder what I am doing, Margaret thought again. "Well, one of these days, anyway," she said.

And she put off the separation for a while. Where would she go, for one thing? And then, she was used to Edward and his ways. She ignored him and he ignored her and she worked on her book and on her new project, an essay entitled "Culture and Teeth."

EDWARD ADHERED to his schedule and Margaret did not. She had no schedule of her own to take its place, so she got up later and later each morning. She ate lunch at four or five o'clock, if at all. She skipped dinner. She spent a fair amount of time interviewing Dr. Lipi.

For Dr. Lipi, every man was his smile, and every woman hers. And when Dr. Lipi entered a room, every smile seemed to cry out to him, "Is there a doctor in the house?" He loved talking about teeth and assumed others loved listening. To Dr. Lipi, there was nothing surprising about Margaret questioning him for her essay.

One evening, Margaret went to his office as the last patient was leaving. Feeling shy and unsteady, she followed him into an examining room, where he showed her several x-rays of decaying gums.

Not for the first time, she wondered why anyone would choose to become a dentist. It was not a romantic calling: a dentist did not save lives, the way a doctor did. There was nothing heroic about a dentist. He was necessary, perhaps, but somehow not important. The popular image of a dentist was never a romantic figure. He was a villain, like the dentist in *Marathon Man*. Or a buffoon, she thought, envisioning

W. C. Fields with pliers, leaning over his patient, a woman whose legs began flapping wildly, then suddenly wrapped themselves violently, obscenely, around him. Yes, she would have to discuss that in her essay.

"My name is really Lipinsky," said Dr. Lipi. "But I didn't want to cash in on my heritage. I wanted to make it on my own. No special pleading."

Margaret looked at the row of x-rays clipped to the white, lit screen and tried to remember how to flirt. Well, she could just pretend she was Till or Edward. For them, talking was a kind of flirtation, a flirtation with existence, preparatory to fucking its brains out. At the notion of fucking someone's brains out, even existence's, she felt herself suddenly aroused, and frightened in that cold room with Dr. Samuel Lipinsky. She shivered a little.

"Cold?" asked Dr. Lipinsky-Lipi. He gently laid a rubber-coated, lead-heavy x-ray apron across her shoulders. He had moved very close and stayed there. He likes me, Margaret thought. He likes me, too. Perched on the arm of the dental chair with the lead apron on her shoulders, she was at eye level with his charms of gold dangling teeth, with his white polo shirt, with his chest. He stayed where he was, saying nothing. This was it. This was her opportunity. What should she do? How to flirt? Show interest in what someone cares about? She'd been doing that shamelessly. Was there any aspect of the role of the tooth in Western civilization that she had not touched upon?

Flattery, passionate flattery, too. That was flirting, wasn't it? But not really a skill within her grasp, flattery.

"Teeth," she blurted out, "teeth are such ambivalent signs. They smile, yes, but they also bite. They can express friendliness, or they can be weapons."

She sat sideways on the edge of the dentist chair, and the dentist stood before her, against her. His legs in their loose, soft linen pants were just touching her knees. Had they been touching before? Or had Dr. Lipi moved closer?

"The dentist's existence *qua* dentist," Margaret continued in a quick, nervous, strangled voice, "is determined by his relationship to teeth, and so to what teeth signify."

She looked hopefully into his eyes, then quickly away.

"If teeth can be used to express friendliness," she went on bravely, "then the dentist's assault on them is a rejection of friendliness." If only Edward were there. He could do this for her. He would know just what to say. "If, however, teeth are weapons, then the dentist's assault is an attempt at disarmament, at castration."

Dr. Lipi, almost imperceptibly, moved back, just a little bit, just enough.

"But then the dentist is an ambivalent symbol independently, too," Margaret continued, hanging on to a last shred of hope. "For, on the one hand, he is the enemy, a stranger from outside attempting to disarm his patient, his victim, to strip away the defenses. On the other hand, he is a caring health professional, a healer, relieving pain."

Dr. Lipi cleared his throat. He stepped away from her. "Precisely," he said. "Precisely."

MARGARET LAY IN bed watching *Claire's Knee* on Channel 13 and thinking of Lily's knee, Dr. Lipi's knee, Martin's knee. She turned the TV off, unable to concentrate on French witticisms. I'm not making sufficient progress, she thought. I'm stagnating. That's because I'm suffocating. Because Edward is always here, in this apartment, always around, always talking to me, at least he used to always talk to me, always listening to me when I talked, attentive, bringing me coffee, giving me encouraging kisses when I worked. No wonder I'm making so little progress! He has no consideration. And now, he's never even around! Just because I barely speak to him does not mean it's right for him to come home late, to devote so much time to his students and his sordid little didactic love affairs with pretty girls.

It was no one's fault. That's just the way it was, irresponsibility and betrayal on his side; the simple search for independence on hers. She would have to stop fooling around and tell him. The fruit was ripe, ready to fall from the trees. Quit standing around in the shade palms up, waiting. Shake the branches, Margaret.

She would have to leave Edward. She'd already put it off too long, out of inertia, nostalgia, whatever. But you're a big girl now, Margaret, she thought. You're a big grown up girl with an inquiring mind and a roving eye.

She looked forlornly around her bedroom, at the curtains, the toppling pile of books, the chest of drawers, the basket overflowing with dirty laundry. But our dirty laundry will mingle no longer, she thought. She began to cry.

When Edward went out to run, Margaret called Richard at his house in the Berkshires and woke him up.

"It's Sunday morning," he said, his lovely voice heavy with sleep and with sadness at being awakened. "Early Sunday morning."

"Can I stay at your apartment for a while? I won't bother you. I need a place to go."

"Don't you have a mother?"

"Come on, Richard. It's important."

Reluctantly, and only because he himself would at least be gone for several days and wanted at that moment to go back to sleep, he agreed and arranged with a neighbor to give her the keys.

Hurriedly, so she wouldn't weaken and change her mind, Margaret wrote out a note to Edward. It said, "I can't stay here. I need some peace and quiet and isolation to finish this book. Without having someone around all the time. You're *never* home. So you won't mind if I leave. I will be staying in Richard's maid's room. Margaret." There! She had done it. She had left Edward. She quickly packed a box of books and papers, a small suitcase, and took a cab across town.

Margaret got the keys and lugged her stuff, as she had been instructed, back to the maid's room, a dreary slot painted yellow in a misguided attempt to cheer it up.

"You know," Lily had said on the phone, "you were always like this in college, dumping guys for no good reason, but you were also with them for no good reason. But this is not college, and Edward is different. Be careful, Margaret. He might not take you back."

"I might not want to go back."

Especially when I can stay here in this charming little hideaway! she added now, to herself. She stood on the threshold of the maid's room. Inside was a sagging cot, a sink, and a wastebasket.

Margaret dropped her box and suitcase with a thump, set up a card table that took up almost the whole room, and put out her books. Rameau's niece didn't have these problems, she thought. She just motioned to the gardener, and he did as he was told.

EDWARD. She had left him. Just an hour or so ago. This, this is what they mean by a heavy heart, she thought.

Margaret tried to make herself comfortable in Richard's apartment, although she knew just how uncomfortable her comfort would have made him. As uncomfortable as it made her. She was in a forbidden place. She was on the wrong side of his desk.

She walked from room to room almost on tiptoe, almost afraid, furtive, glancing at the furniture and the pictures, then sneaking back to her own squalid room. The apartment, as much as she could see from the corner of her guilty eye, was decorated with piles of books and a few pieces of nondescript furniture and some Audubon prints that she was sure were real and dozens of large, old, loudly ticking clocks.

It was very clean, Richard's apartment. Tick, tock. Tick, tock. The clocks rattled and clattered. Maybe I should just stay here, she thought. Live with Richard. He could devote himself to me. A life of forever-unfulfilled pedagogical, sexual tension. Editing, editing *me* from morning till night. A life of flirtation. An exquisite life.

But Richard could not be depended upon for a lifetime of editorial flirtation. Richard had other fish to fry, uncles and other writers and friends and boyfriends and assistants and a mother and sisters and brothers to fry. A grandmother, too, no doubt, to fry.

The horrible clocks began to chime and bong. They were everywhere. They hung from the walls. They stood on the floor. They perched on the countertops. Margaret tried to count the chimes, but there were so many clocks calling out from so many places that their hollow rhythmic noise blended and swelled into one awful, echoing voice. No, she could not stay here for very long.

What time is it, anyway? Margaret wondered when the noise had subsided, for the only room without a clock was the maid's room. She looked at her watch and saw that it was still only eleven. I have miles to go before I sleep, she thought. Sleep with whom, though? Sleep with whom?

Forget Richard and his horrible house of clocks. She must clarify the three propositions. Which one represented reality? Experience must teach what reason cannot.

She went into Richard's room, sat down on his bed, and looked at some magazines — gray quarterlies, a *Publishers Weekly*. She flipped through, shyly looking up at Richard's bedroom now and then, a pleasant, simple, white bedroom with far too many clocks. Hickory dickory dock. Her gaze retreated to the magazine, and something there caught her eye. An ad. An ad for a book by Art Turner. Art Turner? *Her* Art Turner? He had finished and actually published this famous book? The long-awaited work of his entire adult life was available between two cardboard covers, available to the scrutiny and scorn (scorn, surely) of the public, to the scrutiny and scorn of her, Margaret, his beneficiary and secret sworn enemy?

Of course, Art had spoken of his book being almost finished, about to come out. Months ago, when she'd last seen him. But he'd been doing that for years, for as long as Margaret had known him. Margaret grinned helplessly, malevolently. It is not enough that I succeed, said someone, someone French. My best friend must fail. Art is a monster and must fail, and he is not even my best friend.

Margaret went into her new home, the grimy rectangle, which, she now noticed, had a mop and bucket in the corner. She listened to the clocks, rattling like a drawer of tin pots. She went to the window and looked down eight stories at a dog straining at its leash, dragging a young woman on high heels, and Margaret could see the heels clicking, for she could not hear them from that distance.

Margaret went into the kitchen and thoughtfully ate a jar of preserved peaches she was sure Richard was saving to give to someone else. Today, she thought. She would begin to experience, to know, today, and she would begin with Martin.

"I will take you to *Katya Kabanova*," he had said, calling her when he returned to New York. "You will read the synopsis. You will see, you will understand, you will understand everything. Then I will take you back to my client's house. My client and friend. He is away in the country while I install my electronics. I will take you home with me there, and you will hear *Katya Kabanova* on a recording. You will hear, and you will understand everything."

At Lincoln Center, Martin stood by the fountain, holding a small nosegay of violets.

Margaret's heart beat faster. I must be in love. No one brings you flowers unless you're in love with him.

"Marguerite, my darling girl." He kissed her, first on one cheek, then the other. The feel of him, and the scent, reminded her of the airplane, when he was a stranger, silent and sprawled across her, his face buried in her breast.

"You are so kind to accompany me on my little visits here and there, and so I bring to you these flowers."

Margaret held them, wondering what to do with them during the opera, and thanked him, taking the opportunity to kiss him again, lingering there against his cheek, against him for a second too long, then self-consciously pulling away.

Maybe I can check the flowers, she thought.

"Again you have forgotten the book for my father? Marguerite, you are impossible. But at least you have not forgotten me, my friend. Ah, this is really something, to hear such singers today."

They sat down and Margaret put the flowers under her seat. When she sat up, Martin leaned close to her and put his hand on hers. His long eyelashes were half lowered, his lips drawn together in a slight smile.

"Marguerite," he whispered, in a voice almost teasing, "you have forgotten the keepsake for my father. But I have not forgotten you. I have for you a surprise."

Margaret waited as he rummaged in his jacket pocket. Something small. Jewelry-small? No. She watched as he pulled out two triangles of leather attached to elastic straps. They looked like tiny G-strings.

"You like these, Marguerite? For increased pleasure? You will wear them? A friend designed them, asked me to try them out for him. I do not force you. Some people do not like them."

What are these Belgians into? Margaret thought. Wear them? Wear them where? "Where do you wear them?"

"Here. Wear them here, now."

In Lincoln Center? Unhappily, Margaret watched the miniature G-strings dangle from his index finger.

"What I meant was, how do you put them on?" she said finally.

"Oh!" He smiled in a paternal way. "On your ears, Marguerite. On your lovely little ears."

He tenderly strapped the triangles, like little hoods, around the back of her ears. The hall sounded suddenly louder, deeper. The cellos, tuning up, resonated and echoed, and Margaret realized that the little devices were innocent enough, some kind of listening aid, gadgets devised by a high-end hi-fi fetishist.

"Horrible," she said.

"Yes. Horrible. But some people like them. More bass. They like to adjust the concert hall!" He began to laugh, real, bursting laughter, repeating, "To adjust the hall!"

Margaret looked away, embarrassed by his uninhibited laughter. But, she thought, it could have been worse. At least he had not wanted to make love in the orchestra section of the Metropolitan Opera House using tiny leather and elastic triangular sex aids.

Margaret turned to the synopsis. "Well, what do you know?" she said several times as she read. "What do you know?"

The awful woman in black was Katya's mother-in-law. Katya's husband was pussy-whipped by his mother, who also constantly criticized Katya. The other young woman is the housemaid. Katya falls in love with a man who is hollered at by an uncle who controls his inheritance. When Katya's husband goes away on a business trip, Katya goes into the woods with her lover. When the husband comes home, Katya insists on confessing to him even though he doesn't want to know. He wants to forgive her; the mother-in-law doesn't want him to forgive her; the lover is sent away by his uncle. Katya jumps into the Vltava and drowns.

Margaret, listening to the strung-out, taut romanticism of the music, the hysterical, neurotic horn bleats as Katya plunges into the waters of oblivion, nodded her head and thought, Yes, this is just like my life. Should I go back to Prague and jump in the Vltava?

The lights came on and she wiped a tear from her eye.

"No dead baby," she said to Martin.

"No, the dead baby is in *Jenůfa*."

"Ah."

"This is how I knew, you see? On the plane."

"Ah."

THE PLANE. Prague. That was where it had all started. If only Edward had come with her. Then this would not have been necessary. She would not be here now, in a taxi, on her way to her ruin in a rich man's brownstone.

Martin was a large man, and his leg, in beautiful dark green trousers, was touching hers. Her skirt had ridden up. She did not pull it down. She shifted a little to get comfortable. Martin looked down at her leg. He looked at her leg, then at her, then out the window. She thought she heard him sigh.

Edward does not exist, she thought.

But if he does not exist, how come when I ask the question, What is it that does not exist?, the answer is Edward. It's Edward. Doesn't this confer some sort of existence on him?

In other words, doth the lady protest too much? Or is it just that logic makes no sense?

"You are very quiet," Martin said.

Margaret pointed to her throat. "*Laryngite,*" she whispered.

"You are thinking of the trip on the plane," he said. He blushed.

MARGARET LAY on the low couch, a soft, deep couch. How had she gotten there? In the taxi. Up the stairs. A living room with Alex Katz cutouts and wooden venetian blinds. Up the stairs again. A music room with a piano, a plant, a worn Victorian couch, and two speakers, each one the size of a toll-booth. Wine on a low table. Another couch. (You must sit on this couch, said Martin. In the middle. The sweet spot! To get the full effect. Oh, yes, she thought. The sweet spot indeed. The full effect!) Martin, plugging and unplugging, soldering, twisting a screwdriver, yanking a wrench, draping cables, thick cables, cables as thick as, well, as thick as dicks. Margaret burst out laughing.

"It's almost ready," Martin said, looking at her, red in the face. He had already said "It's almost ready" several times. She had drunk the wine. Nothing to eat. Just this wine. Just like France. A man muttering in French and wine. In France with Edward, there had been only Edward. Now there was no Edward. Edward did not exist, except logically, of course. Good-bye, Edward. *Bonjour,* Martin.

Margaret lay on her side and gazed at the antique Chinese carpet. What Eastern despot or Western imperialist trod this rug before it ended up here? Martin's crepe-soled shoes went by, the cuffs of his beautifully draped pants swinging jauntily. Margaret lolled on the soft pillows of the sweet-spot couch. Quit caressing your tube amplifiers, Martin. Quit pacing. Thank God, Edward doesn't pace. Pacing makes me dizzy. I'm dizzy, Martin. Dizzy with drink. Dizzy with desire.

"Records," Martin said. "You must play records. CDs, they are shrill, an evil invention, a conspiracy."

She reached lazily down to one foot, took off a shoe, and threw it at him.

"I'm drunk," she said.

"Well, now at last I'm finished," he said, putting away his tools. "Now, we try my equipment, yes?"

Your equipment, Margaret thought, as the sounds of *Katya Kabanova* came on. Yes, what about your equipment? God, when did I become such a vulgarian? she wondered. Well, I'm only seeking the truth, seeking the good, seeking happiness. The good is happiness. The rational and appetitive, together, seek happiness. The rational is appetitive.

The music rolled through the room like a wave, bigger than a live orchestra. The floor beneath her vibrated. They listened, Martin pacing, standing here, then over there, checking a wire, turning a knob, while Margaret lay on the couch. After a few minutes, Martin lifted the arm from the record, switched off the turntable and said, "Now listen, I play for you a CD. One of my friend's CDs. I don't know what this is. They are all the same. All horrible. Listen . . ."

Margaret heard the rhythm of scratching records and a harsh voice.

"Face down, ass up, that's the way we like to fuck —"

Martin turned it off.

"I am sorry," he said. "I did not know."

"That record caused the French Revolution," Margaret said.

Martin kneeled beside her.

"Are you well, Marguerite?"

"Don't I look well?"

"Yes, of course, again, but —"

"You look well, Martin."

She put her hand up, curled it around the back of his neck,

felt the soft, longish hair there. She pulled him down to her. "I have to know," she said.

"Know what?"

"The truth."

She took his glasses, the thick-framed, oddly shaped glasses, and put them down beside her.

"Marguerite —"

"Can you see?" she said.

"A little. I can see you."

"And I can see you." She put both arms around his neck and pulled his face to hers. She kissed him on the lips.

"Ah, you really are drunk," he said.

"Yes."

She kissed him again. His lips, the moist, thin lips shaped in a slight, superior pout.

"Marguerite, I think it is time I took you to bed."

"Yes," she whispered, kissing his neck. "Yes, do."

He lifted her up. He was carrying her. Her head was pressed against his shoulder. She felt his belly. He breathed heavily.

He carried her across a little hall and deposited her in a soft bed.

"Martin," she said, holding his hands as he sat on the edge of the bed. She ran one hand across the smooth pink shirt, taut across his belly. She felt the silky material of his pants against her arm. His glasses were still in the other room. His hair hung down, straight down, as he leaned above her.

"I have neglected you, my poor little girl," he said. "Fooling with my wires. You have been so patient." He ran his hand over her forehead. "But now I will take care of you. Relax, Marguerite, and I will take care of you."

"I'm very relaxed," she said. "Very relaxed." She moved her head in the pillow to show how very relaxed she was. The room began to spin. "Very, very, very relaxed." She held his arm tightly as the room spun faster. "Very, very . . ." She held him now with both hands, as if she were drowning, which she was, she just wasn't sure what she was drowning in. It was too light to be water, too thick to be air, too invisible, too murky . . .

"Darling . . ." he said urgently.

"Relaxed . . ."

WHEN SHE woke up, she was alone in a soft bed in a small room bright with sunshine. A pigeon cooed outside. Her head pounded. She sat up slowly.

Where the hell am I?

She remembered. She was in a rich man's house. A house with speakers the size of tollbooths. A house with couches and wine, much too much wine. Maybe I'm an alcoholic, as well as a lesbian and an adulterer, she thought.

An adulterer? What had it been like? Had she enjoyed it? She couldn't remember. It was a curse, this memory of hers. Here she had gone to all this trouble, had betrayed her husband, her wonderful husband (he had been wonderful, hadn't he?), had ventured out on a perilous road in pursuit of wisdom and truth, had waited for hours, hungry and bored, while her lover soldered wires together, had surrendered her virtue shamelessly — and now she couldn't remember?

Her skirt and blouse and jacket and stockings were hung neatly over the back of a chair. She seemed still to be wearing her underwear. Interesting.

The sun came in through the sheer white curtains. She closed her burning eyes. She heard footsteps and opened them.

"You're awake?"

She mumbled. Or grunted. Maybe it was more like a groan.

"You need to recover, yes? It was quite a night. You are really something!"

"I am?" she said thickly. I feel like really something. Really something left to rot really somewhere.

Martin had brought her some orange juice. Sweet of him. But as Margaret looked at him, she thought, over and over again, What have I done? And why have I done it? I am in the wrong bed with the wrong man. I'm not even in the right house. Or in my right mind. I have made my wrong bed. Now I must lie in it. Is it a lie? Or is this truth? Who cares, anyway? I want to go home and rest my head. But I have no home. Not anymore.

"You should not drink wine, Margaret."

"No."

"You did some things you would not do without wine, I think."

Uh-oh.

"But now, you must get up, eat some small something, drink some coffee —"

"Coffee."

"I will make you coffee."

He kissed her on the forehead and went downstairs.

Margaret pulled her wrinkled clothes on. Her stockings bagged at the knees. She saw a bathroom off the bedroom and went in to splash water on her face. Things I wouldn't do without wine? Things so shocking I have blocked them out entirely!

She rubbed toothpaste across her teeth with her finger. She looked in the medicine cabinet for aspirin but found only bottle after bottle of Xanax. She considered taking one, then rummaged in her bag, thinking there might be an old aspirin floating around in there. She found a lipstick. Maybe later for that. It seemed hopelessly inadequate now. She found a fuzzy peppermint Life Saver, which she ate. A pen. Dr. Lipi's card. A piece of paper on which was written, "I can't stay here. I need some peace and quiet and isolation —"

She stopped reading, horrified. Oh God. What had she done? What had she failed to do?

"Martin!" she said when she found him in the kitchen. "The phone! I must call Edward! I forgot to tell him that I left him!"

Martin looked puzzled.

"I left my husband and he doesn't know!" she cried. "He must be so worried. Oh, poor Edward. How could I have been so inconsiderate. I left him a note to tell him I'd left him, and then I left him, but I forgot to leave the note —"

"Please, please. Do not worry. I have called Edward. Do you think I would not let him know what has happened here?"

Well, yes, Margaret thought, actually I did think you would not let him know what has happened here.

"I told him you were here with me," Martin said. He patted her back gently. His beautiful green-and-white shirt was back. Margaret looked at it in alarm.

"You told him?"

"He was so very much relieved." Martin smiled in a satisfied way. "Here. Sit down. Drink this coffee. He is happy. I am happy. All are happy."

Yeah? Well, happiness ain't all it's cracked up to be, then, she thought. "Happy," she said, full of scorn.

Martin looked at her in confusion. He stood silent for a moment. Then he smiled, as if he understood something.

"Marguerite, did you think that we, that I, what is the word . . ."

Margaret, staring into her coffee cup, felt a familiar burning shame. Fuck, she thought. The word you are looking for is *fuck. Baiser* in French, is it not? And yes, I thought. But now I see that I was mistaken, as I so often am, and that I have suffered the humiliation and guilt of adultery without even getting to commit adultery. It's an outrage. I've made a complete fool of myself.

"How *could* you?" she said.

"But I didn't . . ."

"That's what I mean."

Martin came toward her, put his hands on her head, and stroked it. His beautiful clothes rustled. His light brown hair fell over his face. His long eyelashes covered his downcast eyes.

"Marguerite, you are as young as my daughter."

"Yeah, yeah."

"You looked so pale, lying there, so innocent and pale, and then you passed out — "

"Christ, I passed out? Did I fucking throw up, too?"

"No, no."

"Good."

"Yes, good."

"I remember kissing you," Margaret said.

"Ah."

"I like you."

"*Oui*? Still?"

"*Oui*. Still."

"You are very fine guide, Marguerite." He smiled slightly, hesitantly. "Mar-gar-et."

"Oh, yeah," Margaret said, burying her face in her hands. "A fine guide." Which way to the Vltava?

MARGARET stood on the corner in her wrinkled silk skirt and blouse and the wrath of humiliation and misapprehension.

Where to, Virgil?

I don't know. Where do you want to go?

Gee, I don't know. I thought you knew. You're the guide.

Who said I was the guide, why aren't you the guide, why do I always have to be the guide?

It was the first truly hot day, the June sun bright and ferocious on the yellow taxis. Margaret marched forward, looking in shoe stores. Where to, where to, where to? Home was enemy territory, occupied by a stranger who thought everything was all right. Everything was not all right. It enraged her to think that even for one mistaken moment Edward thought that everything was all right. She refused to let everything be all right. It wouldn't be right if everything were all right. After all she'd done, imagine everything being all right. Only Edward could think everything was all right. What did she have to do, send him a telegram? "EVERYTHING NOT ALL RIGHT STOP WIFE WANTS DENTIST STOP TRIED TO SEDUCE BELGIAN BUT TOO DRUNK STOP LESBIAN STOP."

And she'd already left a note. At least, she'd meant to leave a note. What more did a person have to do?

Where to, where to, where to? Richard's maid's room? Narrow, yellow, grim, and mean? That maid's room? Yes, yes. That's your home now, Margaret. You and Richard can grow old together, arguing about who left the ripe, fragrant strawberries out overnight to spoil. As the clocks toll the hours, all the hours at once.

What's going on? Margaret wondered. I used to be a happy, scholarly housewife. Now I am a frustrated adulteress wandering the streets, seeking shelter in shoe stores. She sat down and tried on a pair of oxfords. Now that she was a lesbian, she supposed she would need more oxfords. A whole closetful. Of course, she already had a closetful of oxfords, so there wouldn't be much point.

She had forgotten for a while that she was a lesbian, what with all the excitement of passing out in a strange man's bed. But she thought about it now, thought of Lily as she'd last seen her, and she knew it must be true. She could recall vividly the shape of Lily's breasts through a silk blouse — large, curved, a small round nipple showing, pop, in the middle of each one. Those breasts and nipples in white silk were part of a language, a language that, like all language, said something about the world, and Margaret had heard the language and she understood. To find the meaning, understand the use. She looked, she understood the use, she understood the meaning. Maybe, yes maybe, her understanding was not always all that it might be. Martin had clearly been speaking a different language, playing a different game from the one she had been playing, checkers to her chess. But with Lily, she would be more careful. She would limit herself to seeing what was really there. Descriptions, Margaret, not explanations. Then perhaps she would see the truth of the proposition: I am a lesbian, I am Lily's lover.

Martin was not the true end of her quest. That much she had demonstrated. The path led clearly now to Lily. And she felt anew the force of the odd, giddy determination she had experienced for the last few months, the cold desire. I must know; I *will* find out. Her failure with Martin made her more avid, rather than less. I must seek, and I must have, she thought. Fuck you, you fake frog. A world of women awaits me!

She went to Richard's to shower and eat some frozen brownies she found beneath the ice cube tray. And change her clothes. What did one wear? she wondered. For an encounter such as this? This was the other side of the moon. One took a step and flew, high in the air, waiting, waiting to land in the rocky darkness.

She wore jeans, how butch, and anyway she had nothing else with her except the wrinkled skirt of the night before, a night of confusion and inebriated solecism best left rumpled, with the skirt, on the floor.

Outside, the heat had diminished slightly and there was a breeze of just below body temperature. The sun was low and the buildings glowed with pink, as if they were healthy buildings. What a beautiful afternoon, almost evening, really. A beautiful time of day. Just right for a seduction.

Margaret took the bus across town, into the setting sun. She squinted and she felt warm, in spite of the air-conditioning. The sun was low but everywhere, poking its nose in where it didn't belong. Go away, this is a bus, a city bus. Go to Kansas. Or Abu Dhabi. Margaret put her arm over her eyes.

Uncomfortable in the sunlight, hung over, and nervous about Lily, she was breathing in a shallow, unsatisfying way and tried to catch her breath. Was it necessary, she wondered, to do what she was about to do? Simply because she thought Lily was attractive? Her collie had been a beautiful collie, but she had never tried to kiss it on the lips.

Margaret, Lily would say, you're in denial.

You lived in a dream with Edward, Margaret told herself, allowing him to look at you with his icy blue eyes and make you think that the reflection you saw there was really you. Now you can't look in his eyes, there is no reflection to bask in. You yourself must observe and let others bask in what they see in your eyes. Maybe you should teach more, stand in front of a room and look out at eyes waiting for you to speak, wanting something from you, demanding that you guide them, fill them with knowledge, make them whole.

She remembered going to a talk of Edward's, just after they'd met. She remembered how he walked to the front of the room, how he stood absolutely still for a fraction of a second, how his stillness caught the attention and the imagination of the entire roomful of young men and women, how they stared at him, how he seemed to grow as they stared, how he suddenly, absurdly, held out his arms.

He stood in front of his audience with his arms out as if he were greeting the dawn, as if a crowd were cheering him, as if Margaret were running toward him to be embraced, which she longed to do. Her heart had beat faster; her heart had literally beat faster then.

"Goood mooorning," he had bellowed in his richest accent. And he had started to speak and never stopped for the next two hours as Margaret watched, tense and overwhelmed.

I observed then, she thought. I observed every nuance of every sweep of his arm. I observed him and the air around him, the air he breathed.

Well, those days are over. Not a student anymore. Thank God and Madame de Montigny, not a teacher either, but not a student enthralled in a class. Now my husband has other students and I must make my own classes. Lily will be my class. I will study Lily.

Lily's buzzer was broken as usual, the front door unlocked,

and Margaret hurried up the flight of dark stairs. Lily opened her door, and Margaret forgot Edward, forgot her reservations. Lily's eyes looked bigger and darker. The scent of roses, faint and uncertain, was on Lily's cheek when Margaret kissed it, a hello kiss, familiar, but not the same now. Lily's cheek was soft, softer than a man's, softer even than a boy's, Margaret thought. As soft as a woman's cheek, genius.

Lily's lips touched her cheek lightly. "Margaret, why didn't you call?"

The last time I saw you, Margaret thought, I said to myself, I am walking toward Lily and I am going to kiss her on the lips. Everything dissolved but that one thought: I am walking toward Lily and I am going to kiss her on the lips. Then I didn't. But now I will.

Lily closed the door and began to say something but stopped. Perhaps she stopped because Margaret put her hand on Lily's waist. Margaret felt the curve of it and found it even more difficult to breathe. She put her other hand on Lily's waist.

"Margaret?" Lily whispered in her tart whisper through her tart lips, a whisper and lips Margaret had always found so amusing in their contrast to what Lily said. But now they didn't seem amusing at all. They didn't seem to be in contrast to anything at all. They seemed like red lips and a soft, questioning whisper.

"Margaret?" Lily whispered again, almost alarmed, almost as alarmed as I am, Margaret thought.

Margaret said, "I, um, well . . ."

She ran her hand up Lily's back, moving closer to her, moving very close to her, thinking, No wonder men like women, no wonder men like to touch women. Lily was wearing a bathrobe. She realized that for the first time now, a vintage satin bathrobe, beneath which she felt Lily, her hands felt Lily. One hand caught in the tie. The robe was opening in the front revealing one of Lily's round, large breasts.

Yikes, Margaret thought.

"Margaret, hold on —"

Hold on? Hold on to what? The room looked funny, dim and far away. Her face was pressed against Lily's short black hair. She could feel a woman's body against hers, a naked female breast, a crushed satin bathrobe, a curved waist beneath her hands, a smooth, rose-scented neck beneath her lips, soft lips beneath her own lips.

"Margaret, for Christ sake, take it easy —"

Take it easy?

Lily stepped back and gently pushed Margaret away.

"Look, Margaret, I mean I never expected this, I didn't know you, well . . . but I'm flattered, sort of, but, what are you" — she bit her lip, her pretty lip — "doing? Exactly?"

Exactly? Margaret thought. Exactly, I am holding on to a half-naked woman's gently curved waist. Exactly!

"Lily?" said a voice.

Whose voice is that? Margaret wondered. It's not Lily's voice. It's not my voice, although it's somehow almost my voice. It's as familiar as my voice. It's a man's voice. It's Edward's voice, actually.

Margaret let go of Lily's waist.

"Lily, I need a towel," said the voice.

The voice needed a towel. Edward's voice needed a towel. Why would Edward's voice be in Lily's apartment and in need of a towel? Well, it wouldn't unless it was wet. Why would Edward's voice be wet? Well, it wouldn't unless it was taking a shower. In Lily's apartment.

"Edward?" Margaret whispered. She looked at Lily, who turned away, tying her robe around her tighter.

"*Edward?*" Margaret said again.

"But, Margaret . . ." Lily said.

Margaret stared at her. She sensed that her mouth was open, that she ought to close it.

"Lily, how could you do this to me?" she said instead.

"But —"

"You hung around flirting with me to get to my husband?"

But even as she said it, Margaret knew it was a meaningless accusation. Lily flirted with everyone, male or female. She smiled and turned her head cunningly, just so, to show her dimples. She didn't have dimples, but it didn't matter. Her life was a flirtation, from morning till dark. At breakfast, the blushing cereal suspected, hoped, but never knew. At bedtime, its heart pounding, her pillow lowered its eyes, speechless and confused.

"With you? Margaret," Lily was saying, "you're *married*."

"So is Edward," Margaret said. "To *me*." She was enraged. She had fallen for the wiles of a girl, and they weren't even wiles! "You've betrayed me and . . . and *all* women."

"Margaret, don't be an ass. Nothing happened."

"Oh, please."

Lily put a hand through her hair and sighed. "Nothing happened, Margaret, okay? Maybe it should have," she added, almost to herself.

Tristesse becomes her, Margaret thought with a mixture of admiration, sympathy, and disgust. As does every other emotion.

Lily twisted the ties of her bathrobe. "Maybe," she said, then squared her shoulders and looked Margaret in the eyes. "Anyway, what do you care if something *did* happen? You told me you were finished with Edward."

"For good reason, as it turns out. And I didn't mean it." Margaret leaned against a chest of drawers painted with yellow birds caught in twisted blue vines. She put her head in her arms. Finished with him? Finished was right. Finished, *finito, fini.* "But I mean it now."

"It was nothing, Margaret. Nothing."

Nothing, Margaret repeated dully to herself. But Lily's words seemed hardly to matter, a traffic report playing on the radio on a day when she was staying home. Observe, Margaret. Observe the roaring in your ears. This is because the blood has rushed there. She lifted her head. The room looks strangely distant, as if you weren't in it. This is because you wish you weren't in it. You shouldn't be in it. Edward shouldn't be in it.

"I'll have to be satisfied with a flannel, I suppose," said the voice from the other room, which she did hear, with terrible clarity. "Or, better yet, evaporation. Quite pleasant, if somewhat immodest . . ."

Edward walked into the room with his sunken chest, her sunken chest, wet above his running shorts.

"Margaret!" he said, walking toward her quickly, his arms out. "My poor Margaret. Are you feeling better, darling?"

"No."

"No?" He bent down to kiss her.

Was this possible? And to think she had once loved him, had once watched him teach and caught her breath, had once, only moments ago, remembered watching him teach, remembered catching her breath, and, remembering, had caught her breath again.

She pulled away from him. "You two-timing slime Brit creep," she said.

"You did have a bad night."

"Yes," Margaret said. "Yours was obviously a lot more eventful."

"Margaret, you're being ridiculous," Lily said.

"Look, Margaret, darling Margaret, wife of my bosom, I'm

sorry you've got a hangover, but I see no reason to take it out on me."

"You don't?"

"Not really."

"Then you're stupid. Isn't he, Lily? Lily sees lots of reasons for me to take it out on you, don't you, Lily?"

"Oh, Margaret," Lily said.

"Margaret, let's not quarrel in front of your friend."

"*My* friend?" she laughed, a snorting sort of laugh.

"Sorry. Our friend."

"Sorry. Your friend."

"*My* friend?"

"Look, I don't care whose fucking friend you're fucking fucking."

"Fucking? I'm taking a fucking shower!"

"Fuck you," Margaret said and turned toward the door.

"Margaret!" Lily said. "Listen —"

I'm done listening, Margaret thought as she rushed for the door. I'm done talking. My senses have failed me. My senses suck.

OH, EDWARD, Edward, snake, reptile, insect, fungus, algae, blue-eyed, silver-haired algae. Margaret stumbled down the hundreds and hundreds and hundreds of flights of brown-stone stairs from the second floor to the ground floor. Where was the street? Would it ever come? She heard Edward behind her, calling her. She heard his footsteps and ran faster. When would she be free of this house of betrayal and sin? Edward. With Lily. Left alone for twenty-four hours and look what happens. Everything was all right, all right.

I knew it all along, she thought. Edward has betrayed me. He has forsaken my aging flesh for — for what? For Lily's aging flesh! Oh, the humiliation. To lose him to some exquisite little girl with long hair flicking like a horse's mane, a student drawn to him and he to her, intoxicated with the wine-dark words of Walt Whitman, yes, okay, that's as it should be. Well, it shouldn't be at all. But at least that's as what shouldn't be should be!

But this!

On the street, the sun was down, the sky was dark blue, and the breeze blew more refreshingly than before. Fuck you, breeze, she thought.

MARGARET RAN EAST through Central Park in the dusk. Edward was no longer behind her. I've lost him, she thought. In every sense of the word. Now I will be mugged and killed. That will show him. That will show everyone. How dare he? He's my husband. How dare she? He's my *husband*.

That Edward might be fooling around with his pretty little students, while a proposition quite certain in Margaret's mind for some time, was nevertheless something for which she really had not the slightest shred of evidence. It was just a truth, a fundamental pillar of her belief system, a given, a fact, a fate. Her fate. But this! This was real!

Margaret realized she was panting with anger, like a dragon. Through her nose. That swine. No wonder she'd left him. She stopped running, walking quickly, though, and far, and after three-quarters of an hour she knew where she was walking to, because she saw it before her.

The home of Dr. Samuel Lipi rose above her, tall, modern, circular, just the sort of home Dr. Lipi should have. He had pointed it out to her proudly as they left his office together one evening, and she had wondered if he had a circular bed.

She rushed into the building. "It's an emergency!" she said

to the doorman, aware suddenly that she was flushed and out of breath, that she was talking to herself and still panting through her nose like an angry dragon. "An emergency!"

The elevator brought her closer and closer in a sickening rush, jerked to a halt, and deposited her, staggering, with blocked ears, on the twenty-eighth floor. Twenty-eight, she thought. Aha! Aha, what? She didn't really care.

She stood for a moment and looked around, trying to calm down. Then a door down the hall opened, and Dr. Lipi's handsome head poked out. "Margaret?" he said. "Is that really you? What is it? The inlay?" He looked at her with concern and held out his arm. "Come in. Come in. Welcome to my little cave."

She looked around and realized that when she had imagined a circular bed, she had snobbishly underestimated him. His apartment was furnished in expensive Italian pieces, so contemporary a few years ago that they were now already dated. All the walls had been knocked down so that it looked like a loft, a tunnellike low-ceilinged loft.

Margaret could not yet bring herself to look at Dr. Lipi himself, so she gazed out his window at the city, the nighttime skyline softened by a pearly gray cloud of damp June filth. The ceiling loomed just above her head, it seemed, as close and intimate as a large hat. In her ceiling hat, up so high, looking down so low, she felt queasy and weak. She had to sit down. She turned. Dr. Lipi was watching her. She saw a black couch with large leather cushions. She went to it, lowering herself carefully, closing her eyes for a moment, then opening them suddenly, feeling strangely vulnerable.

"It's not the inlay," she said.

Dr. Lipi was not wearing his white shirt, she noticed, which disappointed her. He was wearing a blue T-shirt. Didn't anyone understand anything about erotic fantasy anymore?

"It's not even an emergency."

An Englishman would have known to wear a white dentist shirt. Always. Just in case someone should drop by. Even if he wasn't a dentist.

"It's not even about my teeth."

Why, the English liked women in little maids' uniforms, didn't they? Well, not Edward, actually, thank God.

"You're out of uniform," she said.

He smiled, then turned toward a large mirror as if to make sure.

Margaret followed his gaze. Well, she thought, looking at his beautiful reflection, maybe we can do without the white shirt after all. He was wearing shorts, tight-fitting gym shorts. She stared at his bare legs, at his bare arms.

"Nice place, Dr. Lipi," she said, not taking her eyes off his body.

"Sam."

"Sam. Right."

"I'm glad you like it, Margaret," he said. "And I'm glad you're here. Whatever the reason, Margaret, I'm glad you're here."

"You are?"

Dr. Lipi went over to a platform in one corner of the large room that seemed to be a kitchen, a kitchen so streamlined and technologically advanced that it could, with few alterations, have flown to Paris in under four hours.

"Are you really all right, Margaret? Do you want a drink?"

"Don't I look all right?" Margaret said.

"Well, yes, you look wonderful, you always look wonderful, I just meant, well, you know, you come over and say it's an emergency, and I guess you look as though you don't *feel* all right . . ."

Margaret sighed. "You're right," she said. "I'm not all right. I needed some company. And no thank you. I don't drink. Ever. Again."

Dr. Lipi took a beer out of the refrigerator for himself and stood on his platform and looked down at her, across at her, looked at her for a long time. He was uncharacteristically silent. No mention of the dental pulp chamber or the mechanics of mastication.

Well, well, well, Margaret thought. Good. So drop dead, Edward. Pleasure, Edward, is the only thing desired. Therefore, pleasure is the only thing desirable. I desire Dr. Lipi, Edward, therefore he is desirable. If he is desirable, he is pleasure, therefore he is the only thing desirable. Right?

She carefully watched the muscles of Dr. Lipi's thighs as he walked toward her.

Right.

"Margaret," he said, approaching slowly.

Observe and clarify through logic. He has slim, strong legs, practically hairless. Does he have them waxed or what? Why are they so tan? Observe, observe, Margaret. She stared at his thighs and then, helplessly, at his crotch. Ah, and from what I observe, I can logically deduce a great deal. This proposition really is a proposition. This is not a joke. This is no longer a joke.

He stared at her in a way she could not mistake and said her name again.

Why, we don't need uniforms, after all, she thought.

He stood before her in his Michelangelo pose, the beer bottle dangling by the neck from his slender fingers with their dentist-clean fingernails. She looked up at him, unable to speak, unable to move.

So there, Edward, she thought. You see, pleasure is a state of the soul. And to each man, that which he is said to be a lover of is pleasant. Are you pleasant to me, Dr. Lipi? As pleasant as Lily was to Edward?

She continued to stare at him, speechless and without any thought of what to do next, or even that there was a next. He looked back at her, and for a moment she thought he would begin to explain to her what they were about to do, with special emphasis on the role of teeth in foreplay. But all he said was, "Margaret, you understand me."

You? she thought. What do *you* have to do with it? It's not you I'm trying to understand.

He reached out and held her arm tightly. He took her other arm too and pulled her up. He was standing so close to the couch, to her, that she had no room to stand, no way to keep her balance. She felt his chest against her, the gym shorts hard against her. She tipped and fell back onto the couch. He stepped back and pulled her to him again.

Margaret, her face pressed against his smooth cheek, thought, Perception must be in some degree an effect of the object perceived. The object perceived is hard and muscular. The object's hands are pressing into my back. He is rolling slightly, rolling his hips, backward and forward.

He pulled off his own shirt and unbuttoned hers. His hands were on her breasts. Her flesh against his flesh. He was kissing her neck. He kissed her on the lips. This was no longer a reflection in a mirror, not a copy of which she could have only an opinion but not knowledge. This was an actual form, of which she could have knowledge.

Slipping her hand beneath the elastic waistband in the front of his shorts and running it admiringly over the form inside — a gesture to the activity of clarification — Margaret gained knowledge of it, gasped, and bit her lip.

The soul is like an eye; when resting upon that on which truth and being shine, the soul perceives and understands, and is radiant with intelligence.

But then, like an unexpected cold, damp breeze, a sudden quiver of revulsion passed through her. Dr. Lipi? Connoisseur of the curve of the lower dental arch? A droning stranger who now had his strange arms around her? What was she doing? What could she have been thinking of?

When resting not on the truth, but on a mere copy of the truth, the soul goes blinking about, and is first of one opinion and then another, and seems to have no intelligence.

So this is probably not truth, Margaret thought, pressing her lips to his neck, running her hands over his back. It can't be, can it? Pleasure, yes. But also the distinct opposite of pleasure. I hardly know this man. He's my dentist, not my lover. I am disgusted, actually, with this absurd man who has wrapped himself around me, not without encouragement, I admit, but still — if I am disgusted, and I am, then Dr. Lipi, logically speaking, cannot be the only thing desirable, can he? He cannot be truth.

"I'm sorry, Dr. Lipi." She stepped away.

Fool, she thought, looking at him in all his considerable glory. Margaret, you're a fool. Who cares if he's an idiot? And a stranger? Men sleep with idiots and strangers all the time. Yes, but I'm not a man. If Edward wants to sleep with nubile idiots with long silky hair and nearly middle-aged former-lesbian idiots with short black, tousled hair, that's his problem. Dr. Lipi, Dr. Lipi, if only the reality of you had not interfered with the idea of you, the idea of you as mere physical being. You are a mere shadow of yourself, Dr. Lipi.

"Margaret, what's wrong?" He put his hand gently on her face and stroked her cheek. "Don't clench your jaw, darling," he whispered. "Your lovely jaw."

His voice startled her. He stood before her, magnificent and now quite naked, his clothes in a puddle at his tanned feet. Oh, fool, fool. Look at this gorgeous creature, as beautiful as any statue, a man of truly heroic proportions. But statues, bless them, do not speak. And Dr. Lipi does speak. And when Dr. Lipi speaks, I remember that he and not just his perfect body and overcharged eyes exists. I remember that Dr. Lipi's personality is one of his parts.

"Margaret," he said, taking her hands and putting them on his flat stomach, then pushing them down, and then down some more.

On the other hand, she thought, "Dr. Lipi," after all, is just a name, a linguistic convenience. There is no Dr. Lipi over and above his various parts, and Margaret contemplated his various parts with increasing interest and enthusiasm.

This is not real, she thought finally. This is just an illusion of perfection. But what an illusion! She held the illusion. Dr. Lipi's hands were pushing down her jeans. The illusion was pushed between her legs.

"This is just an illusion," she said.

"Yes. It's all a wonderful dream."

MARGARET lay on Dr. Lipi's bed and looked out the window at the sparkling murk of the city sky. Perfection is perfect, she thought. That much I have established to be true. A perfect performance by a perfect performer. Why don't I care?

Dr. Lipi slept peacefully beside her, golden and relaxed in his naked sleep. She looked at him with distaste. Big deal. Big fucking deal. Senses, bah! Without senses there would be no needs. Hey! Lipi! Did I need this? Are you necessary, Dr. Lipi? Did you follow unavoidably from certain conditions? Are you an a priori kind of guy?

Where was Edward? she wondered. Had he stayed at Lily's? What a sordid affair. Two sordid affairs. Dr. Lipi, the sleeping statue, stirred. Margaret moved away from him and tried not to cry. His beauty appalled her. Strange and abstract, it glowed before her; and yet Dr. Lipi and his beauty were not strange and abstract, not to her, not anymore. Dr. Lipi was concrete and familiar now. Which made it all seem that much more strange and abstract.

This is not my bed, she thought, staring resentfully at his face resting peacefully on the pillow. You are not the man beside whom I sleep.

For once, her memory did not fail her, would not fail her. The failure of her memory failed her. She could not forget what she had done. She could only remember it. In perfect detail. And she could not forget Edward, dripping wet, dripping the drops of the guilty, a husband stepping from a shower that was not his own, cleansed but not clean. She could not forget Lily, either, the feel of her, and her own dizzy uneasiness as she grasped the waist of the girl she then discovered had been boffing her husband. She could not forget Dr. Lipi, the ardent dentist, a man so devoted to his art that he saw himself as more than himself, as an exemplar, an exemplar that must proselytize its own cause, that must proselytize itself. If he awoke now, he would talk of the art of love, his love. He would earnestly relate to her exactly what she wanted to forget. He would look at her with those odd, narrow eyes and kiss her with those curvaceous lips, and he would narrate and explain the significance of his use of eyes and lips in terms of endowing her with pleasure, and through pleasure, oral and emotional health. In terms of the oral and emotional health of the nation, too. Nay, the world!

Oh, I should have stayed safely coiled among Martin's speaker cables. Or lain on my narrow cot, harangued by the tolling of Richard's clocks. Or better yet, I should have stayed at home. With Edward. Where I belong. Where he belongs. But now, there is no home. There is no Edward. Edward does not exist. Not even logically.

Margaret quietly slipped into her clothes and wrote Dr. Lipi a note. "Organs produce needs; and conversely, needs produce organs. But I can't see you anymore. I'm married. Teeth be with you, Margaret."

I'M MARRIED. A true statement. I am an adulteress married to an adulterer. You can't be an adulteress without being married. I'm married, all right.

She went back to Richard's, back to the narrow, bumpy, sagging cot among the chaotic chimes, and she wept. She wept all night, getting up now and then to look at her swollen face in the mirror, a sight that filled her with such intense self-pity that she began to weep again, harder than before.

The sun would soon come up, or so one would assume from the weak light that made it through the dirty window of Richard's maid's room. But then, the truth of whether the sun would come up or not was impossible for her to determine, wasn't it? She had not yet actually seen it come up, had she? So, she thought, what is the nature of the evidence that assures us, lying swollen-eyed on our pallet, of any real existence or matter of fact beyond the present testimony of our senses or the records of our memory? Even if I have seen the sun come up a thousand times before, even if I have read books about it coming up, even if I have it on the best authority that it comes up every single day, it is possible that today is the day the sun does not come up. Causes and effects are discoverable not by reason but by experience. I cannot reason with certainty that the sun will come up. So there is no certainty.

Margaret, that's just stupid, Margaret thought. Your life is over, but the fucking sun will come up and you know it. The desire for knowledge is a *folie à une*. And you are a fool.

Observe, observe. You observed Dr. Lipi. You observed for half the night, didn't you? And what did you see? Things you had no business seeing. And how about observing your husband shtupping your friend? How about observing that without Edward you are nothing? You feel like nothing, you want nothing, you are nothing.

ഗ ഗ ഗ

Even in my disconsolate state, I considered going to my pupil in an attempt to turn her away from her false ideas, to take her hand and lead her with me toward the bright lamps of knowledge and truth. But all my previous attempts, my tireless efforts to instruct her and encourage the autonomy of her mind, seemed to mock me cruelly.

Defeated and confused, with the excuse that I suffered from the fatigue of my journey from Geneva, I repaired to my room. Alas, little rest did I find there, so closely in my mind did I link it with Rameau's niece and the lessons we had shared in that place.

Unable to remain still, walking up and down, sitting, then rising again, I determined to leave the house of the Marquise de——, to return to Paris immediately.

My things had yet to be completely unpacked, and so very little preparation was necessary. I waited for the mail to arrive, then informed my hostess and the assembled company, which included my promising, ah, too promising, pupil, that I had received notice that I was wanted right away in Paris on further business, and I was not questioned.

Farewell, little pupil, I thought. And good-bye as well to philosophy. No longer would the thrill of enlightening a young mind be mine. No longer would I struggle with a problem of understanding, tired but persevering until, at last, truth broke through ignorance, bursting forth as the sun bursts from the clouds.

∽∾ ∽∾ ∽∾

MARGARET FELT her forehead. Surely she had a fever. No, she didn't have a fever. No such luck. She was just hot and miserable and nothing. The phone rang, but she didn't answer it. She took a shower. Just like Edward, she thought. Then she took another. Neither shower worked. Edward was still gone. She was still a fool.

What had she been doing all these months, chasing after men and women, running away from Edward? Why? Well, if one hopes to find the answer, to find the meaning, one must understand the use. But what use was it?

The phone kept ringing, on and off, all day, six rings each time before the machine answered. Margaret couldn't stand it. It interrupted her woe. Ding-a-ling-a-ling. Ding-a-ling-a-ling. It rang as the clocks chimed. It rang after the clocks had signed off. She finally turned down all the bells on all the phones. Then, having taken two showers, she realized she had to do something different, so she took a bath.

She lay in Richard's tub in his bathroom with the black and white tiles and looked at her feet. She had looked at her feet in the bathtub in Prague. Now they were the feet of a fool.

There was nothing to eat. Margaret had not eaten anything but peaches and brownies and wine for two days. Imagine someone who actually cleaned out the refrigerator before going away, who edited the refrigerator. Nothing. Not a frozen pea. She'd have to go out. But she couldn't go out to a restaurant, crying and throwing herself dramatically on couches here and there. Restaurants didn't have couches.

I will have to order in. Just like the old days. From the

Greek coffee shop. Surely there is a Greek coffee shop nearby. But what is it called? She looked in the phone book under American Restaurant, Athens Restaurant, Three Guys, Two Guys, Four Guys Restaurant. What do they call coffee shops on the East Side? One Guy?

She lay down on Richard's bed, exhausted. His room had air-conditioning. His bedroom was large and clean and charming, and she would stay here forever and watch the hands on the clocks make their endless journeys. Richard could stay in the maid's room. He wouldn't mind. He would understand. She smiled. Richard loved her and looked after her in a bustling, disapproving way, but even in her present mood, she had to smile at the absurdity of the thought of Richard sacrificing his beautiful bedroom to her and moving into the maid's room.

The phone must be ringing again. Margaret heard the click as the machine answered it. It was right by the bed, but she had turned the volume all the way down. She didn't want to hear any of Richard's conversations with anyone but herself. The fact that Richard was anything other than her editor continued to diminish him in her eyes.

She went back into the maid's room and sat at the card table. She looked through her notebooks. In a margin, she had written out a quotation about empiricism but had not written where it came from: "Naive realism leads to physics," it said, "and physics, if true, shows that naive realism is false. Therefore naive realism, if true, is false; therefore it is false." You can say that again, Margaret thought.

"Margaret?"

It was Richard, home from the Berkshires. She heard keys, paper bags crinkling, footsteps.

"Margaret, are you here?"

Margaret sat on the bed at the card table and hoped Richard would not notice she had been crying. Had she left wet towels on his bed? How puffy were her eyes? Of course he'd notice, and then she'd have to explain.

Richard appeared in the doorway of the hideous slave quarters. At the sound of his sweet, questioning voice, at the sight of him, Margaret felt the loneliness of her miserable state with an abrupt, sickening clarity. Here was Richard, her friend, the only friend she had left.

"Oh, Richard!" she cried out. She threw herself into his arms and wept. "Richard, what am I going to do?"

"Margaret," he said, "you have no clothes on."

That was true, Margaret thought, sobbing, her face buried in Richard's neck. Buck naked. Well, at least he hadn't noticed her puffy eyes.

"Richard!" called a voice. A familiar voice. Whose voice? Not Richard's voice. Not hers, although it was almost her voice. Oh, yes, it was Edward's voice again. "You left the door open . . . Margaret!" said Edward's voice.

Margaret jumped back from Richard. The room was quiet. The clocks, even, were quiet. Margaret wondered if she ought to blush. If she did blush, would the blush spread all over her body?

"Margaret," Edward said in a horrifyingly hushed, controlled voice. "I never expected this."

Which *this*? she wondered lazily. She felt as if she were under water.

Edward gestured toward Richard.

Oh, *that* this, she thought.

"I have *my* clothes on," Richard said.

"I'm sorry," she said. She was still crying. "I'm sorry, Edward, sorry about everything."

"Sorry? You're both insane," Richard said. "There's nothing to be sorry about!"

Nothing, she thought. She put her face in her hands. Nothing at all.

The two men stared at her as she stood before them, naked and weeping. Like a Renaissance Eve, she thought. Poor old Eve.

Margaret reached for a crumpled silk ball on the floor, her skirt. Cover thyself, she thought. She pulled it on and looked down at her still naked breasts.

"Oh, well, *that's* better," Richard said, as he too looked at Margaret's breasts, his face registering the kind of hostile despair Margaret had noticed on the faces of people stepping over homeless derelicts and their bare, filthy feet.

"I've been looking all over for you," Edward said. "I've called everyone I could think of. I called here. I called everywhere. I've been running around the city looking for you."

"You have?" Margaret said. He had? He had been looking for her? Why? Surely not to tell her what she already knew, that he was having an affair with Lily. She trembled with humiliation, then remembered Dr. Lipi, and her humiliation increased. She sniffed and wiped her eyes with the back of her hand.

"Now I've found you, haven't I?" said Edward, his voice soft, almost sad.

He had been looking for her. All over. You look for someone when you want to find them. You want to find them when you want them. You want them when you love them. Did that mean he still loved her? He loved her after all? Edward loved her! And she loved him! She didn't care what had happened. To either of them. She cared only that he loved her, he had searched for her, he wanted her, and he had found her.

"Yes, Edward," she whispered. "You found me."

"Finders keepers," muttered Richard, and he retreated to his own room, closing the door loudly behind him.

Thank God you found me. She looked up at him. He was so beautiful to look at, his voice was so beautiful to listen to. He knew everything. He taught everything. He took everything. He shared everything. And now he was back. Back to take her back. He had searched for her and he had found her.

"Edward," she said. But as she moved toward him, Edward shook his head, turned, and walked out of the room.

"Edward?" she said, following him with a startled, scurrying gait. "Where are you going? You found me. I found you. What are you doing?"

At the front door, she caught up with him. She stood halfnaked in her silk skirt, holding his arm, pulling on it.

Edward turned around, slowly, fixed his eyes on her like locks, padlocks, click, no keys, caught forever. "Margaret," he said, then he turned away, but the locks held tight. "Margaret," he said as he walked out the door, as he left her, left her locked in his gaze forever, as her husband walked out the door and left her, "I have eyes. I have eyes, and I can see."

∽ ∽ ∽

I went up the stairs to gather my personal belongings and to supervise the removal of my trunk, and then sadly I made my way to the carriage. I sat down with a heavy sigh. I had stepped down from that carriage only hours before, and with what a light heart, what hopes for nocturnal discussion and debate! Now I was back in the conveyance, on my way to Paris, stripped of every aspiration; every inclination to pursue knowledge and truth had been dampened in my cold breast. The truth? The awful truth. Truth was more than a human being ought ever have to bear.

There was in that carriage, on the seat beside me, a large blanket provided by some overzealous servant. It was a warm day, but in my state of unhappiness I should not have cared if it had been a cold one. I had no interest in comfort. Comfort, the idea of comfort, seemed to me at that moment to be an affront, and in my unsettled state of mind that blanket appeared to ridicule me. Useless and unwanted, it was a blanket that reminded me of myself. I pushed it impatiently away.

THE BLANKET: Sir!
MYSELF: Who is under there? What sort of mischief is this?
THE BLANKET: Sir, it is I, your pupil, Rameau's niece.

She uncovered herself and, in spite of my anger and disappointment and general misery, the sight of her, so close to me, so disheveled among the folds of the blanket, caused a stirring of intellectual interest that I had thought I should never experience again. She brushed her hair from her flushed face, and her eyes, always bright, seemed to be lit with a new fire; her lips, so sweet to my memory, looked sweeter still than ever I had seen them.

SHE: Do not be angry with me, sir. I could not bear it.
MYSELF: You must not be here. If anyone should find out —
SHE: What care I for the opinion of anyone else when the opinion of the one who has taught me what opinion means is turned against me? What does it matter if every face turns away from me, if only this one dear face would turn back and let me gaze upon it?

As she spoke, her little hand gripped mine with surprising strength. Tears fell from her eyes, wetting her smooth cheeks.

MYSELF: You seem to have enjoyed the gaze of others, one other, at least, with rare enthusiasm. Can the removal of mine really cause you such pain?
SHE: Can you look at me as I am now and ask that question? Is not my distress only too apparent? Have I not risked much to come to you, to be with you, to beg you?
MYSELF: Beg me? And for what do you beg?
SHE: For understanding.
MYSELF: That is all I have ever sought.

I said as much, and as I said it, my anger turned to tears, and my face, far from turning away from my pupil, pressed against her own delicate face, our tears mingling.

SHE: Understand me!
MYSELF: All I have ever wanted is to understand you.
SHE: Understand me here.
MYSELF: Here?

SHE: Now.
MYSELF: Now?

She had thrown the blanket to the floor, and, although the carriage was not ideal for a discussion of this nature, the urgency of the situation required that we make do as best we could under difficult circumstances.

Wherever the repetition of any particular act or operation produces a propensity to renew the same act or operation, without being impelled by any reasoning or process of the understanding, we always say that this propensity is the effect of custom. And so custom dictated that we renew an act, an operation dear to us both, and so we were impelled to begin, and so began with joyous familiarity the act.

MYSELF: There are two ways of investigating and discovering truth.
SHE: I urge you to demonstrate them to me with the full weight of your considerable intellect.
MYSELF: The one way hurries on rapidly, leaping from the senses and particulars to the most general axioms. This is the one now in use.
SHE: Yes, that is so.
MYSELF: It is not a satisfactory method.
SHE: No, as I discovered when I sought truth with another, less learned guide.
MYSELF: The other method, my method, constructs its axioms from the senses and particulars by ascending continually . . .

My pupil was agreeing with my proposition in a most enthusiastic way, which, while gratifying, was somewhat alarming considering our position, that is traveling in a carriage on the public highway.

MYSELF: Continually and gradually . . .

The noise of our discussion was quite audible, and, fearing discovery, I urged discretion by placing my hand across her little mouth, an act that seemed only to intensify her excitement at our endeavor, for she continued her unmistakable sounds, and her breath on my hand was hot and quick.

MYSELF: Ascending continually and gradually till it finally arrives at the most general axioms.

Only then did we both sink back with a sigh. In the carriage, there was tranquillity.

SHE: Did you arrive?
MYSELF: Did you?
SHE: As a being endowed with sensation, you must know the answer to that question.

After some time and some miles, I addressed my pupil, for she was once again my pupil.

MYSELF: Can you tell me what the existence of a being endowed with sensation means to that being itself?
SHE: It must mean the awareness of having been itself from the first instant of consciousness down to the present moment.
MYSELF: And this awareness is grounded in the memory of its own actions.
SHE: Alas, I should like to forget some of my own actions, that is, those actions that have caused you so much pain and me so little satisfaction.
MYSELF: But if there were no memory, there would be no awareness of self, because if a creature were aware of its existence only during the instant of that awareness, it would have no history of its life.

I looked at Rameau's niece, her dark auburn hair falling over her neck, creating a pleasing distinction of color from the paleness of her tender skin. The strings of her petticoat lay loose, the petticoat itself lifted up, together with her shift, navel high, and I slipped them higher yet.

MYSELF: You are young and still inexperienced, but there is no man or woman so young and inexperienced as not to have formed, from observation, many general and just maxims concerning human affairs and the conduct of life. But it must be confessed that when a man, or in this case a woman, comes to put these in practice, she will be extremely liable to error, till time and further experience both enlarge these maxims and teach her their proper use and application.

It was a long way to Paris, and my student lying there beside me, ever eager to learn, not wishing to squander this opportunity of intimate and secluded pedagogy, began quietly but intently to enlarge the maxim before her, and together we spent some time further investigating its proper use and application.

As our journey neared its close, my student turned her face to mine.

SHE: Does this mean that you forgive me?
MYSELF: The inquiry of truth, which is the lovemaking or wooing of it; the knowledge of truth, which is the presence of it; and the belief of truth, which is the enjoying of it, is the sovereign good of mankind. I have inquired with you, I have known your presence, I believe and enjoy you.
SHE: I have been misled by faulty logic, by the inveterate errors that are founded on vulgar notions. But my search for the truth has at last brought me back to you.

෨෨ ෨෨ ෨෨

MARGARET slept long hours and stared at the walls when she was awake. Forget it, she told herself. Even Edward's egotistical largess could not forgive a wife who ignored him for months, left him, and then, naked, embraced another man. Forget it. But she couldn't forget. She thought of calling him, of course. But sometimes shame held her back, sometimes anger. So what if she had thrown her naked arms around Richard? Did Edward think she was sleeping with that prissy misogynist? What kind of woman did he take her for, anyway? Call him? He could damn well call her. On his knees. She imagined him telephoning on his knees; but then she thought that she had been such a terrible, criminal wife that it was she who should approach Edward on her knees, and then she cried into her pillow and went back to sleep.

In this way, she spent a week of a dreary, lonely, maid's-room existence during which she strained Richard's hospitality. Then she went home to Massachusetts, to Mom and Dad, to relive various adolescent disappointments by sitting beneath big suburban trees and contemplating lawns. In her parents' house, she was outraged to find a copy of Art Turner's book, just out, called *Sight Unseen,* which had become an instant best seller. She was further outraged when she read it, for far from the bloated, self-important twaddle she had expected, it turned out to be a brief, rigorous, and peculiarly comic novel about a blind psychiatrist, which she thoroughly enjoyed.

All this time away from Edward, wandering — her mind wandered, at least — had left Margaret more and more homesick for him. Her shamed anger simply grew at first, becoming grander and more intense; and then it stopped growing and seemed to blossom and flower into something else entirely: determination. How dare Edward leave her? He had no right. She loved him, and she would have him. She would get him back. He was hers. She had sought friendship. She had sought lovers. She had sought knowledge, she had sought the truth about things. Now, she would seek Edward.

Seeking truth is the lovemaking or wooing of it, said the philosopher in *Rameau's Niece*. Now Margaret must woo in earnest.

But what about this truth? Who needed truth? Truth didn't pay the rent. If you have your health, her grandmother liked to say, *and* an independent income, you have everything. Truth! Truth is a tautology. A chair is a chair. Logical truth is a tautology.

Yes, but it is not just any truth that one must woo, she thought. "A chair is a chair!" I am no longer interested in such trivialities. Dr. Lipi is attractive, therefore I am attracted to him. So what? Martin is a man and I like men, therefore I like Martin. If Lily is a woman and I like Lily, I like women. So what, so what, so what? I no longer simply seek truth, I no longer seek unimportant tautologies. Such truths exist, but they are of no value to me. I seek interesting and enlightening truth. I seek Edward.

She flew back to New York, to Richard's maid's room, and she felt better now that she knew what she had to do. And she felt better now that she realized what she had done, what had been going on through those months of empirical frenzy. What I have done, she thought, is to test the truth of my attachment to Edward. I have searched for the falsity content of my best theory, that is, Edward. I have done so by trying to refute my best theory, by trying to refute Edward, by trying to test my theory severely in the light of all my subjective knowledge and ingenuity. I have employed the critical scientific method with precision and care. I have tested my theory against a dentist, a Belgian, and a woman. I have discovered there is no certainty, but that I can nevertheless say that Edward, my attachment to Edward, my love of Edward, all are a greater approximation of truth than my attachment to anyone else. In other words, she thought, Edward is the guy for me.

RICHARD WAS barely speaking to her, so intimate had their relationship become.

"Leave me some milk," was all he said when he saw her.

She checked her datebook. It was July 12. Seemed like an auspicious date. A familiar date, too, but why? Margaret could not remember, but what difference did it make? She was going to seek Edward. Where would she find him so that she could seek him? School was out, but she was sure he would be at his office. It was that time of day.

In the rain, a light, cooling rain, Margaret waited for the bus. The clouds were gray and low. She would swoop down and pluck Edward from among the mortals. Just as Jove took Io, Jove wrapped in his cloud. But I will arrive in a bus.

She walked through the halls and realized how long it had been since she'd been to Edward's office, years since she'd gone down this corridor, so quiet and dim. She could hear her footsteps on the linoleum floor. They were as loud as her footsteps had been in the streets of Prague. Through the dingy passage she went, a pilgrim in search of her shrine.

Her determination and need were so stark and plain to her that she began to feel something like confidence, and that confidence grew the more she thought of Edward. How would Edward feel if Edward were seeking Edward? she asked herself. Why, he would feel strong and eager and sure. And so would she.

She imagined his face, all its angles and the deep-set blue eyes, the sudden explosion of a smile. She could hear his loud laugh, his voice resounding with love for his fellow man, who so resembled him.

She strengthened her resolve with these pictures of his face and sounds of his laugh until she realized she was at the office, and his laugh, his real laugh, echoed from within, and his face, his real face, appeared in the gap left by the half-open door. She could see him, and in front of him the back of a head with long silky brown hair, a student's head that faced him and moved only when he moved, to the left a little, to the right, the hair flicking loyally behind, then back to face the smiling, laughing, professorial shrine. My shrine, Margaret thought. Not your shrine.

It was summer. Didn't these girls have homes? Or summer camps? Or generous indiscriminate grants to study the sexual orientation of the figures depicted on Caribbean postage stamps?

Margaret stuck her head in. "Hi!" she said. She waved, wiggling her fingers, and smiled broadly.

"Margaret?" Edward looked startled. She'd caught him off guard, not an easy task. Her smile grew. She felt better just standing in his doorway. Beat it, broad, she thought, glancing quickly at the glossy brown hair, then back at Edward.

The silky head turned to face her. Oh — the pretty pale-skinned girl she had expected to see was not a girl at all but a boy. With a scraggly mustache. Well, all the better. Beat it, buddy. Can't you tell when you're *de trop*?

"Busy?" she said.

Edward stared at her in irritation.

"John," he said, after an awkward silence during which Margaret continued to smile blandly, thinking an insipid innocence to be her best opening ploy, "this is Margaret Nathan." He motioned toward her dismissively.

"Wow! Hi!" said the boy.

And Edward continued in a tone of voice that Margaret did not recognize and that did not become him, she thought. Edward bitter and pompous? Edward disappointed and therefore affecting superiority? Edward *was* superior! Didn't he know that anymore?

"Margaret, this is John Marsh. And the conference you have burst in upon with such uncharacteristic zeal, at least in regard to your proximity to me, has to do, or I should say had to do, with John's difficulty in deciding whether to return here next year or to take a year off to seek a higher understanding."

"Ah," Margaret said. "You mean riding across the country on a motorcycle."

"How did you know?" John said, eager and earnest as a dog. He stood up and began to shake her hand heartily. "Wow! Margaret Nathan! It's totally an honor to meet you."

Gee, Margaret thought. Look at how he's looking at me. He's heard of me. He's excited to meet me. Why, he adores me! And isn't he cute, behind that little tufty scrap he thinks is a mustache. Look at those pretty, wide hands.

"Yes, quite an honor," Edward said.

Margaret was gratified by the boy's attention, but she was becoming alarmed at Edward's manner, and annoyed by it, too. How was she to woo him back if he reacted to her mere presence with petty sarcasm? What if she *was* a bad wife? She was in love with him and wanted him back. Wasn't that enough? She glared at Edward, her smile, and plan to continue smiling vacantly, quite forgotten. Then she turned her eyes back to young John.

"So *this* is why you teach," she said, insinuating, consciously suggestive.

Edward said nothing, but flashed her a look that said, Don't go too far.

She gave him a look that she hoped would say, I've already gone too far, so what's one more little misstep?

But she added, "This is why you teach. A student of such devotion, showing up on such a beautiful July morning."

John grinned.

"It's raining," Edward said.

"Is it?"

"Margaret, we really are busy. Perhaps you could conduct your own tutorial somewhere else."

"Perhaps." And she ostentatiously eyed John again.

There was another silence, then John said, "My mom likes your book, Ms. Nathan."

Well, aren't you sweet, Margaret wanted to say. You and your mom. But she limited herself to a soft thank-you, then ran her eye down his smooth young face to his T-shirt, which was decorated with revealing little rips, to his jeans and pointy cowboy boots.

She felt Edward watching her watch the boy, so she said, "I hope we'll be seeing much more of each other, Mr. Marsh."

"Wait'll I tell my mom," said John, and he shuffled out of the office, mumbling thanks and a promise to Edward to think over his advice and a shy good-bye to Margaret.

Edward looked at her. He leaned back and put his feet on the desk. "His mom. How nice. Well, my darling, welcome. Leaving so soon? You needn't tarry on my account. I know why you've come, so let's get on with it, shall we?"

"You know why I've come? You know what I want?"

"Such delicacy, Margaret. Such consideration. But I have another student coming. Shall we conclude our business quickly, then?"

What does he mean? A quick hump beneath the desk? Hardly. He was sarcastic and distant and bitter, an unfamiliar, eerie state of affairs. Margaret's confidence of moments before hardened into willfulness. She felt reckless and glib.

"Professor Ehrenwerth?"

Margaret turned toward the quiet greeting and saw the girl from the dinner party, the silky brown-haired girl who read Walt Whitman in the library. The girl, the one. Oh, really. That's why you want me out of here. Well, too bad, chump. I'm not budging.

"Professor Ehrenwerth, am I interrupting you? I just wanted to come by and wish you a happy birthday and drop off this paper for my incomplete."

"Come in, Eve."

Eve? Yes, that was her name. Naturally.

"You remember my wife?"

"Oh, yes, hello, Ms. Nathan."

"Hello, Eve. And please call me Margaret."

"Margaret also came to wish me a happy birthday, didn't you, dear?" Edward said.

The twelfth. Yes, yes. Edward's birthday. Yes, she supposed she had come to wish him a happy birthday. And she, Margaret, was the gift. Surprise! No returns, Edward. And no exchanges.

She looked at Eve. How did this wide-eyed child know

about his birthday? Well, of course she knew. She was the one. But not for long, sister, Margaret thought. You're finished in this burg.

"So thank you and good-bye, Margaret," Edward said.

"Eve," Margaret said, putting her hand on the girl's arm. "Would you mind if I stayed and observed your discussion? I'm researching a new book about the relationship between teacher and student in Western culture. It's called *From Socrates to Mr. Chips: Pedagogy and Desire.*"

"Margaret —"

"Oh, no, that's okay, Professor Ehrenwerth," Eve said. "It sounds so interesting. And if listening would really help . . ."

Margaret sat down on the one extra chair and crossed her legs.

Eve looked around for another, then shrugged and stood in front of Edward's desk.

"It's just that I really didn't have that much to say," Eve said. She put her paper on Edward's desk.

"Did you know that Professor Ehrenwerth was forty today, Eve? He certainly doesn't look it, does he?"

"No. But these days forty's young," said Eve. "The prime of life. I sometimes wish I were forty."

"You will be," Edward said.

"Yes, and I'm sure it will be wonderful for you," said Margaret. "The prime of life. Mid-life, in fact."

"My paper's about mid-life, Margaret!" Eve said. " 'Twenty-eight young men bathe by the shore'? You know it? And see, she's twenty-eight, the woman who's watching, and it's like a mid-life crisis? Because in those days twenty-eight was like mid-life?"

Margaret looked at Edward.

"Go away, Margaret," he said.

"Actually, I've got to go," Eve said cheerfully. "I'm leaving for Paris tonight. Are you going anywhere this summer?"

"Yes," Margaret said. "We're going to Paris, too."

"Are we?" Edward said.

"Mmm. We'll also drive around to other places, of course, stop here and there. Avignon, Les Baux."

"Ah, yes, of course, how could I forget," Edward said.

"Yes, how could you? Well, age does have a way of catching up with us, doesn't it, Eve?"

"I guess so. I hope we bump into each other, anyway."

"Where?" Margaret asked.

"In Paris!"

"Ah! Paris. Of course," Margaret said.

"Well, *au revoir!*"

"Yes, bye-bye," said Margaret. "Close the door, dear, would you?" And Eve was gone, leaving Margaret and Edward alone in the small, dusty office.

"Whitman and the Mid-Life Crisis?" Margaret said. "The Self-Help School of Criticism?"

"An unfortunate interpretation, I quite agree."

"Gosh, Edward, now that you're forty, you too can have a mid-life crisis, a full-blown mid-life crisis. Shower your seed upon the young —"

"Really, Margaret."

Margaret got up, sat on his desk, and pretended to look at some papers.

"So what is this about France? You're going to France?" Edward said.

"Why not?"

Edward was silent, tapping his finger on the desk.

"Look, Edward, why not?" Margaret said suddenly, softly. "Let's go. Tomorrow."

He continued to tap his finger on the big scratched desk, then stopped and leaned back in his chair. Margaret heard a jackhammer outside. And a bird. She slid back, off the desk, into the straight wooden chair. I have been waiting to see you, she thought. For weeks. I've been planning what to say. I want to say that I'm sorry, that I see you and hear you when you're nowhere around, that I have no one to talk to and nothing to talk about without you, that the days have no shape and the nights have no end. That I have been a fool.

"Why not?" she said again. She was in earnest now. She wanted him to smile and laugh loudly and lead her off to a drunken landscape of castles and inns and drafty museums.

She looked at him as he sat across the desk from her. There was no laugh, no smile. His pale blue eyes gazed at her steadily. She could hear herself breathing. She turned away. There's one every semester, she thought. Me. I'm the one. Your only one. And you're mine. These students are just students. Lily is just Lily. I am the wife.

But the memory of sitting just like this, herself a student, not a wife, in other offices at other times was strong and surrounded her like a perfume.

"I feel like a student, sitting here," she said. And he was her teacher and her subject. The desire to know was just like desire. Desire was just like the desire to know. She looked at Edward, at his dissident hair, his face of angles and creases, his coldly knowing eyes, which looked back at her, unblinking, and she knew that these statements were true.

She reached for Eve's paper. "'An unseen hand also pass'd over their bodies,'" she read. "'It descended tremblingly from their temples and ribs.'"

"Why did you run off, Margaret?" Edward said. He said it not in the brittle voice he'd used earlier, but in a stern and earnest voice that made her feel very sad, although not quite sad enough to lose wholly her own sense of being wronged.

"Well, you *were* sleeping with my best friend," she said.

His eyes opened in wide skepticism.

"Okay, not my best friend," she said. "You're my best

friend. Or were. So Lily was sleeping with my best friend. Not to mention my husband."

"Margaret," Edward said. He was rocking forward and backward on his chair, in patient disgust. "Richard is your best friend. So it was you who were sleeping with your best friend."

"Richard? I wasn't sleeping with him. And you were."

"I never slept with Richard."

"Of course not. You were sleeping with Lily."

"No I wasn't."

He wasn't?

"Just bathing?" she asked sarcastically.

"She wanted me to take her running."

"In the shower?" She was stalling, trying to catch up. What did this mean? That he had never slept with Lily? Was it possible? The shower was just a shower? She heard his voice indistinctly through her own panic. He was explaining what had happened. Did that mean she had to explain what had happened? Did she have to tell him what had happened with Dr. Lipi? Was she supposed to confess? To the Vltava, driver! And step on it!

"I couldn't run in the morning," Edward was saying. "I'd been up so late waiting for you before Martin finally called." Martin! A gentleman and a papa. How improbable he seemed now, now that her life was over. "So we ran in the afternoon," Edward was saying, "and I brought a change of clothes for my class . . ." Yes, think ahead, Edward. No crumpled silk skirts for you. ". . . and I was going to shower in the gym, and then Lily offered her shower." Lily's shower. Yes, that part she remembered. She noticed he was wearing her favorite suit, a terrible old brown suit, the one he'd worn to Europe on their first trip, much too hot for summer. He was deteriorating without her. "I'm guilty!" he said. "I took a shower!"

He shook his head. "Margaret, did you actually think I was throwing a leg over your coy little friend?"

In that moment, Margaret realized he would never have thrown his leg over anyone but her. His sense of order, of his own power, would not permit it. His egotism made sure that his generosity was not squandered but celebrated. To his students he gave what was due them — his bountiful teaching. His largess was in quantity and quality, not in the diversity of his gifts. It would have been unseemly, in his own eyes, for him to pop his adoring students. He was their teacher. He gave them teachings. To Lily, he gave his companionship and running tips. Oh Christ, he was just an innocent jogger. While she! She!

"Did you actually think I was, was fucking *Richard*? Richard the homo?" she blurted out in a tone of as much ironic outrage as she could muster. "I was just taking a bath."

And, you know, I also fucked an Adonis. Same difference.

"A bath?" Edward said, laughing. "That's the truth?"

Is it the truth? Margaret wondered. What is truth? Is it true to say "I was innocently taking a bath" without also saying "after a roll in the hay? With the fabulous physique of Dr. Lipi? With my dentist?" Is it true that I slept with Dr. Lipi, is that truth, or is this truth, that I'm here with you, that you're everything? If I rely solely on my senses at this moment, Dr. Lipi does not exist. There is only Edward. If I rely on reason, still Dr. Lipi doesn't exist, never did exist, never could exist. There is only Edward.

It is true that I threw myself into another man's bed. I did it. I experienced it. I remember it. I know it. It is a true statement. But there are an infinity of true statements. They are not all equal in value. A statement is true if and only if it corresponds to facts. A statement that conveys more information has a greater informative or logical content than a statement that conveys less information. It is a better statement. The greater the content of a true statement, the better it is as an approach to the truth. "I love you, Edward" has greater content than "I fucked Dr. Lipi." So "I love you, Edward" is a better statement.

"The truth, Edward, the real truth is that I love you." She said it so quietly she almost couldn't hear the words herself. Edward stared at her, steadily and seriously, until, unnerved, she looked away.

"Margaret," he said, and he sounded angry. "Are you quite certain? This time?"

"Well, there can be no certainty —"

"For Christ's sake, Margaret . . ."

Which of the young men does she like best? asked Walt Whitman. Which of the young men does Margaret like best? asked Margaret, and she knew the answer. An unseen hand pass'd over their bodies, over Edward's body. It descended tremblingly from their temples and ribs, from his temples and ribs as she looked at him, at his temples and ribs and his terrible, relentless eyes. Perhaps he thought of the poem, too, for he leaned over the desk toward her, just a little, and very slowly. Margaret saw his hand lying on the desk just inches from hers, and, as she watched, her hand reached across those inches to touch him, to pull him toward her as she stood and leaned across the desk until he stood, too, his face against hers, his hands descending tremblingly, her hands descending tremblingly, until they had both descended tremblingly and completely onto the scarred desktop. Pencils and pens, books and journals and Styrofoam cups, Eve's preposterous paper on the twenty-eight-year-old woman and her twenty-eight young men all gave way to their pedagogic struggle.

The growth of all knowledge consists in the modification of previous knowledge, she thought in a last wild gesture toward reason. Kant said our intellect imposes its laws on our sensations. But how rarely it succeeds!

"Edward . . ." Reality resists our laws, she wanted to say, her face pressed into his chest, her hands pulling his jacket away, his shirt. We make mistakes again and again. Karl Popper says so.

"Popper," she gasped, unaware she had spoken.

We modify our laws, Edward, we modify our knowledge.

He looked down at her and smiled.

I made mistakes again and again, she thought. I modified. And now I know.

"The method of science is the method of bold conjecture," she gasped, feeling a bold conjecture pressed suddenly down upon her.

"Do shut up, Margaret."

Bold conjectures and the ingenious and severe attempts to refute them, she thought.

Her shirt had dropped somewhere onto the floor with several periodicals. Edward's narrow chest was against her, her face was against his, their legs tangled, the world back in its proper orbit.

He was her bold conjecture. She could not refute him.

"Thorough," she whispered.

This was a thorough critical discussion. Severe and ingenious testing.

"Severe and ingenious."

"Yes, Margaret," Edward said, his voice hoarse in her ear. "Whatever, darling."

THEY LAY QUIETLY, wet with sweat, uncomfortable, their position absurd, their pleasure infinite.

In light of this critical discussion, in light of this severe testing, this ingenious testing, this modification of knowledge, this redemption, this remarriage, this lesson, this search for truth, this fucking on a desktop in an airless office, you seem by far to be the best, Edward, the best tested, the strongest. You seem to be the one nearest to truth.

"You're the best," Margaret whispered to her husband. "Of all my theories, Edward, you are the best."

സ സ സ

MYSELF: And so, if you think carefully about it, you will agree that in the end our truest opinions are not the ones we have never changed, but those to which we have most often returned.

സ സ സ

EPILOGUE

Margaret Nathan's book, *Rameau's Niece and the Satin Underground,* was eventually published, and while early reviews were on the whole respectful, even enthusiastic, a certain contradiction — some called it an egregious error — was soon widely noticed. "Ms. Nathan discusses the obvious connection between the eighteenth-century text *Rameau's Niece* and Diderot's *Rameau's Nephew,*" one typical review remarked. "What she (incredibly!) fails to mention is that though Diderot wrote *Rameau's Nephew* in 1761 or thereabouts, he showed it to no one, as far as we know. It was not published until 1805, posthumously, and then only in a German translation made by Goethe from a transcription of a manuscript discovered in St. Petersburg."

"Oh God!" said Margaret. "I forgot."

How did the anonymous author borrow from a book that did not exist? Margaret asked herself this question, the obvious question, the question that would have brought her great scholarly renown had she thought to ask it before. Discovering a historical diamond, she had held it up to the light and marveled only at a prism.

Was Diderot himself the author? Did one of his friends, shown *Rameau's Nephew* in confidence, write his own unpublished response? Or was it Diderot's mistress? One of his students, perhaps, one with silky brown hair. Maybe Rameau's niece wrote *Rameau's Niece*! Rising from her bed, where she had spent the last several weeks in speechless mortification, Margaret began her research. And, dimly, she recalled something Diderot had said. Perhaps it was Diderot, anyway; perhaps it was what he said: It is my job to seek truth, not to find it.